Who Killed
Cock Robin?

Also by Margaret Duffy:

Brass Eagle
Death of a Raven
A Murder of Crows

Who Killed Cock Robin?

Margaret Duffy

St. Martin's Press
New York

Library of Congress Cataloging-in-Publication Data

Duffy, Margaret.
    Who killed Cock Robin? / Margaret Duffy.
      p. cm.
    ISBN 0-312-04988-9
    I. Title.
    PR6054.U397W48   1990
    823'.914—dc20
                                          90-8626
                                          CIP

First published in Great Britain by Judy Piatkus Limited

First U.S. Edition: October 1990
10 9 8 7 6 5 4 3 2

Requiem

The crematorium chimney was emitting thick black smoke. I parked the car so that it was facing away from the building and sat still, trying to dispel the images of horror being presented to me by my cursed writer's imagination. Without success. Gazing, on this perfect June morning, across the Gardens of Remembrance – neatly trimmed paths, weeping willow trees, flowerbeds – all I could see were flames engulfing a man, a young man, trapped in his car.

Terry's car had been his coffin, the beloved sports car that had, cruelly, first been turned into a murder weapon by his unknown killers. The murdered man's thoughtful and considerate nature had undoubtedly saved the lives of a few other people, friends who had waved him off from the restaurant car park. For it was very late and he had driven more quietly and slowly than he might otherwise have done. Thus what had presumably been a tilt-firing mechanism had not been activated until he braked hard in a suburban road a few minutes later, possibly to avoid hitting a cat or dog. This was guesswork, there had been no witnesses.

Several windows in nearby houses had been broken, a woman cut by flying glass as she stood by her dressing table. A few people, mostly elderly, had been treated for shock. But nothing could have been done to help Terry, who had died – and no one had said they had heard him screaming – in the car. You do die quickly, don't you? I asked myself, finding that I was tightly gripping the wheel of the car. Hadn't I read somewhere that you die very swiftly from suffocation in that kind of fierce blaze? That is, what is left

1

to die of a body mangled by the blast.

No, don't think about it. Think instead of his girlfriend Alison who was still alive because they had had an argument and Terry had gone to another friend's birthday celebrations without her. Think of that and forget lingering horrors.

In the accounts of his death in the newspapers he had been described as a civil servant. This of course was perfectly true. But details of the staff of D12, a small unit within MI5, are not openly discussed. Official reaction to recent questioning from the media, after certain activites of the department were unaccountably leaked, was that its inauguration had been an experiment and it had been disbanded. The truth is that D12 – created to investigate foreign interference with MI5 – has gone to ground, lost to outsiders in the labyrinths of Whitehall. And it is now larger and with more power, its controller, Colonel Richard Daws, answerable only to Number 10. Its brief too has been extended and we now investigate all incidents likely to result in a security lapse within the MI5 framework. Directly beneath Daws's command is the main investigative team. This consists of three operatives; an army officer, Major Patrick Gillard; his wife, who is a novelist for most of the time; and Terry Meadows. I am Ingrid Langley, the novelist, and today I was attending Terry's funeral. I still couldn't believe it.

We had been a well-knit team, Patrick finding exactly the right blend of authority, humour and occasional plain bloody-mindedness to bring out maximum efficiency. Well, nearly always. I could imagine Patrick's reaction to the murder of his lieutenant but had had no opportunity to speak to him as he had been in the States when it happened. All I knew was that the time of his flight arrival would enable him to act as pallbearer if he broke speed limits all the way from the airport.

A small group of people were emerging from the crematorium, shaking hands with a priest in the entrance. They all seemed to be elderly, some walking with great difficulty using sticks or being supported by relatives. We should all be old when we die, I thought as I locked the car, not in our late twenties with the best of life to come.

In truth I had been reluctant to attend. For one thing it was

2

doubtful if Terry's family knew the exact nature of his work. I had a horror of them imagining me to be not an office colleague but an old flame, with the emphasis on 'old'. I don't look like an office person. The problem would be eased if Patrick turned up on time, for then I could merely tell the truth and say that I am the wife of Terry's boss. It shows my state of mind that I was worrying about this at all; I'm the wife of his boss whether the plane was on time or not. With all this useless mental agitation I went slowly over to where newly arrived cars were parking on the gravel. I was also fretting that Patrick had not had a dark suit and tie with him, he had not gone to the States on D12's business but mine, for he is also my agent.

One of those arriving was Richard Daws. It came as a slight shock to see him for I had been fairly convinced he would not come. His cover being of necessity profound, I had imagined him concerned that too many operatives of D12 were in attendance already. Perhaps, on the other hand, he had reasoned that not too many newshounds would be wandering around Reigate.

We shook hands and for a moment neither of us spoke.

'I feel . . .' said the colonel, uncharacteristically hesitant, 'helplessly angry.'

I said, 'I just don't know why it had to be Terry.'

'No,' he replied pensively. In an undertone he added, 'Fields thinks it might have been the IRA.'

Colin Fields is an explosives expert with Scotland Yard's Anti-Terrorist Branch.

'From the method used?'

'He's not had time to evaluate the evidence yet. Just a hunch.'

'He does tend to blame the IRA for everything.'

'I'm aware of that. We'll just have to see.'

'But Terry never had any connection with Northern Ireland,' I persisted. 'As far as I know he's never even been there.'

'That's right,' Daws agreed. 'I checked with his file. Not even on holiday.'

'You don't think they mixed him up with Patrick?' Patrick had done several tours of duty in the province while serving in

3

an undercover unit during his active army days. 'It's not likely, is it? And I should imagine they'd be far more interested in me as a target. I did a lot of damage to that organisation while the major was still in short trousers.' And with that he turned to greet Mr and Mrs Meadows, who were approaching us diffidently.

I had never met Terry's parents before. Smoothly, Daws made the introductions and I tried to smile a little at them through sudden blinding tears. The Meadowses were still a comparatively young couple, in their late forties, and there was a daughter with them, Louise, with her husband.

'Do you know anything about this?' said the latter, furiously, to Daws.

'Martin!' his wife remonstrated quietly.

But Martin's pent-up anger could not be so easily checked. 'I mean, it stands to reason some bastard had it in for him. And all the police are doing is spouting a lot of rubbish about checking number plates of people who might be on terrorists' hit lists to see if there's one close to Terry's and they mixed them up. What about that oaf Alison used to go out with? That pin-brained weight-lifter? Has anyone asked him about his movements that night?'

'I'm not in touch with the latest police investigations,' Daws observed calmly. 'Did the man detest your brother-in-law sufficiently to want to kill him?'

'No,' Mr Meadows answered shortly. 'And the insult aside, Maurice has neither the inclination nor wherewithal to make bombs.'

'He threatened him,' said Martin. 'You damn well know he did. On the evening they bumped into each other at – '

'All this argument isn't going to bring my son back,' interrupted Mrs Meadows. 'Martin, you have no right to speak to Terry's senior colleague like that.'

'I take it the police have interviewed you,' Daws said to her, smiling briefly to acknowledge Martin's muttered apology.

She nodded. 'There was nothing we could tell them that was the slightest bit of use. As you know, he had his own flat in town to avoid a long journey to work.' She paused, frowning slightly. 'I've never been quite sure what Terry did in the course of his job and I've never pried. But I've always

4

wondered what happened when he was shot in the shoulder a while back. He said it was a shooting accident in Scotland but then again most folk go after pheasants with shotguns, don't they? Not high-velocity rifles. I didn't mention that to the police but . . . ' Her voice trailed away and she smiled at Daws, the intelligence behind the steady gaze belying the outward appearance of weak, grieving womanhood.

Just then a strong clue to the answer to her riddle arrived at speed in his BMW and braked hard, slewing to a standstill.

'Who's this?' Martin demanded to know as Patrick got out of the car. 'There's an awful lot of people here I don't know.'

Daws said, 'Terry's immediate superior, Major Gillard. By the look of him I'd say you two have a lot in common right now.' He took Mrs Meadows by the arm and steered her away from the group for a short distance and I heard him say, 'It might help if I give you a few details.'

Perhaps it was a mistake to take her away, I thought. It would have done her good to see someone who obviously really cared about Terry and did not hide his feelings for the sake of polite convention. It was doubtful too that Martin would look at Patrick to see his own emotions exactly mirrored; rather, I felt that he had rarely, if ever, seen anything so *dangerous*. Indeed there was every likelihood that, had one of those whose names are on Patrick's own hit list put in an appearance, the gathering would have been treated to the sight of one man killing another with his bare hands.

And all this of course was an appalling breach of security. Those in charge of ordinary civil servants do not arrive at the funerals of their underlings with murder and mayhem writ large in their normally sane grey eyes. Perhaps Daws, on the other hand, had realised the state of affairs and had merely been trying to prevent Mrs Meadows from experiencing a severe fright.

Louise turned to me in slight alarm.

'We were both very fond of Terry,' I told her, somewhat lamely, I'm afraid.

Then Louise seemed to remember something and said to the new arrival, 'Are you the Patrick Terry sometimes mentioned?' She had her late brother's brown wavy hair, brown

5

eyes and an air of no-nonsense competence that would stop wild bulls in their tracks.

'Louise,' Patrick murmured after a pause when he appeared to emerge from his black mood. 'Yes, I should imagine so.' They shook hands and he came over and kissed my cheek.

Louise introduced him to her family, but before any more could be said the hearse arrived. The Meadowses seemed grateful that Patrick organised everything. He chose five others, the youngest and strongest, including Steve Lindley who also works for D12. The quiet, concise instructions ensured that everything went off perfectly. Patrick is a clergyman's son as well as a military man so is familiar with such unhappy occasions and knows how they should be arranged.

I saw very little of the short service, my vision blurred with tears. The utter finality of death came home to me. Terry was dead and soon would be no more than a small pile of ashes.

The clergyman's son read the lesson, his voice bleak but calm, hardly needing to glance at the Bible. He had heard the words so many times before, hadn't he? He concluded with a quotation purely from memory and I saw the officiating priest stare at him in surprise and wondered if he had been about to utter the same words.

'I am sure that neither death, nor life, nor angels, nor principalities, nor powers, nor things present, nor things to come, nor height, nor depth, nor anything else in all creation, will be able to separate us from the love of God in Jesus Christ our Lord.'

It is understood in the Gillard family that one day Patrick may take up his father's vocation.

So Terry slid through the final curtain and we all went outside again into that perfect summer morning, not one of us looking up at the chimney.

In passing, Daws observed to me mildly, 'I was waiting for him to add, "Vengeance is mine. I will repay."'

6

Chapter One

There was to be little time to grieve or feel anger. The phone was ringing as we entered our Devon cottage. It was the colonel who, naturally, had had plenty of time to return to his London office while we were on the road. Watching Patrick's face as he assimilated what was obviously important information and also orders, I decided to go for a walk in the garden. No, not another assignment! Not just now.

There had been a note in the kitchen from Dawn, our baby son Justin's nanny, informing us that she had taken him into Plymouth to do some shopping and to buy him some clothes. She hoped I didn't mind but he had grown out of practically everything suitable for warmer weather. Mind? The girl was an angel.

I had a lot of work to do. At last I had completed *Echoes of Murder*, my latest novel, in rough, and could now go ahead with the final draft. (No one yet has talked me into buying a word processor.) I was hoping to finish this in time to be able to accept an invitation to watch the commencement of filming of the screen adaptation of another novel, as yet only published in the States, *A Man Called Céleste*, which had unfortunately been retitled *The Immortality Man*.

'Where are you going?' Patrick called when I was some yards from the front door.

Damn. 'Just round the garden for some fresh air.'

He came out, leaving the door open, walking slowly with a slight limp, very tired. 'Westfield's been murdered.'

I went back. 'Sir John Westfield?'

'Yes, he's been found battered to death at his sister's home near Petworth.'

Sir John Westfield had been a senior man in MI5. Westfield was a codename, not his real surname, taken from the village where he lived in Sussex. He was referred to as Westfield by everyone within the security services, to confuse enemies of the state and eavesdroppers. I had never met him.

I asked the first question that came into my mind. 'Does Daws think there might be a connection between that and what happened to Terry?'

Patrick shrugged. 'He didn't say.' He wasn't giving the issue his full attention, not wanting to, not caring about anything but Terry's death right then. He pulled himself together. 'It's too early to say. Daws wants me to go down to Sussex in a couple of days. After the police and forensic people have gone over the place. You know what they're like if anyone gets under their feet.' He stopped speaking, surveying me closely. 'Daws is sending us Steve Lindley. He's to take over Terry's job until someone else is found.'

Terry had been more than our assistant. Patrick had been grooming him to take over from him one day. Tragedy, murder and outrage aside, it was over three years' work wasted.

I leaned on the barn wall, knowing I was going to cry again. 'Please tell me he didn't suffer,' I whispered. 'Say something that will banish the pictures I have in my mind of him sitting in that car with his limbs blown off, screaming as he burned to death.'

Patrick, who had been horribly injured by a grenade during the Falklands War, came to me and put his hands on my shoulders. 'You mustn't torture yourself like this. It would have been over in seconds.'

'I suppose he should have checked.'

'We're all supposed to check. The device would have been placed near the petrol tank. If he'd checked he'd be alive today.'

'Do you?' I asked through tears. 'Every time you use the car? Do you get down on your hands and knees in your best suit and peer underneath?'

8

He took a breath and let it go slowly. 'No,' he said softly. 'And perhaps I'm blaming myself for not impressing it on him often enough.'

'Are we really targets?'

His hands slid from my shoulders and he rammed them in his pockets and commenced to wander listlessly up and down. 'I wouldn't have thought so. Officially D12 doesn't exist. I can understand a group of terrorists gunning for Daws or me, but Terry . . . ? It doesn't make a lot of sense, does it?'

There was a short silence. Then Patrick said, 'In a way I wish it had been me.' He added quickly, 'Leaving out you and Justin for a moment. I've done things that probably deserve some kind of retribution. You can't help it when you're a soldier. I've killed and maimed. There have been occasions when I've interrogated people and used my hands when it should have been just my voice and brains. Just to get quick results. Terry enjoyed a bit of muscle when the job demanded it of him but there was no malice in the lad. No thought of making the world a better place all on his own by personally kicking the ungodly in the teeth.'

I had my walk round the garden, taking my time. There you have it, I thought, the reason that people like Patrick, in possession of a quirk, or perhaps a flaw in their natures, are put in positions of power to investigate crime or treason. But wanting to put the world to rights didn't make you a superbeing who never shed bitter tears of grief.

'I gather Lindley doesn't want the job,' Patrick said later. 'They put him in charge of the small surveillance section he works for last month.'

During my wanderings on the riverbank Patrick had taken a phone call from my publisher, Thorpe and Gittenburg, a tentative enquiry about a possible date for the delivery of *Echoes of Murder*. I had an idea he had been rather abrupt in his reply. Then Daws had rung again with further information about the new temporary team member.

I said, 'Steve didn't mention it at the funeral this morning.'

'He didn't know then. Daws had only just sprung it on him when he rang the first time.'

'When is he joining us?'

'Tomorrow.'

'But tomorrow's Saturday and it's our weekend off.'

'Yes, I know. Daws wondered if we minded Lindley coming for the weekend so we could get to know each other. It was tantamount to an order so what could I say? This morning was the first time I've so much as spoken to the man.'

'Is he coming by train?'

'No, flying. Daws has arranged some kind of military transport for him. I made it quite clear that he could get a taxi from the airport and the department could pay.'

'That's not very friendly,' I commented.

'Right now I don't *feel* all that friendly,' he snapped.

Just then Dawn returned with Justin. Our son is now eighteen months old and very much like his father. That is, of slender build — one day he will also be tall and wiry — with grey eyes, black hair and a rare line in rages. Dawn is very good with him but sometimes I know he is beyond her patience and she puts him in his cot and goes away, firmly shutting the door, until he has roared himself out of it. Hot, hungry and tired right now, he appeared to be well on the way to earning this temporary banishment. Carried in under his nanny's arm, for he was kicking and screaming and generally being so awful I was ashamed of him, he found himself fielded by a strong grip.

An impending and louder yell died in Justin's throat as he discovered himself eye to eye with the only person on this planet who can cope with him other than his paternal grandmother. Patrick has never smacked him. There was no need, a tiny vibrant shake said it all. Seconds later Justin had capitulated and was being cuddled, sucking his thumb.

'I'll get his tea ready,' I said, as I helped Dawn unload the car. 'I hope he hasn't been like this all day.'

'Goodness, no,' she said. 'The real trouble was being held up in a traffic jam at Mutley. I think there'd been an accident.' She hefted the pushchair out of the hatchback. 'I've been thinking about you all day. I can't believe Terry's dead. It's only a week since I spoke to him on the phone.'

I suddenly realised that she was near to tears.

'Was Alison at the funeral?' Dawn asked.

10

'No,' I replied. 'Now you come to mention it, she wasn't. Too upset, I expect.'

Dawn sniffed but I wasn't sure if this was a comment or a result of her distress. She knew of course that Patrick and I were connected with national security. This was vital for both her and Justin's sake. Patrick had made her aware that owing to the nature of our work there was a slight risk to her charge's safety. He had impressed on her the importance of never doing things to routine, never being in the same place at the same time every day or even every week. She had a car with a phone in it and had been given numbers she could use if she was out on her own with Justin and had any cause for concern. So far she had only had recourse to this once, when a man had tried to force his way into the car one evening when she had stopped at traffic lights. The result of pressing a few buttons on the phone had surprised Dawn greatly and the man even more. In no time at all, probably less than a minute — by which time the man had succeeded in wrenching open the door and was trying to drag her out — the police arrived in two squad cars, one motorbike, two on foot, one on horseback and an unknown number in a helicopter hovering overhead. No one had minded when the man had turned out to be merely a drunk vagrant, least of all when she produced the special ID card she carries. And for all this added responsibility and excitement Dawn is exceedingly well paid.

'Why should anyone want to kill Terry?' Dawn said, blowing her nose.

'It looks as though it might be a ghastly mistake,' I told her, anxious that she shouldn't worry that the danger was coming any closer. 'It's been suggested that the IRA might have been involved but Terry has never had anything to do with Northern Ireland.'

She turned away, again fumbling for a tissue. 'I just can't bear the thought . . .'

I comforted her as best I could, feeling helpless and angry in a numb sort of way. Naturally, I could understand her grief. She had met Terry only a few times, tending to stay in Devon with Justin, the country air being better for a young baby, but he had after all been good-looking and with a crazy sense of humour. I had a sudden thought that she might have

11

been fonder of him than I had imagined.

In the end Patrick brought us mugs of tea, telling us that the world had to go on and where the hell was the peanut butter so he could give Justin something to keep him going until someone fixed his tea?

Later, when Justin was in bed, I cooked the dinner even though no one was really hungry. Dawn usually prefers to prepare her own meals and eat in her room watching television, mainly because she always seems to be on a diet. But tonight she clearly had no heart to do anything at all so I opened a large bottle of Soave and invited her to eat with us. Alcohol is not a good idea when you are miserable but I knew that the wine would get Patrick talking – about anything, everything – and he is always worth listening to, even when less than happy.

When we were well into the cheese course, everyone still remarkably quiet, Dawn said, 'This MI5 man who's been murdered ... was he very important?' The story had been headlines in the evening papers and on the television news.

Patrick delicately speared a morsel of Stilton with the cheese knife and transferred it to his plate before answering. 'It depends, Miss Clark, who is doing the asking. Now, are you wearing the guise of a Red beneath a bed or honestly our true-blue Justin minder?' He glanced up with a hint of a twinkle in his eyes.

'True blue,' declared Dawn, who, joking apart, has signed the Official Secrets Act. It was imperative. Neither Patrick nor I can stand whispering and warning glances within a household. You have to be able to relax in your own home and there is very little that we do not discuss in her presence. The girl is most definitely not a security risk.

'He was important,' began Patrick slowly, 'in the sense that he had good contacts, the sort that come from going to the right schools and belonging to the best clubs. So far as I know he worked in connection with the positive vetting of firms engaged on sensitive defence contracts.'

'Would he have gone any higher?' I asked.

'According to Daws, probably not. One grade perhaps, no more. He would never have been made head of MI5.'

'In other words the system won't collapse without him.'

12

'Oh no. Not that anyone's *that* vital. It's deliberately structured that way.'

'Who would take over from you if you retired tomorrow?' Dawn wanted to know, probably emboldened by the wine.

'A very wicked man,' Patrick whispered conspiratorially. 'With stainless-steel dentures and a glass eye. The other one emits death rays. His right kneecap fires ground-to-air missiles, the left CS-gas canisters and plastic bullets. But only on Tuesdays and Thursdays.'

'And Mondays, Wednesdays and Fridays?' Dawn enquired loftily.

'In a cupboard having his batteries recharged. Don't ask me what he does at weekends — it's not at all nice. No, seriously, I haven't a clue. There must be quite a few people who could do it. Daws said at the start, when D12 was set up, that he wanted a soldier, mainly I think because he thought he'd have a lot in common with whoever it was and wouldn't have to explain overmuch what he wanted doing. It's a soldier's job in a way and, without sounding too conceited, he got a bonus with me because I'm rather good at asking people tricky questions as well as usually knowing when they're lying.'

I said, 'Terry was to have taken over eventually.' There seemed no point in not mentioning him just to try to keep ourselves cheerful, that was immoral.

'Yes,' Patrick agreed with a sad smile. 'And the first thing that had to be done to a graduate with high courage and an enquiring mind was to turn him into a soldier. Of course I didn't undertake to give him the initial training, he had spent six months with a regiment before I even clapped eyes on him. Then came the delicate part — undoing just a little of the "yes, sir, no, sir" thing that had been drummed into him so he started to think for himself, ask me *why*.'

'That was easy with Terry if I remember rightly,' I said.

'Oh yes. The enquiring mind conquered all, even me sometimes.'

'Are you worried about working with Steve?'

'Absolutely,' Patrick replied soberly. 'Worried as hell. He was given his own section and now it's been taken away from him for a while. He's older than Terry, an ex-chief petty officer, Royal Navy, and apparently in possession of a *very*

13

enquiring mind. But Daws was quite emphatic. He's mine to use and if he doesn't want to toe the line then ...' He shrugged and changed the subject and over dessert regaled us with stories from his early army days. I had heard most of them before but he is such a superb mimic that Dawn and I were helpless with laughter.

I felt guilty, laughing, but knew that Terry wouldn't have minded.

It seemed thoroughly churlish not to meet Steve so the next morning I left Patrick in charge of Justin — it being Dawn's day off — and drove the fifteen miles or thereabouts to Plymouth airport. He had already arrived, walking towards the taxi rank.

'Just in time,' I called.

It occurred to me as I watched him approach that I had not noticed when I had seen him before how like Terry he was. It was almost uncanny. He was the same height and build; slightly shorter than Patrick's lanky six foot two and with broader shoulders. Like Terry also he had thick light-brown hair and brown eyes.

We did not say much on the first few miles of the journey home once I had dispelled his discomfiture at Daws foisting him on us for the weekend. Once or twice I glanced quickly at him but the quiet profile gave nothing away, he seemed to be enjoying gazing at the scenery.

'How's the major?' Steve said all at once when we had left Tavistock behind and were heading over the open moor.

'Inwardly howling for blood,' I told him and wondering if my role of occasional fender between the men with whom I work would have to continue.

'That's a very honest thing to say.' He sounded slightly surprised.

'You have to be honest in this game,' I remarked. 'A lot depends on it.'

'I suppose you're right,' he replied a little grudgingly. 'He got on well with Meadows, I understand.'

I was silent for a moment, gathering my thoughts. 'I think you realise you're skating around reality when you make statements like that about my husband. No one gets on with

14

Patrick in the sense that life becomes a series of "hail fellow, well met's". You must have heard enough about him over the grapevine to know that. Terry had learned to treat him with the greatest respect for Patrick expects it. On the other hand I've seen them clowning to the point of lunacy. Five minutes later Patrick might have taken him apart for forgetting something he'd told him.'

'He's an army officer. Some army people are like that.'

'Possibly. But what you must remember is that Patrick would have been quite prepared to die for him if the need had arisen.' I pulled up by Lydford post office. 'I've just a couple of things to get. I won't be a minute.'

'It's a bit quaint these days . . . dying for people,' Steve said as I rummaged for my purse in my bag.

'Then you'll find Patrick quaint,' I said, finding what I was looking for. 'Horribly quaint.'

It was very hot when we arrived and Patrick was in the garden. Lounging in a deck chair he was wearing only shorts and Justin's sunhat tilted over his eyes against the brilliant midday sun − the rightful owner of the latter asleep in his pram in the shade of the apple tree. This, I realised, wincing for Steve's sake, was probably test number one.

'Mornin', major,' said Steve, apparently not at all fazed by this bizarre apparition.

The sunhat was pushed up a couple of inches and then removed altogether. Patrick had, I now saw, been genuinely dozing. Perhaps he hadn't intended to appear thus, the battle-scarred man.

Without doubt, Steve must have already known that Patrick had lost the lower part of his right leg following injuries received during the Falklands War. The only outward sign of this when he is fully dressed is a slight limp when tired, the artificial replacement being sophisticated and very, very expensive. But it is not a cosmetic affair, tending to catch the sun, blindingly, where it is made of metal and allowing glimpses of the garden through it where − with a view to keeping the limb lightweight − it is not of solid construction. The new assistant might also have been aware that a year previously he had suffered an appalling beating at the hands of self-styled Hell's Angels. Applied with the buckle ends of

15

studded belts, this left Patrick's back badly scarred. I have a feeling he will be scarred forever but he *is* regaining his former strength. Slowly.

The two shook hands.

'Sit down,' Patrick said, indicating a couple of deck chairs leaning on the back of the barn.

Steve obediently erected both chairs, placing one for me to sit on.

'Beer?'

'Thanks.'

'There are several tins cooling in the river. And some lemonade for Ingrid.'

When we were settled, the lady novelist clutching her can of drink and as taut as an overwound clock spring, Patrick said, 'Nothing like carrying your predecessor's coffin, eh?'

'He was a good friend,' Steve replied quietly, thus, by not flying off the handle, effortlessly passing test number two concerning comments deliberately designed to offend.

'Did he say anything about threats to himself?'

'Not to me. I guess he'd have gone straight to you with things like that.'

'What about the man who used to go out with his girlfriend, Alison?'

Steve uttered a humourless chuckle. 'That musclebound wally? He'd run a mile if you popped a balloon in his face.'

'Not the kind of bloke to mess around with explosives, then?'

'You've said it, boss.'

Patrick gave him one of his stock-in-trade heavy stares. 'Call me Patrick when we're just talking, sir when we're on a job and people can hear, and what the bloody hell you like behind my back.'

Steve's surprise showed, a little glimpse behind the calm exterior. I knew Patrick wouldn't be happy until he had discovered exactly what lay beneath, even if it meant Steve losing his temper. It occurred to me that Steve might be bent on doing the same.

'What d'you make of this Westfield business?' Steve asked.

'Have you any further gen? Daws just said that he'd been

battered to death with some kind of blunt instrument and so far the police hadn't found it.'

I began to feel slightly annoyed. After all, I was the third member of the team. They were talking as though I wasn't there. And here was I sitting sipping my lemonade like a good little girl when I would much rather have been putting a glass of dry white wine to good use.

'They had frogmen in the lily pond the last I heard,' Steve murmured. 'But Daws briefed me last night, I didn't see him before I left this morning. What was Westfield working on?'

'Before I answer that, tell me about your security clearance.'

'Didn't Daws make that clear to you?'

'No, for some reason he didn't mention it.'

A spark of irritation glittered briefly in Steve's eyes. 'Nevertheless I would have thought it pretty obvious that — '

'He was screwing around,' I interrupted, monumentally bored with both of them. I am a firm believer in bombshells.

'Westfield?' Patrick enquired politely.

'Westfield,' I agreed.

'Where did you get that gem of intelligence?'

'Babs. Daws's secretary.'

The look of scorn faded, to be replaced by one of interest. For obvious reasons Babs's gossip tends to have a firm grounding of truth in it. 'Any details?'

'No. You'll have to ask Babs.'

'Do you mind telling me how the subject arose?'

'Not at all. We were discussing which men in the building we'd even *consider* going to bed with.'

Steve choked on his beer.

'I see,' Patrick said weakly. 'And I take it Westfield wasn't on either of your lists.'

'I've never met him,' I said. 'But Babs had. She said he gave her the creeps. Toadsbreath, she called him.'

Whereupon Steve started to hum the first few bars of '*A frog he would a-wooing go*'. He desisted after Patrick had given him a look.

'Lunch?' I asked brightly, having resoundingly sabotaged what might have developed into an acrimonious first meeting between the two men.

17

Chapter Two

I was quite unrepentant. Right then emotions were running too high for anything useful to be achieved. So I prepared a good lunch and then pleaded, distraught, that as I had forgotten about a starter for dinner would they try for a few brown trout in the river? (I have a theory that men never fall out when they're fishing.) Amazingly, they went off, meek as lambs, with rod and line. And despite nodding off in the sultry afternoon heat, they caught seven.

I continued with low cunning, giving them, after the fish, a steak, kidney and oyster pie, a bottle of fine claret to accompany it. Cheese followed; Shropshire Blue sent by a friend and mature farmhouse Cheddar. We finished with raspberry sorbet. I placed a bottle of ten-year-old Glenlivet on the dresser and then went into the kitchen to make coffee and load the dishwasher, humming lightly.

It worked. When I took the coffee into the living room Patrick was crying with laughter at a navy yarn Steve had just told him. Steve repeated it for my benefit.

'No one could ever work out how the captain's steward managed to climb up to the bridge without spilling a drop of the old man's cocoa. Even in the roughest seas he'd arrive with the mug brimming, not a drop spilt. Then one day when he'd had a few too many pints in the mess someone asked him for the secret. He said he took a big mouthful when he left the galley and spat it back in the mug just before he arrived at his destination.'

For the sake of the captain's peace of mind I shall not reveal the name of the ship in which this gem of ingenuity served.

'How do you feel,' said Patrick thoughtfully, a while later when he had recounted a few stories of his own, 'about a little sortie into the countryside around Petworth tomorrow?'

'To the scene of the murder?' I asked. 'Daws said – '

'I know what Daws said,' he interrupted placidly, always genial after a few measures of his favourite tipple. 'I was thinking of an undercover operation. Itinerants perhaps. A fairground group that had lost their way? A bearded lady? No? All right, no.'

'But you *are* serious,' Steve said, not at all sure.

'Oh yes, I'm always serious,' Patrick observed, straight-faced.

'We'd never pass as hippies.'

'My son, we would pass as anything,' he was told with a beatific smile. 'Ask Ingrid. She will tell you that we have been bikers, tramps, security advisers and tourists. All kinds of things. But I think I know what is at the back of your mind. There is no point in turning up at what one gathers is a high-class establishment in the kind of guise that will only ensure we'll get a dose of birdshot in our backsides. Whatever it is must *fit.*'

'Fencing contractors?' I suggested. 'You've done that before too.'

'On a Sunday?'

'Surely there are emergency services for fields fronting on to roads.'

Patrick studied Steve's broad shoulders. 'Can you use a maul? You know, the – '

'I know what a maul is,' Steve cut in, smiling. 'A bloody great hammer that's used to bang in the post with. Yes, I can. My second cousin bought a farm in Wales and there always seems to be a lot of fencing to do when I visit him.'

Patrick got on the phone to the warehouse in London where all kinds of vehicles and equipment are kept, well maintained for the sole use of the security services. If he had wanted them he could have had an army lorry, a British Telecom lookalike van, a fork-lift truck or a low loader. Just about anything. He settled for the battered Land-Rover pick-up he had used on the previous occasion and asked for it to be loaded with two peeled ash end posts, one and a half

19

dozen smaller posts, sheep netting and a roll of straining wire.
'You have to have the right kit in case you're challenged,'
Patrick said as he hung up. 'But of course you both know
that.'

'I do a nice line in repairing phones myself,' Steve said. 'I
had to go on a three-day course with the folk who really do the
job so I don't foul things up when I'm fiddling around.'

'You're modest,' Patrick said. 'I happen to know that
you're D12's star of the show when it comes to bugs, taps and
listening devices.'

'What about me?' I asked into this glow of mutual
admiration. 'What shall I do?'

Patrick frowned. 'Fencing blokes don't usually have camp
followers.'

'I think I'd worked that out all by myself,' I commented
tartly.

He gave it some thought. 'Drive down — not with us of
course — and case the joint, as they say in bad movies. I leave
it entirely up to you how you do it. The easiest cover is to be
yourself, a writer gathering material and atmosphere from a
village.'

'In view of the fact that we've been ordered to be there early
next week anyway — ' Steve began.

'I want to watch them for twenty-four hours when they're
not expecting to be watched,' Patrick explained. 'And, to put
your mind at rest, I haven't been *forbidden* to arrive until
Monday, Daws simply made it plain that the police want a
clear road until then.'

He briefed us, informing us that the house was called
Bitterns. It was set in several acres of grounds. Jan, John
Westfield's sister, had married a property developer by the
name of Miles Hurst. The marriage was Hurst's third, his
first wife having been killed in a car crash, the second
divorcing him when she had discovered that he was having
an affair with Jan, who at the time had been a model.
Patrick concluded by saying that, from the tone of the
colonel's voice when he had mentioned the young lady's
choice of career, he had gathered that she had in fact been
less a model and more a page-three girl. Sometimes Daws
can be infuriatingly coy.

'Set your alarm for five,' Patrick said, permitting himself another drop of whisky.

Since Justin's birth and the arrival of his nanny, our cottage is simply too small, the third bedroom being where I write. To avoid moving we have had the barn on the other side of the courtyard converted into living accommodation. There is a single large living room on the ground floor with a tiny kitchen at one end screened by plants. Above this are two bedrooms with sloping ceilings, and a shower and toilet.

'You've forgotten something,' I said, having shifted Justin, sound asleep, from his nursery to our room in the barn. 'I gave Dawn extra time off.'

'I haven't,' Patrick replied from the inside of the sweater he was pulling off. He emerged, tousled. 'Lynne said she'd have him until Dawn comes back just after lunch.'

'But we're going from here at six a.m.!'

'She doesn't mind. I asked her earlier while you were in the bath. Anyway, she's a GP's wife. She's used to everything being a bit chaotic.'

Lynne does often step into the breach and always says she loves looking after Justin, her own children having grown up. I nevertheless made a resolution to buy her something rather special when I next had the opportunity.

I refrained from telling Patrick that he sometimes uses people, even when he got into bed and didn't ask if I was tired before making it clear what was uppermost in his mind. Sometimes men want sex because they want sex. Not because they particularly love you at that moment or because you are their wife, mistress or whatever and lovemaking has become a habit. They don't even need to be comforted or forget their worries for a while. They are male and you are female and available and that's that. Sometimes females have to put up with it.

The old chestnut cob had a mouth like iron but the day was hot and he felt lazy so this state of affairs was not bothering me unduly. I had wondered, as I gave the woman at the riding school the information that I had not done any serious riding for ten years, whether she would haul out an animal that hadn't been ridden for ten years. But Warwick was very good,

21

I had been assured, 'just don't let him eat the hedges as he is prone to colic'. He had attempted a couple of cunning forays into the hawthorn but had desisted after I had reminded him with my riding crop that such fare was very bad for him.

The village of Longcoombe, five miles from Petworth, was very pretty. It was exactly the sort of village to which a writer might repair to imbue herself with the characteristics of rural Sussex. The High Street had probably been photographed a hundred times to illustrate calendars for the month of June; thatched brick and flint cottages, a war memorial with a tiny garden around it, a horse trough planted with pale-blue pansies and yellow snapdragons. Regrettably, one end of the street had been ruined by the construction of an ugly modern shopping precinct. But soon this would be partially hidden when the newly planted trees grew, at present no more than green lollipops.

While quickly looking at the Ordnance Survey map for the area that morning with Patrick and Steve, I had noticed that Bitterns was virtually encircled by what were probably bridle paths. So I had raked out my riding hat, breeches and boots from the bottom of the wardrobe and put them in my car. The men had left first in Patrick's car. Arrangements had been made for them to take delivery of the pick-up at Pulborough, some seven miles from Petworth, where Patrick had booked us in at the Martlet Arms Hotel.

It was now two p.m. and to be honest I was tired after the long drive. I had to force myself to concentrate as I approached what I knew to be the entrance to the house I was looking for. Consulting the map now of course was out of the question but I had committed the important details to memory.

There was a police car parked near the wide wrought-iron gates. I tried to exhibit just normal curiosity while taking in as much as I could. It was a Regency-style house just visible through an avenue of chestnut trees that bordered the long straight drive. There were about ten bedrooms, I guessed. A few yards farther along and over the neat beech hedge I got a much better view, unimpeded by trees. A wing that had at one time almost certainly been a stable block and coach house had been turned into garaging for four cars, one of which, a Rolls-

22

Royce, was being hosed down by a man wearing blue overalls. Around the side of the house I could see what was probably the top of a covered swimming pool.

Two hundred yards farther on I came to a road junction. I turned left on to a wide verge which, judging by the track down the centre pitted with hoof prints, was a regular route for the riding school. Warwick seemed to think so anyway and broke into a trot. I reined him back as I prefer to choose my own paces. Before you know where you are with some horses they've galloped you all the way home.

I knew from my map that a bridle path meandered through the woods to the rear and side of Bitterns. I hoped this would provide a better view than where I was now. The road curved away from the house and the hedges were overgrown and impossible to see over. I passed a farm, an untidy nightmare of a place awash with manure, the yard littered with broken machinery and sheets of rusting corrugated iron. A sorry-looking collie tied to a length of frayed rope lifted the corner of its lip in a silent snarl. Then it barked and a man — presumably the owner of this example of bucolic ecstasy — shouted at it from within a byre.

I pushed Warwick on, anxious to get on with the job in hand, and he broke into a slow, bouncing canter, his head in the air, snorting. We progressed thus for a short distance, mostly sideways, cars hooting and their drivers shouting not so helpful suggestions. I sat tight, making growling noises. My mount soon became tired of these antics and decided to behave himself for a while. Truly, I thought, tomorrow I shall be so stiff I won't be able to move.

Warwick found the path for us, swinging without warning into a narrow gap in a hedge. We were met by a large cloud of flies that rose from a stinking pool in a gateway and he had an answer to that too. We left them behind. It was a memorable gallop, mostly because I couldn't stop him. All I could do was lean forward on his neck to avoid being swept from the saddle by low branches. I realised that I was enjoying myself immensely; the horse was too old a hand to do anything really suicidal.

We tore along, my mission almost forgotten. I had no idea of the whereabouts of Patrick and Steve, the former having hoped he could work so as to keep close surveillance of the house. The plan was that he would find a suitable stretch of poor fencing and start work. If challenged by the owner of the land, he would discover that repairs were being carried out on the wrong farm. And of course, the old fence having been removed, there was nothing for it but to replace it. Patrick has never yet found a farmer who objected to his finishing the job gratis.

The path left the cover of the trees and joined another, a wider one going uphill, fields on either side. There were a lot of puddles and Warwick jumped them all. Then, ahead, I saw the pick-up, rolls of wire and a tumbled pile of fence posts on the ground. There was no room to get round and suddenly Warwick seemed to remember an awful lot about cross-country courses. His head came up again, ears pricked, and he bounded towards the obstacle as though it was the Irish Bank at Hickstead.

And, right at the last moment, Patrick dashed from behind the pick-up waving his arms.

It was one of those ploughing stops that horses do in cowboy films. My out-of-condition riding muscles were no match for this kind of activity and I found myself airborne. There was a collision with something soft and yet solid and then I met rather a lot of mud.

Something was underneath me in the mud. Or, to be more precise, someone.

Steve.

'Ingrid . . .' Patrick began remarkably patiently, holding Warwick's reins, when Steve and I had picked ourselves up and I had apologised. Behind the one word his tone spoke reams. We were D12's crack team. Any doubts that Steve might have about the efficiency of a man-and-wife partnership must be dispelled and we had to show him that we were a force to be reckoned with. Our future working relationship depended heavily on this. And lastly, we were engaged on a surveillance assignment where not drawing attention to ourselves was of paramount importance.

'You had no business to block the entire path with this stuff,' I said, aggrieved. 'There are other people who ride along here besides me. If you hadn't rushed out like that he'd have jumped everything.'

24

There was a short silence broken only by Steve trying to spit the mud from his mouth. Then he began to laugh. It was the sort of laugh that promised to go on for quite a while so I snatched the reins from Patrick, mounted and rode off. I could still hear him laughing when I was a couple of hundred yards away. They were still in view when I met a woman riding a handsome bay thoroughbred.

'You've had a fall,' she said sympathetically, pulling up.

I complained bitterly about men who block public rights of way with fencing materials and we agreed that, sometimes, the male sex are beneath contempt.

'Do I know you?' she asked, eyeing me closely.

'Probably not,' I said. 'But you might have seen my photo on the dust jacket of a book.' I introduced myself, adding that I was on holiday in the district.

'Ingrid Langley,' she repeated. 'How exciting to meet a writer!' She nudged her mount closer and held out a hand. 'I'm Jessica Campbell. I enjoyed your books *One for Sorrow* and *Two for Joy*. Is there another story about the Harrison family in the pipeline?'

'Coming out next month,' I told her. '*Three Bells for the Cat*. But it's the last one about the Harrisons, I'm afraid. I'm working on a crime story at the moment — I haven't done one since *The Brandy Glass Murder* some years ago.'

As I had hoped, this brought the subject around to the one in which I was really interested. Jessica glanced involuntarily down into the grounds of Bitterns which lay in full view slightly below us. Indeed, the ground had risen more sharply than I had thought and the rear of the house was visible above a stand of young beech trees that marked the boundary, the northern one.

'A man was killed ... murdered at that house on Thursday,' Jessica said. 'At least, his body was found there. The police aren't sure yet whether he was killed there or somewhere else.' She gave a little shudder. 'Such a ghastly thing to happen. I mean, you read books about murders and it's all rather fun. And then it happens on your own doorstep. He worked for MI5. You must have read about it in the papers.'

'So you live close by?'

25

'No distance away at all. As you can see, there's a field between the house and the next one. Going towards Long-coombe, that is. A retired RAF officer lives there. I live on the other side of the road about halfway towards the village. You can't really see the house from the road.'

'Did you know the man who was murdered?'

'Only by sight. He was the brother of Jan Hurst. That's her and her husband's house. Poor Jan. It was she who found him, apparently . . . in her bedroom. He was so horribly battered she didn't even realise who it was until she saw his wristwatch. She'd given it to him and had it inscribed with his initials.'

'Are the Hursts close friends of yours?' I hoped I wasn't sounding too nosy.

She gave a little moue. 'At one time. For a short while. But not what you'd call close friends. They don't really make friends. To be honest one must say that they've gone out of their way not to. They do have friends, though. But not from round here. There are parties sometimes and weekend gatherings and everyone's come to the conclusion that the people are from London.'

I could imagine the resentment. Retired RAF officers and the likes of Jessica Campbell would not like being treated as though they were country bumpkins. 'Was anything stolen from the house? Perhaps he disturbed thieves.'

Jessica checked her horse sharply as it was fidgeting. 'Not according to Grace. She's my daily woman and her sister Rose works for the Hursts. That was one of the first things Rose had to do, check that none of the silver and china ornaments were missing. Miles Hurst has a superb collection of old English china. Nothing had been taken.'

'Is Rose that well acquainted with it?' I wondered aloud.

'Oh yes.' Jessica shot me a smiling but slightly accusing look. 'Just because people help others look after their houses it doesn't mean that they're only charladies. Grace and Rose are retired professional women and have a lot of lovely things of their own. China and glass is one of Rose's interests. No, nothing had been touched. Neither had Jan's jewellery or the safe.' She looked at her watch. 'Look, I must be going. I said I'd ring my mother and she does fret so if I'm even a few

26

minutes late with the call. Our chats mean a lot to her now she can't go out so much.'

'Sorry to have kept you,' I said, a little chastened by her remarks.

Jessica gazed over to where Patrick was holding a post while Steve swung the mawl. 'If those oafs so much as look at me I'll give them a piece of my mind. The farmer is the sort to employ types like that. Everything on the cheap.'

I guessed from this that we were still within the realms of the filthy steading I had seen earlier.

'Give me a ring,' she called, reining back her horse after a few yards. 'Come over for coffee. That's if you'd like to.'

I said that I would love to and we parted after she had given me her phone number.

She had no trouble with the fencing contractors. Both stopped working as she reached them, Patrick doffing his filthy seaman's hat as she went by. It was too far away for me to see if he was smiling at her but when she had gone the look he gave me, I'm prepared to swear, was a raffish leer.

Pondering on the leer and deeming myself forgiven, I consulted my map once more, Warwick now apparently content to plod along on a loose rein after his exertions. I had just under an hour of my ride left and the distance was not great so if I continued in a circle I had time for a little snooping.

The western extremity of Bitterns was marked by a brick wall some seven feet in height. This abutted on to a narrow lane that joined the path that I was riding along and then swung away uphill in a northerly direction. I turned left on to it. After a hundred yards or so I came to a postern gate set in the wall, rank tall grass growing undisturbed on the verge. I edged Warwick up close and lifted the latch of the gate. It wasn't locked and when I pushed it opened a couple of inches.

There was absolutely nothing to be gained by entering and I was hardly of an age where I could pretend to be searching for a lost ball. Peeping through the gap I could see what appeared to be one corner of a neglected orchard. Then, walking towards me along an overgrown path, I saw a man. For a moment I almost panicked as he appeared to be staring straight at me. But it was impossible that he could see me from fifty yards away as I had opened the gate only a little and was gazing at him through the foliage of a Russian vine that was festooned all over this part of the wall.

He stopped and I held my breath. I dared not shut the gate and move off because he would hear the horse's hooves and realise that someone had been spying on him. After a few seconds careful surveillance of his surroundings, he left the path and went through the trees towards a lean-to shed that backed on to an interior wall that I guessed bordered a vegetable or fruit garden. He went inside and I closed the gate, gathered the reins and rode away, keeping to the grass verge.

He was not one to forget quickly. I was almost certain that he was the same man whom I had seen hosing down the Rolls-Royce.

'If this was a film, Warwick,' I said to the large ginger-coloured ears, one of which swivelled in my direction, 'and not real life, that man would not be a chauffeur and general handyman. He looked as though he is handy with his fists. No, in fiction he'd be a minder working for a ruthless man. I wonder.'

Chapter Three

A police car was parked outside the riding stables. For a moment I was a little alarmed but then I realised that the visit could have nothing to do with my opening a gate in a wall and peeping through. I dismounted and led Warwick back into his box. While I was removing his tack, a constable came to lean on the half door.

'Ride regularly here, do you?' he asked.

'This is the first time,' I replied. 'And most people introduce themselves.'

He flushed, I observed by glancing around Warwick's neck, his rather dour expression assuming a stubborn look.

'Parker,' he responded shortly. 'John Parker.'

I gave him my name and said, 'Are you investigating the murder at Bitterns?'

'No, as a matter of fact I'm enquiring into the theft of two horses. So I'm interested in strangers and people who haven't been seen at riding establishments before.'

I heaved the saddle from Warwick's broad back and placed it on the door, forcing Parker to take a step backwards. 'I haven't room at home for a horse,' I told him with my best smile. 'You're looking at a writer who's soaking up rural atmosphere for her next novel.'

He didn't thaw. 'Did you notice anyone behaving suspiciously? You know . . . hanging around fields of livestock. There have been a lot of cattle stolen around here as well lately.'

'Only some men mending a fence,' I said, slaying with great difficulty an unholy temptation to give him the kind of

29

information that might result in Patrick and Steve being picked up for questioning. Deep within me there is a very strong streak of irresponsibility. But it was almost worth it just to see the look on Patrick's face when he was unloaded at the police station.

'About this murder — ' I began.

'Would you care to describe them to me?' said PC Parker.

'Who?'

'The men mending the fence.' His gaze was now drifting over my muddied clothing.

'Oh, them. I didn't notice really. I was going rather fast.'

'Is that when you had a fall?' He was positively oozing suspicion now.

I collected saddle, bridle and my whip and went to open the door but he didn't move aside to allow me passage. 'Yes, I fell off. Warwick shied at some posts they'd left on the path.'

'So if they were close by you must have had a good look at them.'

I was handling this appallingly badly. 'You don't really notice people when you've had a bit of a shake-up.'

Just then Patrick drove the pick-up into the yard.

He had opened the driver's door and put a foot out when the proprietor of the stables, a young woman with a wonderful head of red hair, shouted at him out of the office window.

'Hey! You can't park that there! I've a ride due back at any moment.'

Patrick wound down the window. 'Want any fencing done, darlin'?'

Heaven only knows why he joined the army instead of going on the stage.

'Is that one of them?' Parker hissed, right in my ear, making me jump.

You'll go far, I thought. 'Yes,' I told him, working on the principle that if I lied and he discovered otherwise it would only make things worse. And in reality, of course, and not in my imagination, the worse that *could* happen was that Patrick would have to show his MI5 ID card. This did not mean that he would necessarily so choose. Whatever happened it seemed that my name might be mud with a capital M.

Frankly, right now, the jewel in the crown of the security

30

services was way over the top: chewing gum, insolent wink, inane grin. It was enough to make any self-respecting woman want to throw the manure heap at him, wholesale. Redhead, whose name I was shortly to discover was Libby, did not disgrace her sex.

'Get yourself and that damn rust bucket out of my yard! No, I most certainly don't want any fencing – ' She stopped in mid-sentence, having noticed about the same time as I did the blood-soaked handkerchief wrapped around his left hand. 'What have you done to your hand?'

It was given a cursory glance. 'You can't win 'em all.'

'That's no answer,' she scolded.

He glanced around the yard, took in the presence of PC Parker and then pretended to notice me. 'We met earlier,' he stated, grin back in place.

'How could I forget?' I responded, realising that he was probably taking advantage of what must be literally a painful situation.

'Come in the office,' Libby commanded. 'You need a plaster on that hand.'

'It's nothing,' Patrick replied.

Her eyebrows rose. 'I insist. If you bleed to death here it'll make an awful mess on the concrete.'

Patrick chuckled, climbed out of the pick-up and followed her into the office. I went along, carrying Warwick's saddlery; the tack room was next door. Parker brought up the rear, thumbing through his notebook.

'That's horrible!' Libby was exclaiming when I put my head round the office door.

It was a deep cut in the fleshy part of his thumb, received, Patrick explained, when he was clearing away long grass. A broken bottle had been in the undergrowth.

'Where were your gloves?' Libby asked repressively.

'Took them off to drink coffee and forgot to put them on again,' said the patient.

Libby led him over to a sink in one corner and put his hand under the tap to wash off the blood. 'I think young John suspects that you're involved with the theft of my horses,' she said with a sideways smile. To me she said, 'The first-aid box is in that cupboard. You don't mind, do you? Are you in a hurry?'

31

I said that I had all day and found what she had asked for. Through all this Parker was endeavouring to look like a pillar of the law.

'Horses!' Patrick snorted. 'And don't I spend nearly all my working life keeping the damn things with their owners? Stealing horses? What would I want with — '

'Your name, sir?' Parker interrupted, pencil poised.

'Holy Mother!' said Patrick, who had dropped the Cockney accent in favour of an Irish one. 'And what are all good men from the Emerald Isle called? It's Paddy, man, and I'm proud of it.'

At this point Parker removed his hat as though his head felt hot. He was saved from further overheating when his radio demanded his presence elsewhere and he left, promising to return. Glancing out into the stable yard I saw him take the number of the pick-up before he drove away.

'You are a rogue,' said Libby, pouring some antiseptic lotion into the cut. She ignored Patrick's sudden intake of breath, squeezed on some sticky ointment from a tube, the application of which caused him to expel the air from his lungs through his teeth, hissing, and slapped on a large plaster, the bleeding by this time having stopped. In Libby's presence, one gathered, nothing would dare step out of line.

'Thanks,' said Patrick when he could speak. 'About this fencing — '

'My fences are magnificent,' was the stern reply. 'Besides, I don't employ the kind of people who forget to wear protective gloves.' But she was smiling, looking at him below lowered eyelashes.

'I met a woman called Jessica Campbell,' I said, wondering if Libby was doing her lady-with-the-lamp act because she fancied him. 'We were talking about the murder.'

'Everyone's talking about the murder,' Libby said, handing me the first-aid things to put back in the box. 'He didn't live here, though. Thank God.'

'So he didn't ride, then?'

'Not *horses*,' Libby said meaningfully.

I was receiving loud and clear from Libby that it was about time I paid and went on my way. It is a unique sensation,

32

knowing that another woman is about to proposition your husband.

'Eight pounds?' I enquired, finding my purse.

'Six as he's old and you fell off,' Libby replied.

'*That's* why I fell off,' I told her starchily, pointing at Patrick.

I drove away but not very far, just until I was out of sight of the stables. Five minutes later the pick-up turned out of the entrance, drove past me and then pulled up about fifty yards up the road.

'Well?' I said when I had drawn up near him and approached on foot.

'Well, what?' said owl-like innocence.

Sometimes he makes me *seethe*. 'Patrick...' I began.

He smiled in the way he knows makes me seethe. 'I'm meeting her later for a drink in the Swan. When we've finished work. Info,' he added, perceiving that I was about to explode. 'She knows all the local gossip and I want to pump her about the Hursts.'

'So what will happen when we roll up tomorrow morning as Major Gillard and full team from MI5?' I enquired icily.

'What does it matter? The only people likely to be miffed by a little preliminary snooping on our part are the police.'

'I take it you didn't have all this planned.'

'Of course not. How could I? I thought of going to a local doctor but then decided to find you first.' He gazed at me steadily. 'Why don't you get changed at the hotel and meet Steve and me later for a meal? Well away from here, though. I've told Steve that I don't want us all to be seen together anywhere near this village until we break our own cover. Give me a ring at the Swan at eight.' He glanced around quickly and then kissed me.

Orders are orders.

I didn't feel like staying in the hot and stuffy hotel on such a beautiful evening so I drove out to the village of Hampton. This was on the other side of Pulborough to Longcoombe, to the east, the two villages some ten miles distant. The Dog and Whistle had a garden by a river but within a minute the mosquitoes and midges made life unbearable so I went into the public bar. By then it was about seven-forty-five.

I was by the bar, ordering another orange juice with ice, when Steve strode in and came to stand by me.

'Scram,' I whispered. 'We're not supposed to meet up yet.'

'Chance meeting,' he countered. 'Besides, I'm apologising for having you off your nag, aren't I?'

I was given my drink and found a table in a corner. To my alarm he came and sat down.

'Go away,' I said, trying to keep my voice down. 'If Patrick finds you here he'll hit the roof.'

'No one'll find us,' Steve said when he came up for air from his pint of bitter. 'This is a good ten miles from Longcoombe and he's in the Swan with that riding-stables woman.'

'You followed me, didn't you?'

'What if I did?' he said lightly.

'What are you trying to prove?'

'Nothing.'

'You're not very impressed, are you? By us . . . Patrick and me.'

'I wouldn't go so far as to say that,' he said unconvincingly. After a short silence he added, 'There *is* something I think you ought to know.'

'What?' I snapped.

'The major . . . he cried when he cut himself.'

'You mean he sat down and had a good howl,' I stated baldly.

'No, of course not.' I had shocked him but he was nevertheless puzzled by my reaction.

'Look –' I began, about to tell him that I had to phone Patrick.

'You don't have to explain. Everyone has their off days.'

I almost threw his beer over him. It was quite useless to tell him that Patrick is a very sensitive man and he could not be expected to get over Terry's death quickly. Terry had been his protégé and a lot more besides. When you have worked closely with someone and been in tight corners with them, learned to rely on their courage and integrity, the relationship becomes special. In a way Patrick had almost lost a son.

'Don't worry about it,' said Steve urbanely.

When Steve was halfway through his second pint Patrick

34

blundered in, somewhat the worse for drink. He was still wearing his filthy working clothes and, from the state of them, had fallen in more than one ditch since I had last seen him.

At least, this was what our fellow drinkers were being led to believe.

This was when Steve made his biggest mistake. He stood up politely to make room for Patrick to sit down.

'You bastard,' said Patrick softly as though Steve had in fact made off with his date.

I saw Steve's Adam's apple bob as he swallowed nervously.

'Clear off,' I said to Patrick, praying that Steve would think himself out of his predicament.

Patrick stood there, swaying belligerently.

'You heard me,' I said louder. 'Haven't you done enough damage for one day? I thought you were joking when you said you'd meet me in here − just being offensive after having me off the horse. I'm not with your confounded friend. He sat down and started making a nuisance of himself.'

Terry would have got himself out of this, I thought, waiting for the inevitable. I felt sorry for Steve and yet at the same time furious with him. He had been working inside pseudo-telephone vans for too long.

The inevitable happened. A long arm shot out, grabbed Steve by the collar and hauled him outside. This was just as well for the landlord was moving towards the phone on the bar. I also left, murmuring apologies to nearby customers.

I got in the car and manoeuvred it until I could see what was happening in one of the driving mirrors. It was not spectacular as such things go and no one sitting outside the pub ran inside to call the police. A few youths hooted encouragement to Steve as they witnessed what was a very bad example to their own behaviour. At last Steve picked himself up for the third time and both men got in the pick-up. It roared off.

I followed and when I caught up with them parked in a lane that was signposted to Wisborough Green, World War Three was in progress inside the cab.

'Magic!' Steve was saying, choking with anger as he dabbed at a split lip. I was astounded at how otherwise unmarked he was. 'And when I turn up on Monday morning everybody will know where my thick lip came from. The little erk who disobeyed orders and got his block knocked off.'

'Do you see it differently?' Patrick asked smoothly.

Steve's rather good-looking features suffused with red and for a moment I thought he would lose control of himself. 'I'm supposed to have reached a stage in my career when I can think for myself. There was no harm in my wandering into a pub in the next village.'

'Nevertheless I told you not to be seen with Ingrid.'

'Explain what harm it did. Anyone who saw us from Longcoombe would assume that I was saying sorry for making her fall off the horse.'

'Never assume,' Patrick told him. 'And if I remember correctly it was me who caused her to fall off. Never assume. Never imagine that no one's watching. Never disobey orders when you're working for me. Not unless you can think your way out of it. Why were you watching me in the Swan?'

'I don't think you saw me,' Steve said, dangerously politely.

Patrick sighed. 'A lot of the things you've heard about me over the grapevine are lies. I've no doubt there are a few exaggerations as well. But some of the stories are true. I have exceptionally good eyesight, sense of smell and hearing. I heard you ask for a drink in the next bar – the counter's adjoin, if you remember, with only an archway between the two rooms. I'll ask you again. Why were you keeping tabs on me?'

Steve was silent, dabbing his lip.

'Did you think someone was watching *me*? Or were you following an idea of your own? Do talk. Otherwise I'll only assume you want to carry on where we left off outside the pub.'

'You would too,' Steve said. 'That story wasn't a lie – how you use your fists to get your own way.'

'Truly,' Patrick murmured, getting out, 'I think I'm only trying to thump some sense into you.'

Steve tumbled out of the cab with a sob, probably of rage.

'This is what you should have done in the pub,' Patrick told him, dancing out of range. 'But you dropped your cover. You bloody well stood up and waited for me to sit down. If you're going to disobey me then you must think on your feet to keep the shop front intact. You were so busy congratulating yourself that you didn't even notice me follow you out of the Swan.'

Patrick ducked or parried the first few punches and then deemed one survivable and took it manfully on the side of the jaw. Sitting in the road, shaking his head to clear it, he suddenly chuckled.

'I'm a bastard,' Steve whispered, kneeling down. 'You're not fit to be roughed up.'

'That's what you should have done in the pub,' Patrick repeated. 'Or, *much* better than that, bawled me out right at the beginning that you didn't want to work for me this side of hell. Your resentment stopped you thinking altogether.' He stood up. 'Now tell me why you were watching me tonight.'

'I just wanted to study your methods,' Steve said, no louder.

'That's OK. I believe you. Just remember in future that I expect to know where people are. If they aren't where I thought they were and I have to drop what I'm doing to make sure that my staff aren't being fed to someone's pet shark, then the job suffers. Get that?'

'I get it,' Steve said. 'But — '

'There are no buts,' Patrick said. 'Those are the terms. I've no objection to explaining my methods until I'm blue in the face in quiet moments.'

'Terry wasn't a yes man.'

'No. He would have been a lot better than you in the pub though. He would have hit me first and pretended to be plastered. No one hits a drunk. If you'd played the drunk you wouldn't have a fat lip now.'

'It sounds as though we'll be in competition with each other,' Steve said with a wry grin.

'Isn't that what you wanted?' Patrick said.

'It's a risk,' I said later when Patrick and I were in our hotel room. 'Terry was only just getting to the stage where you were allowing him to challenge your authority.'

'Steve's basically a level-headed bloke,' Patrick replied

37

imperturbably. 'What we saw today was merely him trying me out. I was waiting for it to happen. It always does.'

I changed the subject. 'What did you find out from Libby?'

He laughed from inside a towel, drying his hair, and went over to where his working jacket was draped over a chair. 'She gave me this.' He held up a small object between thumb and forefinger that he had taken from one of the pockets.

'Her doorkey? How touching.'

He ignored the sarcasm. 'In her view the Hursts are a rum lot. They keep themselves to themselves and don't get involved with anything that goes on in the village. Libby reckons Jan is far from happy even though they've only been married for ten months. I didn't get round to asking her about Westfield.'

'Did she say what Miles was like?'

'Fairly odious. According to Libby he's short, fat and balding and she can't see for the life of her why Jan married him unless it was for his money. And, as I've just said, it doesn't seem to be going well. She reckons the guy who drives him around in his Roller is in fact a minder. He's six foot five, built like a rhino and with an intellect to match. Libby's fairly obsessed with their wealth. She's never seen Jan wearing the same outfit twice.'

'A large pinch of salt with that,' I commented. 'A well-dressed woman can wear the same thing lots of times with different accessories and other women are still jealous.'

'I wasn't totally blinded by Libby's winsomeness,' he pointed out, smiling.

'We can check up on Hurst,' I said. 'But he must be above board or surely Westfield would have steered clear of them. In his job he couldn't – '

'Rhubarb,' said my spouse placidly. 'OK, in his job he had to keep his nose clean but he could hardly tell his sister whom to marry and refuse to ever visit her again if she got hitched to a godfather.'

'But the directives – ' I started to say.

'We all know about the directives. But in practice it can't always work. You're not telling me that if your mother got married again and the bloke had funny Swiss bank accounts you'd cut her dead in the street.'

38

The idea of any man being rash enough to engage with my mother now in holy matrimony robbed me of speech for a moment.

'Are you staying?' Patrick asked. 'I'd like you here in the morning but you don't have to be. Steve can take notes and keep his eyes open.'

'Wouldn't you rather he sleuthed in the background and kept his eyes open?'

'Yes. But I know you want to get on with *Echoes of Murder*.'

'Thinking of your 10 per cent?'

'Ingrid. . .' he said in pained tones.

'Sorry. I was teasing. Are you going into Bitterns tonight?'

He laughed in the way he does when he's taken aback. 'You're pinching my methods.'

'I know,' I said. 'Charm, retreat and then pounce. Are you?'

'Yes. At about two a.m. When they're safely in bed.'

'I didn't notice any dogs but the place must be bristling with alarms.'

Patrick snorted contemptuously; domestic burglar alarms hold few terrors for him.

'And there's the minder. They don't need dogs with him around.'

'I'll throw him a bone.'

By the time Patrick had showered, shaved and changed it was too late to wander around the town looking for somewhere to eat so we dined in the hotel restaurant, a subterranean affair residing darkly within the original beer cellars of the building and from which it seemed we would find our way out only with great difficulty, let alone be seen by anyone from Longcoombe.

'Are we bugging the Hursts' phone?' Steve asked over the cheese course.

Patrick pretended to be alarmed, drawing up his jacket collar before he replied. 'Perhaps you shouldn't have said that. Dodgy subject, phone tapping. Now you have mentioned it I'll have to say no.'

'Right,' said Steve. 'Sorry to have mentioned it.'

'Bring your little black bag with you,' Patrick said out of

the corner of his mouth. 'The most fascinating aspect of the job will be to see if there are any bugs there already.'

'I hadn't thought of that,' Steve said. 'Yes, quite.'

I said, 'I really can't see the point in breaking in when you'll be on the doorstep officially at nine the following morning with every right to carve the house into small pieces if you so choose.'

'They know I'm coming to investigate. Yes?'

I nodded.

'So they might not hide anything away they don't want me to see until the morning.'

'The police will have been over the whole place very thoroughly, surely?'

'The police aren't interested in the same things as we are. Ingrid, you know all this. Why are you going on about it?'

'Perhaps I'm worried about you both,' I persisted. 'I've a funny feeling about the Hursts.'

'Your cat's whiskers?' he enquired and leaned over to give me a cheesy kiss.

'My cat's whiskers are often right,' I said when we were in bed, Patrick intent on snatching two hours' sleep. Then, recalling the loan of a certain key, I added, 'Libby's probably wondering where you are.'

'I rang her earlier and said I couldn't make it.'

'While I was in the shower, I suppose.'

'I didn't deliberately wait until you were out of the way,' he replied, beginning to show all the signs of exasperation. 'Look, I simply must get some sleep.'

I hit him over the head with my pillow. This had an odd effect, for he rolled over towards me and said, 'Do you have a sense of total unreality? We're here to investigate a murder but I can't even begin to want to get involved with this man's death. I don't care a bloody damn about him. All I can think of is Terry and him dying in a blazing car.'

'Yes,' I said. 'Every time I close my eyes I see flames and his lovely brown hair burning. Why can't we investigate his murder? Surely if someone places bombs beneath the private cars of D12 operatives it isn't just a matter for the police?'

'You're only putting my own thoughts into words,' Patrick muttered. 'But I can't do a thing about it until Daws orders me to. I'm not quite sure why he hasn't. I intend to ask him next time we meet and I think I'm going to ask him in a manner that'll mean he'll have to come up with a pretty good answer.'

Chapter Four

I came out of a heavy sleep to discover that Patrick was shaking me. At least, I hoped it was him, there were no lights on in the room.

'Wake up!' said that well-remembered voice. 'You'll have to come with me to Bitterns. Steve's ill.'

'Ill!' I exclaimed.

'Shush! Keep your voice down. The walls are thin. Yes, he's been as sick as a dog and has the trots. I told him the meat pie he bought for his lunch had whiskers on it.' He thrust a bundle at me. 'Here's his night-combat kit.'

'Just a teensy bit of light,' I pleaded.

'In the dark,' insisted the stern commander. 'Very good practice.'

'Just so long as the surviving assistant doesn't fall over a chair and break a leg,' I mumbled, trying to find the underwear I had laid out for the morning. Having succeeded with that I hauled on the thick dark-blue sweater, woollen trousers and socks. As might be expected it was all too big for me and very, very warm.

'What about shoes?' I hissed, having pulled off the sweater to put it on the right way round.

'Haven't you brought your trainers?'

'Yes, but they're white. New ones.'

He groaned under his breath. 'You'll just have to muddy them up a bit.'

'You'll be lucky. They were forty quid.'

'And when Hurst's minder sees two white feet coming across the lawn?'

I always lose this kind of argument. However, I knew better than to ask how we would be leaving the building. The fire escape was right outside the window; reaching it involved no more than a slightly hair-raising swing across empty space hanging on to a supporting strut. Patrick, even though by no means up to full fitness, went across with scarcely a pause. Most of his strength is in his arms and fingers. It was very reassuring to feel his strong grip on my sweater, pulling me in to where he was standing.

'Our Richard won't be too happy if we're caught red-handed,' I said when we were in the car heading west.

Patrick just chuckled.

It was decided that we would gain entry into the grounds of the house through the gate I had noticed in the western boundary wall. We parked the car well away from it and walked the rest of the way. By now we had donned dark woollen balaclava helmets that had holes just for the eyes and mouth so we were quite invisible in the night. I was glad that no one was likely to be watching out for intruders using infra-red night sights that picked up body heat. Inside my woollies the temperature was like a Turkish bath.

'If Libby could see you now,' I murmured as we reached the gate. 'Didn't she say anything about Westfield? She did hint that he was a ladies' man.'

'You're over-prim all of a sudden,' Patrick said, hand on the latch. 'Yes, in your own classic words – he screwed around.'

'In Longcoombe?'

'She would only be likely to know about Longcoombe, wouldn't she? Shut up – I want to listen.'

My streak of irresponsibility was still beavering away. Right now it seemed to join forces with my writer's imagin-ation, that useful but also infuriating part of my brain that presents me, in a split second, with several possible scenarios for any given situation. Life, as it were, stepped back from and viewed on a small screen. So, teeth in my lower lip to stifle a possible giggle if the hinges of the gate squeaked *à la* mystery story, my ears cocked for the obligatory hoot from an owl, I wondered what we would do if the minder-cum-chauffeur burst out of the garden shed in a cloud of splinters, having turned into a werewolf at midnight.

'You're shaking,' Patrick said, removing his hand from the latch.

'Nerves,' I spluttered. 'You know silly old me.'

It was too dark to see if he gave me an odd look. Besides, I was too involved with trying not to scream with laughter. I was almost glad when the gate turned out to be locked.

'The were– minder might have seen me,' I said.

'You didn't mention anything about going in.'

'I didn't. I was on Warwick and pushed the gate open just a little bit. The chauffeur or whatever he is was coming down the path. He went into a shed. Perhaps the gate's unlocked for people who work in the garden at certain times of the day and he was coming to – ' I nearly uttered a shriek of pain.

He had gripped my wrist, just between thumb and forefinger, fleetingly, the agony also fleeting but enough to make me feel sick and dizzy. We stood face to face for perhaps ten seconds in utter silence.

'This is not the Upper Fifth's rag night,' said Patrick.

'Sorry.'

'And next time tell me if someone might have seen you.'

'Sorry.'

There was another quite long silence. Then Patrick took my wrist once again but this time he rubbed it. 'Sorry.'

I said, 'I was initially asked to join D12 to help preserve your cover on social occasions. Since then I've branched out a bit and learned to defend myself, climb, shoot, abseil and God knows what besides. But that doesn't mean that I can play the burglar without...'

'Without what?'

'Imagining things.'

'Imagining things! What things?'

'Forget it,' I said.

Whereupon, for at least two minutes, and in a very cold voice, he lectured me on the importance of what we were doing. And I hated him for it.

We resumed the job in question.

Using his cupped hands and a shoulder as steps I climbed on to the top of the wall and, relying on the thick main stem of the Russian vine for handholds, slid down the other side.

Then in the beam of a tiny flashlight I quickly examined the door for security alarms. But all I could detect were spiders, earwigs, rusting hinges and a lot of moss.

The key was hanging on a large nail on the back of the shed door. It grated and groaned in the lock but the door finally opened and Patrick slipped in. Perhaps we were being over-cautious in unlocking the gate but it was to be our escape route if anything went wrong and Patrick is not so agile as he used to be when clambering over high walls.

'Are you going to bug the phone?' I whispered.

'If there's time.' His manner was still decidedly chilly.

'If we find any in place already they might have been put there by Special Branch.'

'So we crunch them underfoot.'

It never ceases to amaze me, the rivalry between people supposed to be working with the same aims in view.

'I forgot to tell you,' Patrick said in an undertone, drawing me into the cover of an apple tree. 'I didn't want to question Libby too closely about Westfield because I felt she has some personal grudge against him. I can ask her about that when I'm wearing my MI5 hat. But when I was waiting for her a scruffy sort of individual sidled up to me in the bar and said it was a pity the police weren't questioning a lot more of what he called the ordinary folk. He said that it was common knowledge that a girl had been raped at one of the Hursts' wild parties and that his secretary had left shortly afterwards. He also told me that the murdered man used to drive a big red Merc and from the way he drove it through the village left no one in any doubt that he hated dogs. More than one ended up crushed to death beneath the wheels, apparently . . . including Libby's pet collie, Muffin.'

An almost full moon had risen over some trees, its pale silvery light just sufficient to show us where we were going. Keeping as much as possible to the thick concealing foliage of trees and shrubs — the garden did seem to be unusually overgrown — we approached the rear of the house. Beneath a large rhododendron we paused. There was only about twenty yards of open lawn now to cross, our proposed point of entry the door that apparently led off a kitchen, according to Patrick usually the weakest area as far as security is concerned.

45

He made the crossing, bent low, and once again I marvelled at how gracefully and silently he moves. He might not be so quick at climbing over walls now but he is still utterly *mobile*. No one watching would begin to guess at the weeks, months, years even, of agonising hard work it took him to achieve such mobility. Recently he had taken dancing lessons — and I don't mean waltzing either — to keep stiff and damaged muscles as supple as possible. All at once I felt very angry with Steve. Try walking with an artificial leg, I mentally told him. Do press-ups, keep-fit routines and dance until you're soaked with sweat and half crying with pain and exhaustion. Then you can talk to us of 'off days'.

The entire house was in darkness. I went to Patrick's side as he stood to one side of the kitchen window. It was a large window and very modern, part of an extension that appeared to include a utility room and pantry. This much Patrick had been able to ascertain with binoculars earlier in the day, the information given to me in a short briefing in the car on the way over.

He touched my hand, drawing my attention to an open top window. It was the work of a moment to stand on a plant tub, insert an arm through the opening and find the latch of the main lower window. Before he grasped it, he carefully felt around the frame, located what he was searching for and utilised a slightly secret item of D12's electronic hardware to nullify the alarm.

'At least it wasn't one of those systems where you only have to breathe on the glass to set it off,' he muttered, more to himself than to me.

A pot plant and an assortment of small objects, including a woman's purse, were silently moved aside and we climbed in, closing the window but not latching it. Then we stood quite still for a long minute while our eyes adjusted to the darkness. We listened but there was no sound except our own quiet breathing.

We crossed the room, our passage illuminated by tiny flashes from Patrick's torch; we dared not bump into anything. A door to the right led to the utility room: washing machine, tumble drier, freezer. We went to another door. This led into a short corridor and thence to a large square hall.

Patrick guided me into a room on our left. It was a dining room. There was a large oval table with at least eighteen chairs around it and an old-fashioned buffet sideboard with an untidy array of bottles thereon; newspapers were strewn on the floor around one of the four armchairs at one end of the room as though the person reading them had flung them aside with impatience. The colour scheme was red throughout. Heavy, overwhelmingly claustrophobic in the light from the tiny torch. In fact a brooding atmosphere seemed to hang over the entire house.

I do not know how he knew it — experience, probably — but the master switches for the alarm system were situated in a box on the wall behind the door. This was opened and subjected to the same treatment as the sensor in the kitchen. But the Hursts would not discover the equipment wrecked, merely switched off. They might blame the police for meddling with it.

There was a telephone on a small card table. Patrick lifted the receiver carefully and, with me holding the torch, took out a tiny screw from one end to dismantle it. Revealed, a small round object was tossed into the glowing embers of the log fire — did someone, somewhere, hear Patrick's hollow chuckle? — and another inserted in its place. This procedure was repeated with another phone in the hall and yet another in a small room that appeared to be Miles Hurst's study.

'I'm content,' Patrick breathed. 'Tomorrow I'll do the ones upstairs.'

We searched the dining room quickly and carefully, having of course drawn on fine gloves before we entered the house. Nothing of interest was found here so we crossed the hall to a sitting room. I jumped violently when a grandfather clock wheezily prepared to strike three, the sonorous chimes echoed somewhat incongruously by a cuckoo clock in the kitchen. Next to the clock was a cabinet full of china.

All the time we listened for sounds of movement upstairs.

The sitting room yielded nothing either so we moved on to a smaller, snug room just inside the front door. There was a large television set and hi-fi equipment, a cabinet filled with hundreds of cassettes and compact discs, a video recorder, a cupboard that turned out to be a bar.

47

'They like their drink,' I heard Patrick mutter, fastidious fingers twisting round a couple of bottles to enable him to read the labels. He sat down on one of the two long sofas against the walls to examine the contents of the cassette cabinet. 'Funny music,' he commented dismissively and I took it that the Hursts' taste didn't extend to Beethoven and Mozart.

We searched the kitchen, deliberately leaving the study until last. This would take quite a long time as there were a desk, several filing cabinets, shelving and a small safe. I left this to Patrick, quite content to do as requested and stand by the door to keep watch so he could concentrate fully.

After a few minutes he brought something to the door for me to see. It was a leather briefcase with the initials J.P.L. on it. The murdered man's, for Westfield's real surname began with L.

There was very little in it; a notebook, new and unused, a pen-and-pencil set in a box, also engraved with his initials, and a file with several sheets of A4 typing paper covered in handwritten notes. These seemed to be the minutes of a Parents' and Teachers' Association meeting.

'D'you think the police took away anything from it?' I whispered.

'We'll find out tomorrow,' Patrick answered. 'The inspector in charge of the case is rumoured to be running his eye over us some time during the morning.'

'What's that under the desk?' I asked when the torch beam passed over a flash of something white.

It was a single sheet of paper, the same size as the ones in the briefcase. Typed on it, underlined and right in the centre were two words, *Spy Triad*.

'I bet it's the title page of the typescript of a short story or novel,' I said.

'Let's not jump to conclusions,' Patrick observed, careful as always.

'A pound to a penny that's what was in the briefcase,' I said. 'He was writing something that would expose people. Spies. Traitors within the security services. That's a good enough reason to silence the author.'

'The writer's imagination,' Patrick said and then glanced at me sideways, his teeth gleaming white as he grinned.

'Then where's the rest of it?' I retorted.

Just then I heard a slow measured tread coming down the stairs.

We froze.

The doorway of the study, where we were standing, was actually beneath the stairs. We backed into the room and held our breath, the torch extinguished.

The sound of footsteps receded in the direction of the kitchen and a light was switched on, sending a long bright rectangle of illumination across the hall floor. I heard what sounded like the fridge door opening and then the rattle of plates.

Patrick thrust the sheet of paper at me and went silently across the hall and into the sitting room. Moments later there was anguished feline yowling. It did not emanate from any earthly cat and was enough to make your hair stand on end. The man's in the kitchen probably did. He emerged at the run − yes, it was the chauffeur-cum-minder − plate in one hand and what looked like a cold sausage in the other, and plunged into the dining room without putting on the light. The 'cat' emerged from his hiding place and gestured to me urgently. I needed no second telling, we were away.

No shouts or sounds of pursuit disturbed the night silence.

'Damn,' said Patrick when we were outside the gate and making for the car. 'I wanted to see the room where Westfield's body was found. But it was too risky to stay.'

'Much better in daylight,' I said thankfully. 'Pity about the safe, though.'

'Oh, I opened that. Just a diamond brooch and earrings to match and some business papers. I didn't expect anything else. No, there's another one somewhere, you can be sure of that.'

'There was something about that house that I didn't like at all. It was creepy.'

'The guy in the pub said something about "strange goings-on". Whatever that means.'

Chapter Five

Miles Hurst frowned. Even though we were expected and he had undertaken to be at home that morning, he still frowned, the look of a busy man who answers the door to find someone selling flags for an obscure charity. The fact that we were a couple of minutes early — the agreed time being ten-fifteen — might have had something to do with it. Whatever the reason, the fleeting petulant puckering of an otherwise smooth and untroubled forehead made it quite clear that we were unwelcome. Libby's description of him as short, fat and balding was highly accurate.

Patrick introduced us both and we were shown into the sitting room.

'Coffee?' Hurst asked. 'I can't contemplate more questions without coffee.' He smiled thinly, perhaps to show that he wasn't serious. 'Do sit down.'

'Thank you,' Patrick said.

I perched on the edge of a chesterfield and took a notebook from my handbag. There had been no question of my going home to write; Steve was still decidedly ill, weak and with a temperature. He appeared to be suffering from gastric flu.

Patrick had smiled politely and somewhat absent-mindedly at Hurst in response to the invitation to seat himself and was roaming the room. This I knew was to put Hurst on edge, something Patrick's very good at doing. I waited for another of his ploys, when he would cease walking for a moment or two, a foot tapping, while he perhaps contemplated some item or other in the room, a frown appearing as, surely, he recalled some part of the police evidence or Hurst's own statement which was now refuted by his own observations.

Sure enough . . .

'Nothing wrong, I hope?' asked Hurst a trifle sharply, pausing in a somewhat fussy rearrangement of the chairs, as he perceived Patrick staring in the gilt-framed mirror over the fireplace, craning his neck and standing on tiptoe as if trying to pick out some detail in the reflected garden.

'Oh no,' Patrick muttered unconvincingly and carried on with his silent perambulations.

'Is there a wastepaper basket?' I enquired, pencil sharpener poised for action.

Miles Hurst went out, presumably into the study, and returned with a small bin, the outside of which was covered with furnishing brocade and decorated with small tassels like those on lampshades.

I commenced to sharpen the first of my six brand-new pencils, bought specially from the post office that morning. I became aware of Hurst giving me an appalled stare.

'You *are* free all day, I hope,' Patrick said, taking the cue.

Hurst looked at his watch to give himself a few moments to think. 'No, I'm afraid there's no question of — '

'You and your wife are the chief suspects,' Patrick interrupted smoothly. 'And until we've satisfied ourselves that — '

This time Hurst cut in. 'That is outrageous! And how can you answer for the police? To my knowledge you haven't even made the acquaintance of Inspector Faversham.'

'I don't believe I mentioned the police. They are carrying out their own inquiry. As far as MI5 are concerned one of their chief executives was murdered in this house. And I think you ought to know that in cases where my department is called in the police have to report all their findings to *me*.'

'In case national security is endangered,' I said, hoping that this made the situation perfectly clear.

Hurst gazed at us angrily for a moment longer and then left the room.

'Don't tread *all* over him,' I said.

Patrick rammed his hands in his pockets as though if unconfined they might throttle someone. 'He's snaky. I don't like him at all.'

'Unbiased is the watchword,' I told him.

51

He turned to me, eyes sparking, but I was smiling broadly for it always amuses me when he displays normal human fallibility. Then he grinned and laughed softly at himself.

Hurst returned just then carrying a tray with the coffee. He was followed by a young woman, Jan, his wife. As might be imagined, she was much younger than her husband, perhaps mid-twenties to his late forties. She was also taller, very high-heeled shoes emphasising this. Whereas both were well dressed I got the impression that she had attired herself carefully for the occasion, a fine red suede trouser suit over a matching blouse that set off her long black glossy hair to perfection and made his grey suit look dull and commonplace. Yes, people do make statements with their clothes.

'Did you like Westfield?' Patrick said to Hurst as he was setting down the tray, after only the briefest greeting to Jan.

'Westfield?' asked Hurst, baffled. 'D'you mean John?'

'It was his codename,' he was crisply informed. 'Shall we refer to him as that and then Ingrid won't have to alter her notes?' He remained looking impassively at Hurst, one eyebrow raised.

'As you wish.'

There was a pause, Jan pouring the coffee.

'I asked you whether you liked him,' Patrick said.

Hurst sat down. 'I'll tell you what I told the police. No, I didn't.'

'I see.'

'I don't suppose you see anything,' Hurst retorted. 'But I believe in being honest. Besides, I've no wish to being taken away in an unmarked car to have hell pasted out of me by a bunch of thugs if you suspect I'm not telling the truth.'

'Heaven forbid,' Patrick murmured, pausing in apparently lining up the angle of the edge of the open door with the left-hand edge of the fireplace. 'You have no cause for fear, Mr Hurst. There's no need to take you anywhere. It's just you and me.' He gave the other what can only be described as a shark's smile. 'Why didn't you like him?'

'No reason,' Hurst said. 'It was a cordial dislike on both our parts. He visited us quite often and I welcomed him because he was Jan's brother. We sometimes went to his home at New Year. It was a clash of personalities, I suppose.'

52

'Did his wife accompany him when he came here?'

'Er – no.'

'Why not?'

Jan answered. She banged down the coffee pot and said, 'Pamela doesn't approve of us. She thinks we're jumped-up tradespeople. I don't want to talk about Pamela. Aren't you supposed to be finding out who killed John?'

'Who killed Cock Robin?' Patrick said sadly, not thinking of a top executive in MI5 at all. He picked up a small, very ornate vase from a shelf and took it over to the window to examine it.

I was writing everything down in shorthand, even this latest dispirited utterance, a reference to Terry who had used the name Robin on an assignment in Canada. The Hursts were probably thinking Patrick slightly mad but this did no harm at all.

Patrick said, 'What was he doing in your house last Thursday night?'

'I would have thought it obvious,' Hurst said. 'He was visiting us.'

'Would he have stayed the weekend?'

'Yes. That's early Coalport if you're interested in china.'

'Did he always arrive on a Thursday evening when he was coming for the weekend?'

'No. As a matter of fact we weren't expecting him until the next day.'

'So he was a whole day early?'

'Not really. He usually arrived after lunch on Friday.'

'And hadn't he phoned to let you know of the change of plan?'

'Hardly. Jan and I wouldn't have gone out otherwise.'

Patrick replaced the vase. 'Perhaps you'd go over your movements for that evening.'

Hurst sighed in long-suffering fashion and drank his coffee for a few moments without speaking. All this time Jan had been staring morosely into her cup, having seated herself on a long padded bench with cushions in the embrasure of the bay window. Suddenly she looked up and, unaccountably, gave Patrick a smile.

'You tell the story again,' her husband said to her,

seemingly nettled by this. 'You must have it all off by heart now.'

'Miles goes to London on Thursdays,' she began, pouting at him.

'On business?' Patrick said quickly.

'Major, I am not the kind of man to go greyhound racing,' Hurst said through his teeth. 'Yes, of course on business.'

Jan continued, 'I usually meet him off the train at about seven-thirty and we have a drink in the hotel by the station. Then we go out for a meal. Last Thursday I met him just the same but when we came out of the hotel it was pouring, absolutely coming down in buckets. We'd have got soaked just running to the car and we hadn't even an unbrella with us. When the rain showed no sign of stopping we went into a little Italian restaurant next door and had a meal. It wasn't really all that special but we were starving by then. Some friends of ours were there and we sat talking over coffee for ages and the evening ended by them asking us back to their place for drinks and more coffee. That was our evening. We got home at a little after one and there was poor John . . .' Here her voice became slightly husky and she cleared her throat before continuing. 'Dead on the floor in my room.'

Patrick asked for the names of the hotel (oddly it was the same one as where we were staying), the restaurant and the friends, and she told him.

'Do you have a cat?' was the next question.

'Yes. Why?'

'Do you always leave the top kitchen window open for it to go in and out?'

'As a matter of fact I do.'

'Even though you've gone to the trouble of having a burglar alarm installed.'

'I told you to get a cat flap fitted to the back door,' Hurst said bad-temperedly.

'Ming's too old to learn to use one,' said Jan with another pout.

To Patrick, Miles Hurst said, 'So you *have* been in contact with the police. Faversham thought a burglar might have got in and my brother-in-law disturbed him before anything was taken.'

54

'It's not very likely. Ingrid and I came here last night. Your security system is quite good. Any casual burglar would have set off the alarm.'

They both registered shock.

'You got into the house!' Hurst shouted. 'That's outrageous!'

'It seems to be a favourite phrase of yours,' Patrick said placidly. 'But think before you lose your temper. The security system is satisfactory but it wouldn't deter a professional. If there *was* an intruder – and I still doubt it – we must look at it from the angle that this person was waiting for him. Someone after your china collection or loose change would hardly bludgeon him to death. He'd run. And if murder was the game, why go to all the bother of getting into the house when all they had to do was attack him on the doorstep or as he got out of his car?'

Silence greeted this.

'So what do you gather from that?' Hurst said at last with heavy sarcasm.

'That either he was killed by someone he knew or was murdered elsewhere and his body brought here.'

Hurst was probably on the point of saying 'That's outrageous', again, but Patrick spoke first.

'I understand you have parties.'

'There's nothing illegal in that.'

'It depends what goes on.'

'What goes on?' Hurst echoed. 'What on earth do you mean?'

Patrick sat down. 'According to people I spoke to, the parties are somewhat riotous.'

'You've been asking the village gossips about us!' Jan said venomously. 'Still, I suppose we have to expect that of MI5. Well, what else would the people around here say? If you don't go to church or join the WI you must be suspect. That's what they've been brought up to think and they'll think it to their dying day.'

'Aren't you just a little out of touch?' Patrick said. 'Your neighbours are hardly timeless yokels who touch their forelocks to the gentry. With the exception of one gentleman, these remarks weren't made to me but to the police making house-to-house enquiries,' he continued, lying or, more likely, guessing blithely. 'Your critics are people like retired publishers, an art historian and folk who for the sake of brevity I'll call yuppies.'

He *had* been in touch with the police, I now realised, writing busily. He always tells the truth about things like this.

'And I suppose one of these upright citizens was Jessica Campbell,' Jan went on in the same scornful tone. 'That woman is in no position to talk about *us*.'

'Leave it!' her husband said. 'The last thing we need now is bitchiness between two women.'

'My brother is dead!' Jan shouted. 'He's dead and everyone hates us!'

'What you must remember,' said Miles as though talking to a child, 'is that he wasn't just your brother but a very senior man in the security services.'

'Did *he*?' Patrick asked. 'Remember his position?'

Man and wife stared at him.

'That's a terrible thing to say!' Jan said, still shouting.

'I'm asking a reasonable question. And frankly, if you insist on this childish and stupid protesting and parading every time I open my mouth, my investigations are likely to take a very long time.'

My aching wrist had a rest while there was another silence.

'He — he liked to forget his responsibilities for a while,' Jan said with a worried look at Miles. 'Surely everyone in that kind of job has to sometimes? Otherwise you go off your rocker. Even you,' she said accusingly to Patrick. 'I should imagine you sometimes drink a little too much just the same as the rest of us.'

'Indeed,' Patrick agreed in a bored voice. 'And some of us play with our children and listen to records. Did you arrange that the parties coincided with his visits?'

'Why are you obsessed with our parties?' Miles said.

'All right. I'll ask you another question. What was the reason for your secretary leaving last year?'

'You *have* been talking to that Campbell creature!' Jan yelled.

'I haven't so much as clapped eyes on the woman,' Patrick assured her.

56

'There were rumours spread around at the time,' Hurst said. 'One made it known that a member of my staff had been assaulted in this house. It was nonsense. In actual fact the truth was almost the reverse. She became very abusive when I was forced to ask her to leave.'

'What was the problem?'

'Her work was bad.'

'She couldn't spell,' Jan said. 'She was bloody useless. I wouldn't be surprised if she started the rumour herself to spite us.'

Patrick said, 'Well, if you'll just give me her address – '

'The police already have it,' Hurst interrupted. 'They asked about any member of staff who had left within the last couple of years.'

' – I'll go and see her,' Patrick finished as if the other had not spoken.

Hurst fumed silently for a moment or two and then left the room. When he returned he handed a small piece of paper to Patrick, who folded it and stowed it in his wallet without thanking him.

Jan lit a cigarette, her movements jerky and nervous. 'How much longer is this going to take?'

'You said you found your brother's body,' Patrick said gently.

'Yes.'

'In your own room.'

'That's right.'

'Did you go straight to your room when you came in the house?'

'Yes.'

'Any particular reason or do you usually go straight upstairs when you've been out?'

She gave him a quizzical look. 'You ask completely different kinds of questions to the police. Yes, as a matter of fact it's my habit to go and change my shoes. I don't like to wear pointed heels or outdoor shoes around indoors as some of our carpets are rather valuable. I usually remove my shoes in the hall and run upstairs carrying them to find a pair of slippers. Silly not to put my slippers by the front door, I suppose.'

57

She was thawing towards her interrogator, I noticed. I made a note of it in the margin.

'Do you mind telling me what you saw?'

'She saw her brother dead and a lot of blood,' Hurst ground out. 'I would have thought that perfectly obvious.'

'Shut up, Miles,' said Jan. 'I can't think straight when you keep interrupting.' She reseated herself so that she was facing away from him and did not speak for about a minute, staring out of the window. Patrick made no move to prompt her.

'I didn't realise it was John,' she said finally. 'Not at first, I mean. I just saw a man's body and the blood and screamed. It was a terrible shock. I shall never be able to sleep in that room again. It was rather pretty and feminine with a lot of rather silly ruffles on the bed cover and lampshades. But I loved it. It was my little corner. Now all I can see in there is violence and murder.' She stubbed out the partly smoked cigarette and fumbled for her handkerchief.

She wouldn't have been candid like this with the police.

'And your husband came running when he heard you scream?'

'No, he didn't hear. He was in the downstairs cloakroom.'

I caught Patrick's eye.

'Where is that?' Patrick asked.

'Off his study. You'd never know it was there. The door's behind a dummy bookcase. I think the previous owners put it in as a joke.'

'So what did you do when he didn't come?'

'I'm not sure *exactly* what I did. I think I ran out on the landing and called him. Then I went back into my room again. That's when I saw that it was John. From his watch. I gave it to him, you see. I'd never have known ...' Here she cried openly.

When Miles made no move to comfort her, Patrick went to stand by her chair, a hand patting her shoulder in the most natural fashion. He gazed into space, eyes slitted, concentrating.

'I *did* hear her call me,' Hurst said, resentment in his tone. 'It was most unfortunate for I must have flushed the toilet just as she screamed. I'd closed the doors for some reason. I heard

58

her call and ran up the stairs. There was nothing either of us could do, of course.'

Patrick said, 'Mr Hurst, is anyone blackmailing you?'

Hurst's already pale face lost all its colour.

'It would be a cunning move,' Patrick went on. 'To leave a body in a house where it would be found by the person most likely to be upset by the discovery. The victim so close to the family, too.'

'I understand your thinking,' Hurst said. 'But no.'

'No threats?'

'None.'

'And yet it seems that the people round here don't exactly like you.'

'We've done nothing to anyone that would result in revenge of this kind.'

'Perhaps not,' Patrick muttered and walked over to the window. 'Mrs Hurst, can you bring yourself to show me the room in question?'

'No!' both said together.

'My wife will never go in there again.' Hurst continued emphatically. 'How could you even suggest such a thing? She is still under sedation as it is. It will take years for her to recover.'

'Only if you say so,' Patrick countered.

'No, I absolutely forbid it. A room in which someone was killed has dangerous vibrations and it could do great harm to someone nervous like Jan. Until the murderer is found and brought to justice John's spirit will have no rest. Unquiet spirits can do a great deal of harm if — '

'Rubbish!' Patrick declared.

'If you don't mind,' Jan said hesitantly, 'I'd rather not go in there. I know it sounds silly in this day and age but this house is old and parts of it do give you a strange feeling. And this morning I couldn't find John's picture — a photo I took of him last year and had framed. It's usually on a table in here. I looked everywhere and then found it in the wardrobe in the room I'm using now. Who knows — perhaps John's trying to tell me something.'

In deference to her Patrick didn't give vent to an even more damning comment, just smiled sadly and requested permission to look around the house. The note-taker went with him.

'It's unhealthy, isn't it?' Patrick murmured as we mounted the stairs. 'I've a feeling that bastard has her right under his thumb.'

'It's not like you to get so personally involved,' I told him. 'Just because you come from a religious background and believe in God it doesn't mean that people who appear not to and waffle on about unquiet spirits and dangerous vibrations are ...'

'Good,' he said when I stopped speaking. 'Your brain caught up with your tongue. I only said it was *unhealthy*. I didn't accuse him of murder or even witchcraft. I'm not sure that he does go in for boiling cats up in cauldrons and muttering incantations. People who do that are fools and Miles Hurst is not a fool. He's something else and I haven't pinpointed what it is yet.'

There was no difficulty in finding the room where the murdered man had been found, for the police had sealed the door with tape printed with a warning that it was not to be removed. Patrick unstuck one end carefully from the woodwork, opened the door and went in.

And at that moment I began to feel very, very afraid.

Chapter Six

Although, of course, the body of John Westfield had been removed and there was only a chalked outline on the floor to mark where it had been, I had a sudden nightmarish vision of how he had looked. The face was just pulped flesh, what features remained were hidden by a curtain of blood. Only the mouth was visible, half-open in a kind of last silent snarl. To me, just then, the mouth seemed to move.

I found myself praying – a shock in itself – and leaning on the wall.

'Are you all right?' I heard Patrick say, his voice sounding as though he was a long way off.

Even the walls were oozing blood and it trickled slowly, in glistening globules, to form congealing puddles on the pale-pink carpet.

'Ingrid!'

I knew now why Jan did not ever want to enter this room again. I didn't want to but my fate was never to leave and to stand there for the rest of eternity, staring at a scene of endless murder.

'No!' my own voice gasped. 'No! I can't stand it!' Dimly, I realised that I was blundering around blindly, trying to find the door. I stumbled into Patrick and it seemed that even his clothes were slimy and viscous.

I'm told that I became hysterical. I have no idea what happened for I was plunged headlong into my nightmare, swimming in a great vortex of scarlet ever closer to that twisted mouth. As I was sucked closer I saw that the teeth were broken and pointed like rocks on a reef, sinking and rising again in the sea of red.

Then came total and merciful oblivion.

'It's me, Patrick,' said his voice out of the blackness. 'If you hear what I'm saying, then squeeze my hand.'

Yes, it *was* his hand that I was holding, warm and strong. I could even feel the slight scar tissue on the back where the tattoo he had had applied for the Hell's Angel assignment had been removed by a Harley Street plastic surgeon — a friend of Daws — who had been looking for volunteers to test a new method.

'Right, now I'm going to bathe your face with cold water. When I've done that I want you to open your eyes.'

I had a horror that all I would see was the face of a murdered man but there was no going against that commanding voice. Blessedly cool water sluiced over my face.

'OK?' he asked when I was looking up at him.

'OK,' I answered in a husky croak.

I saw then that I was lying on the floor of a bathroom, Miles and Jan Hurst gazing down on me, Jan white and shaking.

'The last time this happened,' Patrick said to the Hursts, 'she was pregnant.'

'Jan's right,' I said. 'She mustn't go in that room.'

There was a ring at the doorbell.

'I'll go,' Hurst said. 'I gave all the staff the day off.'

'I'll come too,' Jan said and hurried after him.

'I'm not pregnant,' I said, annoyed with him for making me sound like a woman prone to idiotic behaviour.

'No doubt,' he said and offered me a hand to rise. 'So I'm going to act the brute and make you go back in there.'

'Patrick ...' I pleaded.

Inexorably he drew me along the landing.

'Won't you even listen?' I said.

'No,' he replied quietly, 'and for a very good reason.'

'You're a beast,' I complained.

'Your pupils are dilated. You've been nobbled.'

'What?'

'Just be a good girl and co-operate. I'm not sure where it happened — it could have been either here or at the hotel.

62

We'll have to ask a doc to do a blood test on Steve in case he was got at as well.'

The next moment we were standing at the door. Patrick tucked my arm under his and we went in.

'If I shut my eyes,' I said, 'I know it'll come back. Blood – '

'Then don't. See what is really here. As Jan said, a rather pretty room with silly pink ruffles on everything. There are only a few blood stains on the carpet where the body was placed. Yes, placed. There's no way he was killed in here. The stuff would have been everywhere if he had.'

My teeth were chattering now.

'Detect.ve Inspector Faversham,' Hurst said from behind us. 'He'd like to ask you a few questions.'

'Major Gillard, I understand,' said Faversham. 'Someone at the station gave you more information than they ought to have done.'

In my somewhat peculiar state I looked at Faversham and thought of Warwick. For he was a big man with a long horse face and big horselike teeth. His hair was overlong for a senior police officer and hung over his brow in a horsy forelock. It wasn't so clean as Warwick's, though.

Patrick showed him his credentials and, without being asked, I gave him mine, smiling for all I was worth.

'I'm not quite sure why MI5 has to have people on the spot in this case,' Faversham observed.

'Ah,' Patrick said. 'Suffice it to say that my department's brief has been extended to cover all problems concerning those who have signed the Official Secrets Act and not just those cases where foreign interference is suspected.'

'Foreign interference?' echoed an individual who now came from outside the room.

'A rather twee euphemism for words like "traitor" and "spy",' Patrick said. 'Who are you?'

'Grant,' said Faversham. 'Detective Sergeant Grant.'

Grant said, 'Do we defer to you, major, or are we going to be allowed to get on with the job?'

Patrick gave him a sunny smile. 'Sergeant, I do believe they've been telling you nasty things about us. My answer is that I hope we can work together. The ideal situation as I see it is that I tell you anything interesting that I discover as far as solving the murder is concerned and you fill me in with anything you turn up that might involve national security. How's that?'

'That suits me,' Faversham grunted after a pause.

'Sergeant?' Patrick asked.

Grant blushed hotly, nodding.

'Right,' Patrick said. 'Sergeant Grant, be so good as to lie on the floor and pretend you're the deceased for a moment.'

Grant glanced at Faversham, received no guidance, and stretched out on the carpet on his back. One arm, his right, he flung above his head, the fist clenched, the other he tucked behind his back. His left leg remained straight, the right bent at the knee.

'Turn your head to the left,' Faversham ordered.

'What do you make of it, inspector?' Patrick asked.

Faversham cleared his throat. 'I'm working on a theory that he was killed elsewhere and brought here. Before rigor mortis set in. If he'd been killed in here there would have been a lot more blood ... splashes on the walls and even the ceiling. There was plenty on the victim, though. Almost as if ...'

'Yes?' I said.

'Almost as if he'd been stood up again after he was dead and the blood ran down and soaked into his clothing. I'm still waiting for the pathologist's report but Crossley, who was doing it, was rushed off to hospital with a heart attack and someone else has taken over. I don't even know who.'

'Houseman, sir,' said Grant, getting up. 'Not at all happy about it either from what I hear.'

Everyone's voice was booming most oddly inside my head. Nobbled? It seemed so bizarre that I wasn't even sure now whether Patrick had actually said so or if it was another part of the dream world I was living in at the moment. It wasn't possible for people to put spells on others. Or was it? Perhaps I ought to go and talk to Jan. The trouble was that I was frightened. Everything stayed fairly normal if I kept my gaze on Patrick but as soon as I looked away all kinds of things happened. And if I so much as glanced at the walls or floor, that ghastly red flood began to ooze through the paper and carpet.

'From where do you run your business, Mr Hurst?' Patrick was saying.

'Petworth. I have two floors over an estate agent's in the High Street.'

'Also run by you?'

'I'm a partner in the firm. But what this has to do with — '

'Where was your chauffeur on the night of the murder?'

'Thursday is Plummer's day off.'

A kind of impasse seemed to have been reached.

Then Faversham said, 'If you're finished for a while, major, I'd like to clear up one or two points with Mr and Mrs Hurst. Perhaps we ought to go downstairs, Mr Hurst. I'm sure your wife shouldn't be left on her own like this.' And without giving Patrick time to reply he went out.

Giving us a cold look, Hurst followed. Grant remained and from his manner I deduced that he was a little embarrassed by his chief's rudeness.

Patrick said, 'That was an interesting comment — that it looked almost as if the corpse had been stood up again so that the blood ran down into his clothing. I wonder if the body was transported upright? What kind of vehicle might have been involved?'

'Gosh, yes,' Grant exclaimed, seemingly overjoyed that Patrick was speaking to him. 'I see what you mean, sir. Well, I suppose it would have had to have been a truck or van of some kind.'

'Or a cattle truck or horsebox in this part of the world,' I suggested.

'It's worth looking into,' Grant said.

'I'd like a gander at the path report when you have it to hand,' Patrick said. 'It will be interesting to see if there's a mark on the neck where a ligature was tied round.'

'I'll make sure you get a copy,' Grant said, lowering his voice. 'If I can't get it to you personally I'll send someone along.'

'Grant!' Faversham bellowed from downstairs.

The sergeant hurried out.

'Can we leave this place now?' I said, trying to sound casual.

'How do you feel?'

'*Is* there such a thing as black magic?'

'Only in people's imaginations.'

'Patrick, this room is *evil*.'

'No, you were slipped a little acid.'

Nevertheless I went out on the landing. Away from what I could only think as being Patrick's steadying influence the world went mad again, a dreadful brooding *something* seeming to be within the very walls of the building and waiting to manifest itself as soon as I dropped my guard. I had to get *out*.

From inside the room Patrick said, 'I made a right hash of that. Just wasted everyone's time.'

'Not at all,' I said.

He came out. 'I'm going to bug any other phones that are up here. See if you can get Jan on her own and find out what she's really scared of. I'll bet you anything you like it's her husband.' He gave me a clinical sort of look. 'You'll be all right. When you've seen Jan, go and get some fresh air. Someone's trying to put the wind up us.'

'The pathologist had a heart attack,' I reminded him as I went down the stairs.

I had no intention of questioning, or even looking for, Jan Hurst. I had to leave that house. Otherwise I would start screaming all over again.

Grant was on the phone in the hall. Covering the mouthpiece he said, 'We know the time of death now anyway — or as near as it can be estimated. Around ten-fifteen that night, give or take thirty minutes or so. That seems to put this lot in the clear, doesn't it? Their alibis seem pretty solid.'

'Anything else?' I asked when I was by the open front door.

'Mud under his fingernails and a couple of leaves stuck to the blood in his hair. Looks as though the inspector was right. He was killed somewhere in the countryside and brought here. When we find out why we might have a lead.'

'Hurst looked a bit twitchy when Patrick asked him if he was being blackmailed,' I said, going out into the sunshine and not particularly caring what Grant's reaction to this might be.

I had the shaming and utterly juvenile urge to get in touch

66

with Daws and tell him the whole story. I suppose that if I had paused to think about this I might have come to the conclusion that it was not so very unnatural after all. For what I needed, in my rather odd mental state, was a father figure. My own father had died when I was in my early twenties, just before I was married, and was most definitely not the sort to treat extreme fright in his womenfolk, whether drug-induced or otherwise, with a restrained clip on the jaw. As I was fairly convinced Patrick had done. Perhaps on the other hand he had merely applied those wiry, wringing fingers to my neck in a special manner — and exerted pressure for a couple of seconds.

There was no birdsong in the garden, only the same brooding silence. I went to the car and then reflected that, if Patrick was right, I was in no fit state to drive. So I would walk. Not far, just out of sight of this place to where I could muster my thoughts and try to regain my composure.

And what of Steve? *Was* his illness the result of having been given poison? It was strange but, while the idea of those involved with the murder investigation being incapacitated or warned off by those responsible seemed quite ludicrous, I could entertain the idea that, if we were disturbing something infinitely evil, ghastly things might happen.

Ghastly things *had* happened.

Once outside the entrance to Bitterns I sat on a low wall and gazed down the road towards the village. After a short while I got up and wandered in the same direction with vague ideas of finding a café and having something to eat. Perhaps I would overhear interesting gossip. Then, and this really *was* strange, for I had been convinced that she had still been within the house, Jan Hurst came running out of a narrow path not five yards in front of me. We both stopped dead.

'Miles did warn you,' she said as though it had been I who had been running.

'Miles warned *you*,' I corrected.

'He's always right about things like that,' she went on, ignoring my remark. 'Why don't you go and talk to the Campbells?'

'Did your brother write?' I asked.

I did not imagine the crafty look that flitted across her face.

'No.'

'Are you sure? Memoirs? Nothing like that?'

'No. He didn't have the time. He might have done when he retired.' She went to walk past me but I held her arm. 'Let go of me.'

'Jan, why are you so frightened?' On the face of it this was a stupid question for, after all, her brother had been murdered and his body placed in her room. But I had known precisely what Patrick had meant when he had told me to find out. What he was interested in was her *real* fear, the fear that John's death had only made worse.

'Wouldn't you be?' she retorted, snatching her arm from my grasp.

'Look, if there's anything I can do – ' I began.

'Do!' she shrieked. And then, more quietly, 'Just go away. Leave me alone. Take your questions to the Campbells. You'll learn a lot from them.'

She ran off, her dark hair flying.

I continued walking, pondering on whether it had been Patrick's questioning or my hysterics that had further frightened her. Both, probably, and leaving aside the idea that Patrick's air of what I can only call saintly menace had thrown down the challenge to a real and deadly manifestation of evil.

Longcoombe was very quiet for a Monday morning. There was a little light traffic, the distant sound of children in a school playground, and that was all. The church clock struck the half-hour and I glanced at my watch. Twelve-thirty. Where had the morning gone?

I left the modern shopping precinct behind and continued into the older part of the village. In the distance I could see the white ranch-style fencing of the riding stables, a Land-Rover and pony trailer parked in the road outside.

A pony trailer?

I stopped by the little café that I had had in mind but somehow carried on again without going in, my mind fixed only on the trailer. The murdered man might have been transported in such a vehicle. Was it practicable?

It seemed that an animal had just been unloaded from the

68

trailer for the ramp was down and there was fresh manure on the straw within. I could hear the clatter of hooves and voices from the stable yard. At the front end of the trailer was a ring from which hung an almost empty haynet.

There was plenty of room to hang a body from the ring. I went inside to check. Yes, it was quite high up, it had to be or a pony would catch its feet in a haynet hung from it. That much I could remember from horse-mad days in my early teens.

I don't know what made me do it but I bent down and brushed the straw away from beneath the ring. My reaction on perceiving a sticky-looking brown residue in the joins of the floor was total disbelief. I tried to convince myself that it was only dried disinfectant and manure that brushes had not reached.

I took a nailfile from my bag and, with the tip, scraped out some of the deposit. This I carefully placed in a screw of paper that had been a shopping list and put it in my purse.

Then I received an annihilating blow on the head and, as far as I knew, ceased to exist.

Chapter Seven

It took me far too long to work the gag from my mouth and perform the necessary contortions to pull the cord around my neck with the homing beacon on it into a position where I could bite it gently. This would cause it to activate. But the receiver was in the car I had left parked at Bitterns and, anyway, it only had a range of fifty miles. From the speed we were travelling I was halfway to Scotland by now.

For what seemed hours I tried to struggle out of the ropes that bound my hands and feet. Plenty of time to call myself all kinds of careless fool. Not for the first time I was discovering that no training, however realistic, can altogether prepare you for the real thing. No matter how tightly sundry servicemen tie you, chuckling in bloodthirsty fashion, and heave you into army lorries bound for God knows where, there is always a lack of overall *malice*. You know that even if, in the end, all your clothes are stripped off and you're dumped in a river in an effort to make you reveal remembered codewords, or some hooded interrogator is sufficiently keen to slap your face a couple of times, you aren't going to *die* of it. Sooner or later someone will blow the whistle, cups of tea will materialise and almost immediately everyone is friends.

The ropes cutting into my wrists stopped me from trying to free myself. My head hurt agonisingly and I couldn't see very clearly out of my left eye. A little while later we stopped and I thought of kicking the sides of the trailer in case people were ·about and heard me. But what good would it do? Anyone noticing the noise would merely presume that the equine passenger was fed up with travelling.

I must have fainted or slept from exhaustion for the next thing I knew was that it was dark and that the trailer was once again motionless. Someone was lowering the ramp, a man, I heard him swear when one of the fixing pins jammed. He came into the trailer, breathing heavily, and prodded me with one foot. I stayed still. I knew that if I moved or uttered a sound I would be kicked or hit over the head again.

He went away. There was a jolt as the trailer was unhitched and then the Land-Rover was started up and driven away for a short distance. A minute or so later I heard his heavy footfalls coming back, the sound weirdly amplified through the floor of the trailer.

The realisation that he was going to kill me did not cause me to fly into a state of blind panic. Perhaps this is what the training is for, I found myself thinking in a wildly illogical moment, so that I die with a brave smile on my face.

I sat up. To hell with training. I was damned if I was going to go like a dumb animal. When the man's dark shape was silhouetted against the opening I commenced to scream. Then, when he was coming at me, hands outstretched with his fingers like claws in the most horrible fashion, I drew up my legs and kicked out. I hit what I had been aiming for and he doubled up and stumbled backwards down the ramp.

The next time he came at me he had found a piece of wood. He held it high over his head, ready to strike, trying to make me out in the gloom. My only advantage was that I could see him against the night sky. The stick came down, thumping into the straw inches away as I rolled desperately towards the side of the trailer.

It was only a matter of time.

Three times the stick just missed me. I lay panting, my wrists flaring in agony where the ropes were cutting into me. He came at me again and I had no strength to avoid him this time. The stick hit me across the back. He had missed his footing in the slippery straw.

The increased pain from the blow made me see double. There were two of him now. I turned my face away from him and thought of Patrick. No, I'm not dying bravely, I silently told him, I'm cringing all over.

No blows came but the trailer was rocking violently. The

71

man trod heavily on my leg. I looked and there *were* two of them. They fell out of the trailer together and rolled down the ramp, grunting and throwing punches into each other. One got up and fell down again, and the one on the ground flung himself on him, sat on him and banged his head on the ground.

I simply couldn't believe this. I knew it wasn't Patrick, the style was all wrong. The style wasn't like that of anyone I knew. What I was watching — come to think of it — was like two small boys brawling over the ownership of a conker.

It was a ghastly moment when one of the men got up and ran away. I felt faint. I simply didn't know who had won. And for all I knew they were fighting over who would kill me and whether one should rape me first.

The man who was left stayed down, gasping.

Please say something, I pleaded inwardly.

He dragged himself along for a few yards until he could sit on the ramp.

'Steve?' I whispered. 'Is it you?' It couldn't be Terry for I didn't believe in ghosts. Did I?

In the darkness I was vaguely aware of a nod.

'Did Patrick send you?' I promised that gentleman a piece of my mind if he had. It is odd how the human brain can comfortably encompass impending doom and scold in the space of two minutes.

'No,' he gasped, finally. 'Got up . . . felt better . . . sort of. God. Went out the back for some fresh air. The bleeper was going in the fencing wagon.'

'I didn't know it had a receiver,' I said.

'Yeah. Drove to Bitterns. Saw the car . . . bleeper going in that too. No sign of the major. Police car . . . further down the road. Woman screaming that her Land-Rover and trailer had been pinched. Bleeper going loud and clear. Switched on direction finder. Here I am.'

'Have you a knife?

'Yeah . . . somewhere.'

'I'm sure that man's still around here. I haven't heard him drive away.'

'Probably because I hit him hard.'

He was so weak he had to crawl to the pick-up. I could do

72

nothing to help, not even move closer, the ropes were cutting into me so painfully. By the time he returned, walking slowly by now, I was at screaming pitch, expecting at any moment to see a dark figure come at us from the darkness.

'I'm doing my best,' Steve muttered, reading my mind as he sawed at the ropes. 'Can't bloody see what I'm doing, that's the trouble.'

I bit my lip as the knife found flesh but seconds later my hands were free. I took the knife from Steve and cut through the bindings on my ankles. When I stood up I fell over again, no feeling in my feet, and rolled down the ramp on to muddy grass. Steve flopped on to his knees beside me and we sort of picked each other up and stood with our arms around one another.

'What was that?' Steve said sharply.

'What?'

'I thought I heard voices.'

All I could hear were my own nerves jangling.

Then lights came at us through the trees. Someone shouted.

'Come on!' Steve said, hauling me in the direction of the pick-up. 'He went for his oppos. We can't take on the whole damn lot.'

I made up my mind when someone fired a shotgun, lead pellets blasting through the foliage above our heads and clanging into the metal sides of the trailer. We tumbled into the vehicle and somehow I managed to drive it away.

'Where on earth are we?' I said, having to shout the question a second time as my passenger didn't appear to be taking much notice of the proceedings, slumped in his seat.

'Somewhere near Billingshurst,' Steve mumbled. 'I think.'

Only a few miles from Petworth? That seemed crazy. I drove fairly aimlessly for about five miles, keeping to narrow lanes, my only thought that of losing anyone following. Then I pulled up. The adrenalin had run out.

'Sorry,' Steve said. 'I made a real cock-up of that.'

'You were wonderful,' I told him, meaning it. I tried to stop the bleeding from my wrist with my handkerchief. Our first-aid kit was in my car, still presumably parked at Bitterns. No, it couldn't be, I reasoned dully through my headache, Patrick must be looking for me by now. 'Steve, how come it's dark and we're so close to Petworth? I mean, you said you caught up with the trailer and . . . ' I had to stop talking then because of nauseating dizziness.

Steve groaned, more of a comment on the situation than a result of any discomfort of his own. 'Well, he was driving in circles for quite a while. I got lost pretty quickly, what with feeling like death and all. I only had the bleeper to guide me. He stopped once, got out and looked around so I had to drive right past and park up a track a bit further on. My real problem was that I felt so weak. I knew I couldn't tackle a big bloke like that. I thought I'd wait and see where he went. I figured you'd be OK as long as he kept going. I suppose I was hoping the major was on the trail just behind me.'

'He obviously wasn't,' I said, feeling very lonely and lost all of a sudden.

Steve continued, 'He drove down a forest track some time later and it came as a bit of a shock to me that I could see the big TV mast that's on the downs that you can see from Longcoombe. I parked the bus when I saw him leave the track and drive under some trees. I got out. That's when I really failed you. I passed out. When I came round it was almost dark and the guy was just lowering the ramp. You could have been killed a million times.' He switched on the interior light in the cab and his eyes opened wide. 'Oh, bloody hell, Ingrid! That's a terrible head you have.'

'It feels somewhat ghastly,' I admitted.

'You're not fit to drive.'

'Nor are you.'

'We could put a call out.'

By this he meant we could send out a Mayday. The pick-up and my car are both fitted with the means to do so but unfortunately – government cut-backs – not ordinary radios. Patrick's car, parked at Pulborough, has a phone.

'And have half the police and military personnel in Sussex on the spot?' I said. 'Helicopters? Cars? Motorbikes? It doesn't really warrant that, does it?'

'The major wouldn't like it,' said Steve weakly, breathtakingly logical reasoning in the circumstances.

'Quite,' I mumbled.

74

'What were you doing nosing around in the trailer in the first place?'

I swore and he looked at me in surprise.

'I left my bag in the trailer,' I said, starting the engine. 'There was something that might have been blood on the floor of it and I took a sample and put it in my purse. We'll have to go back.'

'You're not fit to drive,' Steve repeated.

'I can't help that,' I told him and drove, following my nose.

'Contact the major first,' he pleaded when the speedometer was hitting sixty.

'How?' I snapped.

'Find a phone box. For God's sake, Ingrid ...'

I had swerved to avoid a car going in the opposite direction. By the light from our vehicle I had noticed something vaguely familiar about it.

'That was your car!' Steve yelled. And when this failed to penetrate, 'Stop! That was the major!' When he had prised himself off the dashboard he asked faintly. 'Who taught you to drive like that?'

I didn't answer, watching the reversing lights of the car in the mirror as it came towards us. They looked like eyes. I had almost convinced myself that they were eyes as they drew level, probably due to my bang on the head.

'I've never been so glad to see you,' I said when Patrick appeared by my wound-down window. 'How did you find us?'

The tiny burglar's torch flashed over us briefly.

'You still have the beacon around your neck,' Patrick said patiently, a hint of a tremor in his voice. He removed it and unscrewed the base to deactivate it.

'You're a genius,' I said. 'Look, we must get back to the trailer. I've left my bag in it with – '

'No chance,' he interrupted. 'By the time I got there it was an inferno. Someone had chucked petrol on it and set light to it.'

'It's no excuse,' I said. 'But people were taking shots at us.'

He opened the driver's door and drew me gently out.

'I'm so sorry,' I told him.

In the lights of the two vehicles I saw him gazing down at me soberly.

75

'This is my fault, Ingrid,' he said softly. 'A leader is supposed to lead, not whinge about his own shortcomings and leave his assistants to go off on their own. A leader is also supposed to define the task, plan, explain, assess, discuss, monitor, support and evaluate. I did none of those things.'

'Then give Steve a medal,' I said, my voice sounding strange to me. 'He fought the man off when he was almost too ill to stand.'

The medal was the first thing I saw when I woke up in bed at the hotel. It was the wheel hub of a car, polished until very bright, a hole bored in the edge so that it could be hung around the neck on a piece of ribbon. Steve was wearing it, grinning widely.

'Is that the Order of Gillard?' I asked, trying not to move my head.

'Gong of gongs,' he replied and drew my attention to a superb arrangement of apricot and cream carnations on the bedside table. 'That's yours.'

'He really mustn't blame himself.'

'No. He mustn't. But nevertheless, he is.' Steve removed the 'medal'. 'I think I understand now. The colonel said working with you both would be different and I took it to mean that everything would be ruthless and super-efficient. You do have this terrific reputation for getting the job done and, frankly, some people have read into this that the major is a real bastard.'

'He can be sometimes,' I said under my breath.

'I've found that out for myself,' Steve went on with feeling. 'But he's a bastard in a *constructive* way − doesn't cut you down to size to boost his own ego.'

You either love him or loathe him, I thought; only his wife is allowed the luxury of both.

'You must have stumbled on something important,' Steve went on. 'Or they wouldn't have burnt out the trailer like that. Oh, by the way, they found out who was shooting at us. The landowner, Colonel Someone or other. He's had a lot of hassle from gypsies camping on his land and cutting down the trees for fuel. One of his gamekeepers reported vehicles in the woods so he got a few blokes together to sort it. I understand

76

that as he's a local JP the police are turning a blind eye to the business of shots being fired.'

'Magic,' I said. 'If he'd been a trade-union activist he'd have been run in so fast his feet wouldn't have touched the ground.'

'You astound me. Thought you'd be for the Establishment and all that.'

I said, 'One of the reasons D12 was set up was to hack away at the old-boy network that's been known to protect those who – what shall I say? – weren't entirely concentrating on what was best for their country. Daws reached the rank of colonel because he's been a fine soldier in his time, not because he belongs to the right clubs. He made it clear when he was looking for someone to lead the main team that he didn't want a G and T man with two black Labradors and a Filofax.' I shut my eyes. 'I'm sure you know all this. I don't want to talk about it any more . . . my head aches. Tell me how someone managed to burn out the trailer with Colonel Blimp's men in the area.'

'They didn't stick around to guard it. Probably *all* went to phone the police. When the law arrived the major had just reached the spot and they found the trailer in flames and the Land-Rover missing. It was discovered later a few miles down the road. The police want to talk to you, by the way, when you feel better.'

Perhaps in five years' time, I thought miserably.

'Would you like some breakfast?'

'Where's Patrick?'

'I *think* he said he was going to call on Colonel Blimp. But that was last night.'

The other side of the bed had not been slept in. Where on earth was he?

'Have something to eat,' Steve urged. 'Say the word and I'll ring room service.' He came close to whisper in my ear. 'A little bird told me that you can always eat – even in the most traumatic situations and while at death's door.'

I smiled. I knew the identity of that bird. 'All right.' I was, after all, ravenously hungry. 'I'll have eggs and bacon with fried bread, tomatoes and kidneys if they have any. Toast, marmalade and a pot of Earl Grey tea.'

Steve had, I now realised, been given orders to watch over me. This left Patrick free to carry on working while Steve and I regained our strength. After I had eaten I shooed Steve from the room and got up. I immediately wished that I hadn't and a glance in the mirror confirmed that I looked as bad as I felt. In a word, ghastly. The doctor had left some pills so I took one, showered and washed my hair. This produced a slight all-round improvement. I had just finished dressing when Steve knocked to say that Sergeant Grant was asking to see me and had a copy of the pathologist's report with him.

'Well, you've certainly got things moving,' Grant said when I had given him my account of what happened. 'Would you recognise this man again?'

'Probably not,' I admitted.

'Tall and well built,' he mused, consulting his notebook. 'Not the Hursts' chauffeur?'

'No. Not so tall and big as him.'

Grant sniffed. 'Pity.'

'Shame on you, officer,' I said.

Unexpectedly, he grinned. 'There *is* a small matter of a previous record.'

'What for?' Steve and I said in unison.

'Assault. Driving while over the limit. Receiving stolen property – a sawn-off shotgun.'

'Peculiar,' Steve commented. 'It's not legal even to possess a sawn-off shotgun.'

'It was peculiar all right. I get the impression that there were a lot more charges but they couldn't make them stick. Faversham's getting in touch with a chum of his in the Met to find out more details.'

I said, 'Presumably this was before he worked for Hurst.'

'Yes. About ten years ago. Except for the drunk-driving charge. That was last year. But in his own car, not the Roller.'

'He's knocked around rough,' Steve said. 'What you've said makes me think of big-city gangs.'

'Makes me think of all kinds of things,' Grant said, closing his notebook with a snap.

He had not noticed the handle of the door moving slowly but Steve and I had. Grant's eyes nearly fell out of his head

78

when Steve pulled his gun from beneath his jacket and silently concealed himself behind the door.

There was a short pause when nothing happened and then the door opened violently. It slammed right back into the wall and would have smashed into Steve if he had not leapt out of the way. He crouched, gun in both hands.

'Bang,' said Steve blithely as Patrick walked in.

'As you were,' Patrick murmured after giving him a Gilbert and Sullivan salute.

'I've got that report, sir,' Grant said, recovering.

''Fraid I'm slightly ahead of you, sergeant,' Patrick said apologetically. 'I went to view the late lamented and had a word with Crossley's stand in, John Houseman. But I'd be interested in having a look at what he wrote if you have it there — it'll refresh my memory.' He sat on the bed, perusing the typewritten report.

Good morning, Ingrid, I thought. How's the head this morning? Did you manage to sleep at all? How lovely you look with those designer bruises. I could ravish you here and now.

Patrick looked up. There *is* such a thing as telepathy between people who are close. 'How's the head?'

'A different shape to what it was before,' I replied.

He carried on reading. His mouth twitched.

'Go on, laugh,' I said. 'You laughed once when I had two black eyes. You were in intensive care at the time with a breathing tube down your throat, another up your nose and others in places that I won't mention. You laughed. When I told one of the doctors he said it was medically impossible.'

Everyone laughed.

Patrick rubbed his hands tiredly over his face. 'God, I need a little levity right now. When you're a soldier you get used to the sight of people who've been hurt or killed. I don't mind telling you that when I came out of the mortuary I threw up. It had been a frenzied attack. One of his eyes had been knocked right out of the socket.' He scanned the report again for a moment. 'There *is* a mark around the neck. First of all Houseman said that attempts might have been made to strangle him but when I mentioned it he agreed that the body had more likely been strung up after he was dead. I won't bore

79

you with things like stomach contents. He had eaten, though ... not all that long before he was killed.'

'A hated man,' Sergeant Grant said thoughtfully. 'The more we ask questions around the village, the more we uncover. One woman in the village was involved in a minor accident with him in her car. She says it was his fault. Apparently he scared the life out of her with his threats and language. Someone else reckoned he tried to kill everyone's dogs ... drove at 'em. Things like that. I wouldn't be all that surprised if the local people didn't club together and hire a contract killer.'

'Who?' Patrick said vibrantly. 'Think! It's highly unlikely that these folk would have any contacts with big-time hit men. Anyone you can think of who might have the know-how? Ex-military people, for example.'

'Jessica Campbell mentioned a retired RAF officer,' I said.

'Wing Commander Gordon,' said Grant. 'He's ninety-two.'

'What about your colonel?' Steve asked Patrick. 'Did you go to see him?'

'I frightened the sweet life out of him,' Patrick said dreamily. 'A serving officer, too. It's only at times like that that I realise how much clout I've been given. By the time I'd shown him my ID card, reminded him that only the Duke of Atholl is permitted to have his own army and told him that he'd nearly blasted two operatives of MI5 from the face of the Earth he was so white you could have ironed him and used him for bedlinen. But I'm a forgiving sort of bloke so when he asked me if I'd care to taste a single malt he'd been saving for a while I was only too happy to oblige.'

'It must have been hellish late when you went round there,' Steve said.

'Almost midnight. But everyone was still up — having some kind of debriefing.'

'You stayed the night,' I declared. 'Too drunk to drive back.'

'Over the limit,' he corrected. 'Yes, I was ordered to. He's a decent bloke beneath all the bluster.'

Grant rose to go. 'I'm going down to that riding school to see if a vehicle parked in the road outside is visible from the

80

yard or office. *If* that stuff in the trailer was blood . . .' He smiled at us. 'Interesting case, isn't it?'

'Have a look from the upstairs of the house,' Patrick suggested. 'There are trees but there must be gaps in the branches.'

'It was Libby's trailer,' I pointed out. 'Is there a husband or boyfriend with bruises? One would like to ask.'

'I will ask,' Grant said. He paused on his way towards the door. 'You mentioned the Campbells. Now Rowan Campbell was a military man. Used to be in the SAS.'

'D'you mind if I follow that one up?' Patrick said.

'Not at all, major.'

Grant left. Patrick said, 'Your car, Ingrid, was low on petrol so I used the pick-up last night. I noticed just now when I parked next to it that there's rather a lot of brake fluid on the ground underneath. Someone tampered with it in the night.' He gave us both a crazy smile. 'Are you ready? It's going to be like in the cowboy films. We're going to walk down the village street with our spurs clinking to show 'em that Gillard and Co. don't frighten easily.'

Chapter Eight

Patrick's BMW, which had been left in the car park behind the police station at Pulborough, had not been tampered with. And, as Patrick pointed out, the case would have taken on quite different aspects if it had, for only the police knew to whom it belonged. Once behind the wheel he relaxed slightly. The vehicle, a 635i, is an automatic model with the pedals adjusted so that he can drive using just his left foot for the brake and accelerator. As he has said more than once, trying to drive with a right foot that has no sensation can be hair-raising.

'You haven't mentioned anything about the result of the blood test you had carried out on me,' Steve said.

'It was negative,' Patrick replied. 'Ingrid's was negative too. That doesn't mean a lot — your bodies probably would have eliminated any foreign substances by the time the tests were done.'

I tried to dismiss from my mind all thoughts of the supernatural.

'I called on the cleaning lady yesterday,' Patrick continued as we wove through the lanes — we were making the journey over minor roads. 'Rose is quite a character. I got the impression that even if the Hursts fried small children for breakfast she wouldn't tell me about it. More people in Longcoombe seem to have been aware of Westfield's connection with MI5 than I personally would have thought possible. Or desirable, for that matter. And you meet a wall of silence. What he was — pretty unpleasant — we undoubtedly must be and that's that. It makes me yearn for the days when

82

I could have arranged sappers to rebuild the village hall as a public-relations exercise.'

Entering the village, Patrick parked by the parish church of Saint Giles. Three women standing outside a grocer's shop stopped talking to watch us as we got out of the car, as did a small group queueing at a bus stop and another in a car park by the Speckled Hen pub – waiting, I was fairly sure, for the arrival of a mobile library. They all watched us. In silence.

'Have you spoken to Plummer, the chauffeur?' Steve said to Patrick, the latter with his hand on the lych gate.

'He's avoiding me,' Patrick said, checking the church clock with his watch. 'He can stew. The police are keeping a fairly close eye on him.'

'Are the Hursts still suspects, then?'

'As far as the police are concerned I don't think they ever have been. From what I can gather Faversham is working on a tentative theory that Plummer and his gangland friends might have had something to do with it.'

'And what do *you* think?' I asked. 'Oysters would appear to be raging gossips compared with you this morning.'

Speaking more quietly Patrick said, 'The Hursts are up to their necks in *something*. But whether it's murder and, if so, whether this can be proved is a different matter altogether.'

'What about the manuscript?' I persisted.

'If it exists.'

'I'm sure it exists.'

'Don't rush me,' was all he said, going up the path to the church door.

'And the business of Rowan Campbell being ex-SAS?' I said, but only to myself.

'Are you going in the church?' Steve called after Patrick.

'Don't you like churches?' he replied without turning round. 'It's an interesting building. It caught my eye yesterday and I thought I'd have a look round when I had a few spare moments.'

Steve caught my eye, shrugged and we both set off after him.

In a low voice I said, 'Patrick's father is rector of Hinton Littlemoor in Somerset.'

'Go on,' Steve exclaimed softly, his tone suggesting that I had let a skeleton out of the cupboard.

I didn't enlighten him further. For one thing my head still hurt terribly when I spoke, each syllable producing a hammer-like blow somewhere behind my eyes. For another, well, Steve was an atheist and proud of it. He was in for a shock.

I hadn't expected the building to be open but the massive oak door swung on oiled hinges to Patrick's touch. Steve and I followed him in, instantly steeped in that heavy peaceful silence smelling of old books and snuffed candles. At the back of the nave were the usual postcards for sale, a visitors' book, several copies of the parish magazine, a posy of fresh garden flowers in a small pot.

Patrick had paused by the tomb of a long-dead nobleman and his wife and the three of us gazed down at the worn stone faces, the morning sun glinting on traces of gilding on their robes and imparting rose and azure hues from the stained-glass windows.

'Death and funerals, superstition and sin,' Steve said, seating himself in a pew.

Patrick set off up the main aisle. 'Christenings, weddings, faith and forgiveness,' he said. Then he went through the gap in the rood screen into the sanctuary and knelt at the altar rail.

'Not a man to make empty gestures of that kind,' Steve whispered.

'You were at Terry's funeral too,' I said. 'No, of course not.'

'I think at the time I assumed him to be wearing his man-from-the-Establishment hat.' He touched my arm. 'Why aren't you up there with him, Mrs Gillard?'

'I'm not sure about it yet.'

Steve shook his head in perplexity. 'When I was in the navy I thought the chaplains good sorts. But out of touch. I've said for years that the whole thing's a load of codswallop but then . . .' He gestured wordlessly in Patrick's direction.

Since entering the building a 'larger than life' feeling had come over me. I wondered if I had a temperature or if residues of whatever drug I had been given were still within me. Or whether I remained under the power of something nameless and utterly evil . . .

'Steve?' I said, the colours of the windows suddenly glaring. 'I'm scared.'

He gave me his full attention. 'What of?'

I stood up. 'I feel that something's watching me. It's like when I was at the Hursts'. We were up in the room where the body had been found and it seemed to me that blood was coming out of the walls. It was everywhere. But something in the house was making it *happen*.'

'It would have no influence here.'

I stared at him. 'But you don't believe in God.'

'No, but . . .' He had gone very pale and I remembered that he was still most unwell.

'I think I'd feel safer . . .' I began and then stopped speaking, feeling the sweat bead on my forehead.

'Outside?'

'No. Up there with Patrick.'

He came with me and we were as little children. It seemed a long way and I was distractedly wondering why we were both suffering from the aftermath of our respective ills and weaknesses while at the same time realising that we were behaving stupidly.

Patrick didn't look up when we knelt at his side but after half a minute or so spoke. 'Did you look on the altar?'

'No,' I replied. I had been looking where I was going.

'No,' said Steve.

'There's a fairly large hammer there and I regret that the blood on it has quite spoilt the white altar cloth.'

My skin crawled.

'Someone's coming,' Patrick said, after what seemed like hours had passed.

We rose to our feet, and my gaze went straight to the item that had been placed in front of the brass cross. It was undoubtedly the murder weapon. Hair and thickly clotted blood was caught in the claw end of the hammer.

'I feel a bit . . .' Steve started to say and then fainted with dramatic thoroughness down the three altar steps.

Patrick and I didn't quite manage to catch him but at least prevented his head from hitting the steps or the floor. We were rolling him over so that he was not lying on his back when the church door boomed open.

When Patrick saw that the man who entered was in his sixties, his hand dropped from where it had been reaching under his jacket for his gun.

Although he was wearing an old, much darned green sweater and equally ancient trousers, this gentleman was undoubtedly the incumbent. A trifle out of breath, high in colour and wielding a pair of edging shears, he came down the aisle towards us, stopping abruptly when he saw Steve on the floor.

Patrick said, 'It would be extremely gratifying, Father, if I could report that my friend here had been zapped by the Holy Spirit. As it is, he caught a glimpse of the sacrilegious object that someone has left on the altar and it was simply too much for him.'

The custodian of the souls of Longcoombe realised that he was still grasping the shears and put them on a front pew with a clatter. 'Someone said there were intruders in the church. Oh, dear.'

'Filthy heathen hordes from MI5?' Patrick said with a crooked smile.

Bright-blue eyes unclouded by age fixed unwaveringly on him. Then, obviously still unsure of what was going on, he transferred his gaze to the altar.

'There might be fingerprints,' Patrick commented quietly. 'I don't advise moving it.'

'I don't think I could bring myself to touch it.' He gave Patrick another searching look. 'Why did you come in the church?'

'Speaking personally, to pray.'

'Do you regard the discovery of this as the answer to your prayers?'

'I thought I'd made my feelings plain. I regard it as desecration.'

The priest sat down in a pew, slumping as though very tired. 'This is a wretched business.' Remembering Steve, he rose again quickly. 'Bring your colleague to the rectory. We'll give him a tot of something and some tea. I'm Ingleton, Cyril Ingleton.'

'I hate to trouble you,' Patrick said after introducing himself.

'There's trouble already, major,' said Ingleton, looking at the hammer. 'A little more can be borne.'

Steve showed no sign of coming round so Patrick carried him in a fireman's lift. The ease with which he did this surprised me and I think it surprised him too for he paused as we left the church to give me a brief smile.

We went round the side of the building and along a gravel path – the gravel being the reason that Patrick had heard Ingleton's approach – then through a narrow gate. There was a short grass path through a small paddock and then we were in the vicarage garden, Mrs Ingleton tending her roses.

'Nothing to be alarmed about, Connie,' called her husband. 'Perhaps you'll put the kettle on while I phone the police.' He turned to Patrick. 'Bring him indoors. We can put him on the sofa.'

'Here'll be better,' Patrick said, lowering Steve on to the soft turf of the lawn.

'Nothing to be alarmed about?' the vicar's wife repeated in some perplexity, pulling off her gardening gloves and dropping them into a trug filled with weeds. 'Cyril never ceases to amaze me. He delivers a body into the garden, runs off to phone the police and tells me there's nothing to be alarmed about!'

'There's no need to worry on *this* one's account,' Patrick told her, loosening Steve's tie. 'He's had the flu and his cruel boss forced him back to work before he was anything like recovered. Give him a squirt of Paraquat and he'll be fighting fit in no time.'

'Something tells me you're the slave-driver in question,' the lady murmured, moistening a clean unfolded handkerchief in the nearby watering can and bathing Steve's forehead. 'Ah – he's with us now. Young man,' she said in peremptory tones, addressing Steve. 'Have no fear. My garden is beautiful but not the Elysian Fields. You are still in the land of the living.'

Steve sat up. 'I must be,' he muttered after glancing at Patrick. 'He's here.'

Forty minutes later we were still in the vicarage sitting room and had been joined by Inspector Faversham – not entranced that we had made things happen again – and Sergeant Grant.

Steve was recovering, very quiet but regaining his spirit and colour as he devoured hot buttered toast as fast as Mrs Ingleton could make it for him.

I was content with personal inactivity, gratefully allowing others to do the talking. For my head still ached as though about to burst and the sight in my left eye remained slightly blurred. I did make a note of a few points I knew Patrick would want to remember: the names of the people living in the cottages and shops that overlooked the church, the hardware shop mentioned by Grant where the hammer might have been purchased, this point raised because the murder weapon looked reasonably new.

After Faversham, Grant and the team who had been working in the church had departed, I stacked cups and plates and took them to the vicar's wife in the kitchen. The vicarage was one of those Gothic structures that are impossible to heat: echoing passages with stone floors, vast cavernous rooms and enormous curving staircases. The kitchen was no exception. There was easily enough room to hold a jumble sale in one end of it and a whist drive in the other while carrying on with normal domestic activities in the centre.

'I've just realised,' Mrs Ingleton gasped when she saw me. 'You were that poor lass who was abducted right here in the village and nearly murdered. Give me that crockery instantly. You shouldn't be carrying anything.'

Meekly, I laid it down on a huge oak table.

'He has no right to keep you both working,' she continued crossly. 'You *are* from MI5, aren't you? Like the man who was murdered? Yes, I thought so. But that's what the rumours said, of course. Well, if I were you I'd tell him.'

She was probably right but I shook my head. 'Patrick's had his share of rough times too.'

'Does he let you call him by his Christian name to his face?'

I had to laugh out loud at this. 'Of course. He's my husband.'

The person under discussion then put in an appearance.

'Tell me,' said Mrs Ingleton. 'Have you come to the village to try to hush everything up? To whitewash the truth in order to protect the security services?'

'Madam,' said Patrick, with a wry sort of smile, 'I work for

88

a department whose sole aim in life is to ferret out irregularities, whether originating from within or without. My brief is to stand them up against the wall and throw darts at them until they squeal for mercy.'

'I'm glad,' she robustly declared. 'I'm glad because when I first saw you I thought what a shame it would be if such a man was involved with shady dealings.'

'I'm blushing,' Patrick said. 'Now, for the love of everything bright and beautiful, tell me what's going on in this village.'

'I wish I knew. We seem to have become crazy people, attacking strangers and tampering with their cars. It was your car the police were talking about earlier, wasn't it? It almost looks as though the community is covering up for someone. I really can't help you – if only I could.'

'Was the murdered man so hated that his killer might be protected by a whole village?'

Mrs Ingleton turned away from him and started to move the crockery I had brought in to the draining board.

'Even you . . .' Patrick began gently.

'No!' She rounded on him and then fell silent, colouring.

'I'm a horrible man,' said Patrick in genial fashion. 'Even my own mother says so and she too is a clergyman's wife.'

'I wouldn't protect a murderer,' she said stiffly after an uncomfortable silence.

'I'd be the last to suggest that you would. But there might be a certain sympathy . . .'

'No,' she said again. 'But I might understand. Just a little.'

'Then I'll repeat the question. Why was he hated so much?'

'Because of his contempt. Open contempt. For the village – the people who live here – everything.'

'Bad temper? Bad language?'

'Oh yes. He swore at me one morning when I nearly bumped into him outside the post office.'

'And the parties at Bitterns?'

'That didn't affect us. What people do in their own homes is their affair.'

'Did you hear the rumour about a girl being raped?' I asked.

'Yes, but villages are always awash with rumours. Someone

said that the girl concerned was the sister of the woman at the riding school. I didn't know she had a sister.'

'What did you hear about the parties?' Patrick said, showing no reaction. When she did not reply immediately he asked, 'Would you rather I asked other people that question?'

Sharply, she said, 'I'm not a prude. When you hear of gatherings with a lot of drink and people from London and there's talk of drugs you have to mind your own business, don't you? And when people hint darkly that there are also prostitutes from town and everyone dresses up in costumes and bites the heads off chickens you thank your lucky stars you know the difference between right and wrong. Either that or dismiss the rumours utterly.'

'Black magic hasn't quite been mentioned,' Patrick remarked.

'Call it sex and frightening ignorant people witless. Then you get it in true perspective. But it's like cancer. Perfectly rational men and women begin to be infected with it when things start to go wrong. Someone's dog dies and the vet isn't sure why. A valuable horse gets caught in barbed wire and has to be destroyed. Things like that. Accidents. Natural disasters. But people look sideways at each other when they know there are others who play at witches and wizards. It's only human nature — we're all slightly superstitious if we'd only admit it.'

'You have a breathtakingly sensible head on your shoulders,' Patrick said. 'One further question: do Jessica and Rowan Campbell come to church?'

'No. But I know the people you mean. She keeps horses, doesn't she? Quite a pretty woman. I'm fairly sure I haven't seen them in church even at Christmas. Some of the wealthy people do come then ... sweep to the front pews as though they were gentry. It affords the regular congregation no end of amusement.'

Absent-mindedly Patrick took a tea towel and began to dry some cups and saucers already washed. 'I can't believe the entire village is protecting a murderer. Whoever attacked Ingrid wasn't just a passer-by who thought that getting rid of Westfield was a good idea. There's more to it than that.'

90

'You'd need to find out who was at the parties,' said Mrs Ingleton, frowning with concentration.

Patrick turned on her a wide, artless gaze. 'Why?'

She stared back at him. 'I'm not sure what made me say that. All I do know is that Longcoombe was a perfectly ordinary place before the Hursts arrived — boring, really. Perhaps they've corrupted us — taught us to hate and kill. Frankly, what has happened here sickens me and I don't just mean the murder. It seems to me that you ought to investigate the source.'

The phone rang but before Mrs Ingleton could reach it — beneath a pile of what looked like hand-spun wool on an overflowing dresser — the call was answered elsewhere in the house. Steve came into the kitchen shortly afterwards.

'That was the police — Grant, actually — to say that your bag has been found, Ingrid. In some bushes on a sports field. The money had been taken but the screw of paper with the sample from the trailer was still there. It was blood all right — the same group as Westfield's. Now they're running tests on the hammer and also putting the fingerprints on the bag through records. Grant wants your fingerprints — yours as well, sir, if you've handled the bag — so they can be discounted.'

'How very odd,' Patrick commented. 'In some bushes on a sports field? Perhaps we have a lead at last.'

'Oh, and a mechanic at the local garage suddenly remembered that he'd written down a couple of car numbers. Two blokes in separate cars bought petrol recently and one of them asked the way to Bitterns. He was so shifty-looking that the mechanic noted down the numbers of the cars — wondered if they'd been stolen.'

Patrick said, 'Let us seek out this genius and heap him with rose petals.'

Chapter Nine

The Campbells were not at home so it was decided that Patrick and Steve would interview Libby at the stables. Dutifully providing the police with my fingerprints — Patrick emphatic that he hadn't laid hands on my bag, ever — I was not present either when the decision was made or during what followed. If I had been, there would have been a different outcome.

Steve, of course, was not aware that Libby had found the elder of the two fencing contractors personable to the extent of giving him the key to her door, Patrick hardly being the sort of man to brag about it. Thus, he uttered no little warning homilies concerning women and the scorning thereof. So when the lady in question saw the visitors in their dark suits, collars and ties and grasped the nearest weapon to hand, a pitchfork, Steve saw that his immediate superior was about to be spitted to the tack-room door.

There is no doubt that had he not flung himself forward Patrick would have been gravely injured, Libby aiming aptly and cunningly low. As it was, all three went down. Patrick's reflexes caused him to leap sideways but he caught his right foot on a ridge in the concrete.

I'm told that charm won the day. When all had righted themselves and Patrick had told her who they were, he offered her the choice of horsewhips at twenty paces, a convivial evening in her favourite pub with the three of us, two tickets for the office raffle, the prize to be announced later, or a ten-franc piece he had found in his pocket. Libby asked for a look at his ID card, eyed him up grimly, walked up and down a few times and then burst into howls of laughter. She was still cackling when she decided on the second option and gave them permission to look around the house.

Walking with Steve into the back door of the Speckled Hen we agreed that Libby's consolation prize was a good idea. It kept us right in the centre of village life and, even if a little risky from the point of view of personal safety, at least gave us the chance to show the people of Longcoombe the kind of folk we really were.

'We're not trying to out-perform the police,' Steve said quietly as we waited for Patrick, who was locking the car. 'And you may depend on it that if Faversham did pop in for a pint he wouldn't learn a damn thing.'

I said, 'No, and most of the things we've discovered so far have been as a result of absolute flukes. If you hadn't fainted we probably wouldn't have spoken to Mrs Ingleton. I wonder if it *was* Libby's sister who was raped?'

'The major intends to ask her some time this evening, I've no doubt.' Steve grinned ruefully. 'That woman's capable of violence. You should have seen the way she went for him with the pitchfork.'

'Violent enough to have killed Westfield?'

'That was going through my mind,' he admitted.

We were all casually dressed — sweaters and jeans — and when Patrick joined us we made for the public bar. There were a couple of seconds of comparative quiet and then everyone commenced talking again, if perhaps in slightly forced fashion.

Libby was late and when she arrived she was very much out of sorts. Not one to hide her feelings, she didn't speak to us at all for about five minutes, finally and with ill grace sipping the drink that Patrick had placed in front of her.

'Are the police making a nuisance of themselves?' I asked, nevertheless wondering if Patrick was still in her bad books.

She glowered at me. 'They virtually accused me of killing the man. I've been in that damn police station for hours — ever since we finished work. At one point I began to think they weren't going to let me go. I mean, it's bad enough having the trailer stolen and burnt out without being accused of murder.'

Her voice was of the carrying variety and I could see that several of our fellow drinkers were all ears, including a whiskered ancient who for some reason reminded me of someone. But I couldn't think whom.

'Anyway,' Libby went on, apparently still peevish. 'Shouldn't people like you be in the lounge bar . . . officer and all that rubbish?'

'I'm a misfit,' Patrick told her solemnly. 'I tend to drink beer — Marston's Pedigree when I can get hold of it. Get me drunk enough and I might lapse into my native Devon dialect.'

This was perfectly true. But to my experience this lapse — if it can be described as such — is not into the lovely rolling burr of the countryside of the South Hams and other areas but pure Plymouth 'Janner', that totally different, thick-as-treacle accent that I personally find very difficult to follow and which Patrick presumably picked up at school. Then again, I am sometimes driven to wonder what *is* his natural manner of articulation, this born mimic utilising sufficient accents to be able to have a different one for every hour of the day.

'*Did* anyone borrow the trailer on the night of the murder?' Steve asked.

'Not to my knowledge,' Libby answered. She was halfway through her drink, shandy, and mellowing a little. 'It's left parked round by the side of the house at night, with the Land-Rover. The police don't like it if you leave things like that in the road at night. It would have been quite possible for someone to push it quietly if they fancied using it for a couple of hours. We didn't chain it up or anything. But I will when I get the new one,' she finished by saying, narrowly eyeing the barmaid, who was openly listening. The girl bustled off and began to wash glasses.

'Don't you keep a dog?' I asked. 'I would have thought with all that valuable tack and — '

'I *had* a dog,' she interrupted. 'Muffin. He was killed on the road a while ago.'

'Who by?' I perservered, suddenly remembering the rumour that it had been Westfield.

'How the hell should I know? The bastard didn't stop.'

94

After a short pause Patrick said, 'The murdered man apparently had a hatred of dogs.'

'Well, he would, wouldn't he? One attacked his wife and she had to have thirteen stitches in her arm.'

Then, I am quite sure, Libby could have bitten off her tongue.

'You've spoken to him,' Patrick said. 'When?'

I thought for a moment that she would throw the rest of her drink over him. But this did not happen. Instead Libby glanced around anxiously and when she spoke it was in a defiant whisper.

'It was a long time ago. Just after the Hursts moved in and he came to stay with them. I met him when I was out for a walk with Muffin and I could see he didn't want him near.'

'Was he abusive?'

'No.'

'And yet people say he was very unpleasant.'

'He wasn't then ... not when he first came. I didn't like him, though − he was creepy.'

'What were you doing on the night of the murder?'

'A convivial evening, you said,' she hissed. 'Ask the police if you want that kind of information. They asked me everything but −' She stopped speaking abruptly, lips pursed.

'If you'd slept with him?' Patrick prompted. 'Did he want you to?'

But Libby was looking over his head at two men who had come in from the lounge bar. They were well dressed in the kind of casual clothes that might be bought from a city gentlemen's outfitters; fine cavalry twill trousers, lambswool sweaters, waxed cotton jackets. They surveyed us all.

'Those two −' Libby started to say and then grabbed her coat and left, not going out of the main door so that she would have to pass them but through the back, out into the car park.

'Want a bet?' Steve breathed in my ear. 'Hurst got on the blower and someone's sent a couple of warlocks to look us over.'

The two men went to a small table in a corner, one of them immediately coming back to stand by the bar. People shuffled aside to make room for him, conversation lapsed but in a

95

different way from when we had entered, the dislike and mistrust was tangible. But not because they were strangers.

I knew then that Libby had met them before and did not want them to see her talking to us. But had Hurst given them our descriptions? It seemed unlikely, for their gaze had not lingered on us. I did not see how we could escape detection for very long and I did not want to be singled out for any attention by this pair; to me they looked murderous.

Then Patrick removed a manic stare from the direction of the ceiling and in the flat and stentorian tones of the profoundly deaf bellowed, 'Corse it depends whether you cuts their throats fust or arterwards.' A finger was drawn across his own throat, the production of revolting sound effects sending him into a paroxysm of coughing.

I leaned my elbows on the table and bent forward as though I was going to speak softly but yelled at the top of my voice, 'You means when you puts them in the pot to git the fur off.'

'Corse that's what I means,' Patrick roared. 'Yer puts them in boiling water — boiling, I say — none of yer middlin' hot'll do. And then when the fur's off yer slit 'em up good. As I said just now — it depends whether yer cuts their throats fust or arterwards how much *noise* they make. Some folk can't handle the noise but when yer've been at it for fifteen year like me you gits used to it, don't ya?'

'Some don't,' I shouted. 'It stands to reason.'

'Call themselves men!' Patrick howled, spitting with great accuracy in the ashtray on the table. 'Call themselves men! Why, I've known wimin with more spine. No, yer gits 'em dead whichever way and then slit 'em up good and git the guts out. Or yer can leave 'em in a while — a few days like — and then do it. More flavour that way. But you git maggits then. My missus can't stand maggits in 'er pie but she always was a bit squeamish. As long as you make sure the oven's 'ot enough to kill 'em off. A pie with *travellin'* maggits ain't everyone's idea of a feast. Now my Uncle Arthur used to — '

'You hold your tongue about that old fool!' I yelled. 'I've heard about your muckin' Uncle Arthur until I'm sick to my stomach. Him and his stinking ferrets. I reckon he used to take 'em to bed with 'im too.'

Patrick uttered a truly filthy laugh. 'That was only to keep his old woman away.'

Morosely, Steve said, 'Ever likely the old cow went and threw 'er drawers over the postman's hedge.'

'Wassat?' Patrick said, ear cupped.

Steve repeated the remark, fortissimo.

The man by the bar paid for his drinks and went back to the table. Out of the corner of one eye I saw him shake his head at his companion, who shrugged. A few words were exchanged and then they both slowly strolled through the bar and back the way they had come.

The old man with the clouds of white whiskers now came and sat himself down in the chair vacated by Libby. 'Your uncle Arthur was a cousin of mine seven times removed,' he brayed into Patrick's left ear.

'He were that,' Patrick replied, nevertheless looking puzzled.

'A real hevil man. I never did blame that woman of his for what she done. The old devil ought to have been strung up.'

I suddenly realised why the old man reminded me of someone. Beneath the hair was Daws.

'What did she do?' Patrick enquired in his own voice.

The laughter started at the table next to us and rippled around the room. Half the gathering appeared to be crying on one another's shoulders.

'Why, went off with postman Fred. Another thing . . . that recipe for ferret pie was once on the radio.'

'He left things all over the bloody place,' I said in disgusted tones.

'No, you daft turnip,' Daws said with withering scorn. '*On* the radio. A lady with a posh Lunnon voice read it out so folk could write it down. It were in the days of they little crystal sets.'

'A bit before my time,' Patrick said, coming up for air from his pint and wiping his mouth on his sleeve. 'Now when – '

He is not easily silenced, let alone in mid-sentence with his mouth hanging open. But at that moment the penny dropped.

Uproar.

The laughter was prolonged. Almost everyone present must have known who we were and that Patrick had failed to

97

recognise a friend of his under a fairly heavy disguise. There were a couple of calls for an encore. Steve borrowed someone's cap and went the rounds with it, dropping the copper coins he had collected into a children's charity box on the bar. He then had to go round again, this time receiving notes and silver instead. The box ended up nearly full.

We made our exit as gracefully as possible. Without being ordered to, Steve took down the numbers of every vehicle in the car park and in the road outside. Discounting cattle trucks and battered four-wheel-drive transport of every kind, even a couple of tractors, this did not amount to very many.

'Oh, those whiskers,' said Patrick with great reverence. 'The faded old gardening trousers ... that hat ...' He stopped speaking again, under the pretext of being struck dumb with admiration.

'Where to now?' Steve asked, giving me back my notebook.

'Can we talk in your car?' Daws said to Patrick.

Steve checked over the BMW thoroughly, wriggling beneath it with a torch.

'Welcome to the team, sir,' Patrick said when we were sitting in the car. 'Correct me if I'm wrong, but it's the first time you've joined us on a mission.'

Daws said, 'You mean at the coalface and not just swanning in in my Savile Row suit to find out how things are going.'

'I wasn't about to put it quite like that,' Patrick murmured.

Daws stroked his false whiskers thoughtfully. 'Major, I discovered long ago that it's not what you say but the way you say it. Now, give me a concise report on what you've discovered so far.'

Patrick spoke for five minutes, leaving nothing out. His army-officer voice, I noted with a smile to myself, clipped, never using long words if short ones would do, almost as if reading from a written report, the kind of voice that could describe atrocity without emotion.

When he had finished, Daws said, 'I think a priority is to discover whether this book he might have written exists and, if so, its whereabouts. I become extremely nervous when civil servants write books. For good reason too, I feel.'

'Mrs Hurst was emphatic that her brother didn't write,' I said.

'But *you* think that a typescript exists.'

'Yes. Even though we only found the title page. It was very neatly typed and with a new ribbon. Not the way you just scribble when you're doing a rough draft.'

'Then find it. Let the police hunt his killer. That needn't stop you interviewing Rowan Campbell if you think it might be useful. As the Campbells used to be friends of the Hursts, they might reveal things that the Hursts would prefer to remain unsaid.'

'What kind of face did Westfield present to London?' Patrick asked.

'Charm,' said Daws. 'Integrity, cultivated tastes. Yes, I find it more than a little puzzling too in view of what you've just told me. Perhaps he led a Jekyll and Hyde existence.'

'Have you spoken to his wife, sir?'

'No, she was on holiday when it happened. But they haven't lived together for a while.'

'Jan Hurst didn't appear to be aware of that,' I said.

'Perhaps he was too proud to mention that his wife had left him.'

Which was highly likely if she had found out about the sort of parties he was attending at his sister's house, I thought. Perhaps on the other hand after many years of marriage she found him no more attractive than Babs and Libby had done.

Into the meditative silence that followed, Patrick said, 'And after this case? I think it's about time, sir, that you gave me some kind of reason why I haven't been permitted to investigate — '

'I know what you're going to say,' Daws told him briskly. 'You want to know why I haven't ordered you to look into Meadow's death. I'll tell you why. You're too emotionally involved.'

'Commitment,' Patrick said quietly. 'Commitment gets results.'

'And if you found his killer? Would there be yet another scandal concerning MI5 being a law unto itself? Major, I was once in your company when you put three bullets into a man who had arranged to have a small child kidnapped. You failed first to ascertain if he was armed and the fact that afterwards he was found to be holding a hand grenade bears little relevance to the point I'm making. At the time, though, it saved *your* skin.'

A thick skin, however. Patrick said, 'I do seem to recollect that he had oppos round him who were busily pointing their Mausers and other ironmongery in our direction. But Meadows was my man. I feel responsible for him and owe it to his family not to just let his death go into oblivion.'

'Nevertheless — ' Daws began.

'There's no one else,' Patrick snapped, angry enough to interrupt. 'No one with that kind of experience. Not in D12. Unless you're going to put the job out to contractors.'

'Someone with several years in the Army Intelligence Unit suit you?' Daws enquired mildly, no sarcasm in his voice at all.

'Who?'

'Me.'

There was rather a long silence.

'I'm sorry,' Patrick said, a little stiffly. 'I didn't dream for one moment that you'd take the time to . . .'

'First and foremost Meadows was *my* man,' Daws continued when Patrick left the rest of what he was about to say unuttered. 'His death needs to be looked into with some urgency to discover if a terrorist organisation is starting at random on its hit list.'

Daws, I thought, could have made this plain before. I couldn't believe that he had meant to put Patrick so brutally in his place, merely teaching him patience perhaps. On the other hand, if the colonel was thinking of finding a successor for the day when he retired he would want someone as cool-headed as himself, even someone he had *forced* to be so. Which was an interesting thought.

'So,' Daws said. 'This little exercise tonight was really so I could bring you up to date with my findings. One of the first things that came to hand was a report from the Anti-Terrorist Branch. They'd experienced a little difficulty so had asked for help from a member of an army bomb-disposal team. He agreed with their findings. There was no sign of the remains of any of the usual explosive devices in the wreckage of Meadow's car.'

'But it bloody blew up!' Steve exclaimed.

100

'Not as a result of a bomb or explosive device having been placed beneath it,' the colonel stressed. 'The only conclusion that can be reached is that some kind of miniature grenade was thrown into it.'

'In a suburban street!' Patrick said. 'I can't see that. London isn't Beirut.'

'What about a petrol bomb?' Steve asked.

'Too much damage to the body,' said Daws. 'My own feelings are that the car had stopped before a grenade was lobbed through an open window.'

'No one saw anything,' I said to myself. 'No one ever does.'

When Patrick spoke his voice shook. 'But ... for God's sake ... Terry wouldn't just stop when any Tom, Dick or Harry flagged him down.'

Daws said, 'I agree. And the remains of Meadows were in the back seat.'

'He wasn't grabbed at the restaurant and driven there,' Steve said. 'Some of his buddies waved him off. And if you're going to kill someone you take them to a piece of waste ground, not suburbia.'

'In the back seat,' Patrick repeated quietly. 'He might have been blown there by the blast. Come to think of it, if it was a grenade bits of him would have been all over the place.'

'Didn't anyone hear anything?' I asked, feeling sick.

'A bang,' Daws said. 'Then a flash as the car went up. One or two people said they heard two bangs. The woman who was slightly hurt by flying glass – just about the only person in the houses nearest as it turned out – was adamant that there were two bangs and then a third with a flash. That was the one which broke her window.'

'Shots?' Patrick said disbelievingly. 'Was he shot and then petrol sloshed everywhere and ignited? The third bang would have been the car's petrol tank exploding.'

'Again not consistent with the injuries,' Daws said. 'The bones of the arms and legs were shattered and there was tremendous damage to the abdomen and head.'

'Just like a bomb,' Steve muttered. 'And yet not a bomb.'

'He's dead,' I said. 'Do we really have to argue over such ghastly niceties?'

'It's distressing,' the colonel agreed. 'One last point I'd like

101

to make is that the same woman thought she heard a car drive away at speed immediately afterwards. If we're to assume that it wasn't someone scared silly by the blast, then that adds more weight to the theory that he was stopped and attacked.'

'There's still no motive as far as I can see,' Patrick observed. 'The lad did great work for us but was never involved with anything you'd call *vicious*. He hasn't been in the game long enough to have had time to really upset anyone. I can't imagine him even being right at the bottom of anyone's hit list.'

'There they are,' Steve said.

It was the two men in the pub. They had left by the rear entrance. For a moment I thought they were about to walk along the lines of cars examining each but after glancing at a couple they got into a large Volvo and drove away.

'Bad lads, those two,' Steve said. 'They had a look about them.'

Chapter Ten

Libby had not gone home. This we discovered when we called at the stables after dropping Daws off near where he had parked his car in a lay-by. There seemed nothing that could be further ventured that night; Patrick was also probably mindful that his assistants were still not up to full strength.

We were having an early breakfast the following morning when a police constable brought a message from Faversham to the effect that a man had been arrested in connection with the discovery of my handbag in the bushes on the sports field. There was to be an identity parade at ten aimed at finding out if the suspect was the man who had driven me away in the trailer.

But none of the men in the line-up remotely resembled my attacker.

'So what have you charged him with?' I asked Faversham as we sat in his office afterwards, drinking coffee. 'The man who hit me on the head definitely wasn't outside just now. None of them was tall or broad enough.'

The inspector pulled a file towards him on his desk and flipped it open. 'That one,' he said, taking out a photograph and handing it to me.

'Yes,' I said. 'The third one along. He's thinner than when this was taken and shaved off his moustache.'

Faversham looked surprised but did not comment. He took back the photo and said, 'His name's Peter Collins. He's one of those who are always involved with something dodgy. Nothing big, you understand. Petty larceny, poaching, stealing the wheels off cars ... that kind of thing. He was involved with a gang of sheep rustlers for a while but we sorted *that* lot — mainly because of their own bungling.'

Patrick grinned at his honesty and I wondered if he was thinking the same as I — that Faversham had received directives from on high, confirming, as it were, our credentials and giving the go-ahead for us to get under his feet. If so, he seemed quite happy; perhaps this was preferable to having to hand over the case to Scotland Yard.

'Can't get anything out of him,' said the inspector ruefully. 'He's trying to wriggle out of the fact that his prints were all over the bag by saying that he saw it on the ground, picked it up, saw there was no money in it and then threw it away again. I don't believe him for a moment. But a chequebook and credit cards *were* still in it when it was found by some children. Usually he's not one to pass up that kind of opportunity.'

Patrick said, 'So you're trying to nail him for the theft of the bag. That seems a trifle precarious to me.'

'Of course it's precarious,' Faversham grunted. 'Mainly because your good lady here didn't — in a matter of law — have her bag stolen. She left it in a horse trailer. But I think Collins is implicated. Possibly in taking away the trailer to move Westfield's body. I intend to question the proprietor of the stables again. Can you see someone going to all the bother of borrowing a trailer when the boot of a car would have done?'

'Only to put the owner of it under suspicion,' Patrick said.

I said, 'Otherwise, surely, it would have been destroyed earlier to hide any evidence. For that matter, why was the murder weapon left in the church?'

I could see no point in relating the rumour that Libby's sister had been raped at one of the Hursts' parties as, so far, it *was* only a rumour. Thoughtless revelations would only bring Libby under deeper suspicion. Patrick obviously thought the same for he said nothing about it. And *he* had been on the receiving end of the pitchfork. I have learned to trust Patrick's judgement of people's characters implicitly. He did, however, now relate to Faversham what had happened in the Speckled Hen the previous evening.

'Did you get the number of their car?' Faversham enquired.

Patrick gave him a slip of paper. 'I'll be honest,' he said, 'I've been ordered to allow you to get on with finding Westfield's killer while I hunt for the lost typescript of a book entitled *Spy Triad*. Not that anyone's convinced it exists.'

'You mean it might have been a motive — he might have been about to reveal classified material?'

'And, if so, I want to know who is in possession of it now.'

'I get your point.' Faversham smiled craftily. 'None of your bunch could have finished him off, I suppose?'

'It has to be borne in mind,' Patrick replied urbanely.

After a short silence Faversham said, 'I was rather hoping you'd question Collins. We haven't had much luck.' When Patrick did not immediately reply he added, 'I was told that you have a lot of success with interrogations. And Collins is no one's lover boy so there'll be no comeback if he gets — what shall I say? — slightly dented.'

Patrick's eyes glittered. 'Any success I have with questioning people isn't as a result of my beating them up.'

'Perhaps not.' Faversham sounded unconvinced. 'But I'm conducting a murder investigation. It matters little who puts the heat on him ... you or a couple of my lads.'

'On my terms then,' Patrick said. 'As if he was the kind of suspect I have to handle — people who might have the KGB paying off their mortgages.'

'Naturally. Anything you want.'

'And I shall require your presence.'

Faversham again produced his slightly sly smile. 'Keep it in the family, eh? I've no objection to that.'

In the interview room Collins was smoking nervously. Faversham dismissed the constable standing by the door and asked for another couple of chairs to be brought.

Collins looked more intelligent than I had expected. In the line-up everyone had adopted a blank expression. When all was ready he ground out his cigarette viciously in the ashtray and said, 'What, the victim as well? Does she enjoy the sight of blood, then?'

Patrick chuckled. 'No, Ingrid is terribly squeamish. She's here to take notes.'

'Why?' Collins demanded to know.

'Because it's her job.'

No, he wasn't slow. He swore vividly and then said, 'So I really hit the jackpot, didn't I? Where's the other member of M15 — putting on the knuckle-dusters?'

'Hardly,' Patrick said. 'Were *you* planning on something violent?'

'Don't play cat and mouse with me!' Collins shouted. 'I've been promised the works if I don't tell you everything. You're the one who beats hell out of those who step out of line at GCHQ.' He smirked. 'A copper told me, and you always have to believe a copper.' He glared at Faversham.

'What time were you arrested?' Patrick asked.

This took Collins back a little. 'At nine-thirty or there-abouts last night. What's it to you?'

'No sleep, no meal, no wash?'

'You must be stupid,' Collins said disgustedly. 'They've been taking it in turns to shout at me ever since I was brought in.'

'Show me your hands,' Patrick ordered.

With nervousness bordering on fear Collins held out both hands. Patrick took them, turned them over, sniffed at the palms and fingertips and then released his hold. Collins, although visibly surprised by the gentleness of the touch, snatched them back and put them out of sight on his lap.

Patrick stood up. 'I don't start interrogating people who are tired and hungry. I'll come back in an hour and a half when you've had a chance to eat and wash and also to think.' He went to the door and Faversham had no choice but to let him out.

'His hands don't smell of petrol,' Patrick said when we were outside in the corridor. 'And he's not the kind of guy who meets soap and water all that often.'

'I thought we'd already decided he wasn't the attacker,' said Faversham.

'He wasn't. I think there were two men involved. A second arrived in another vehicle with all the gear. There were certainly the tracks of another car in the locality, narrow tyres in very poor condition.'

'Then why go to the trouble of taking the Land-Rover away for a short distance?'

'Perhaps they left the scene separately — to confuse anyone following.' Patrick shrugged. 'Perhaps they lived in opposite directions.'

We had more coffee and I took a couple of my headache pills. Steve was keeping a hidden surveillance on Bitterns for a few hours. I envied him, out in the fresh air. It seemed likely that our morning would achieve little more than saving a local ne'er-do-well from a few bad moments with a couple of policemen. It was, I knew, quite the wrong attitude on my part.

'D'you think he'll come clean?' Faversham said.

'Oh yes,' Patrick answered unconcernedly.

'Without resorting to ...'

'Torture?' Patrick finished for him. 'Call it by the right word and then no one's in any doubt. I won't deny that when I was serving in Northern Ireland I hurried things along a little. You have to if people's lives depend on it. And in the Falklands I had a successful interview with a captured Argentinian, the outcome of which probably saved quite a few lives. You don't have to hit people — pressure with the fingers on nerve centres is all that's required. But it's more than my job's worth to do it to a member of the public.'

'So that's why you want me to be present ... in case you're accused of — '

'No,' Patrick said quickly before Faversham could finish.

To be honest, I wasn't at all sure that Faversham had been telling the truth when he had hinted at dark things in store for Collins if he didn't talk, rather that this was a ploy to get Patrick to do his worst to save time. We were, to my mind, entrenched in a double misunderstanding. And I felt that Patrick had stuck his neck out a little. Right then, feeling as I did, I could see no harm in shaking Collins until his teeth rattled.

At the appropriate time we all traipsed back into the interview room. As on the first occasion, Collins was there already. Now he was cleaner, his stringy auburn hair combed, more colour in his face. But a nervous tic was causing his left eyelid to twitch, this occurring with greater rapidity when Patrick removed his jacket, carefully hung it over the back of a chair and stood just to the rear of the man so that he couldn't see him. I took out my notebook and prepared to record the proceedings.

'Where did you find the bag?' Patrick asked without further preamble.

'On the riverbank — just where the sports field joins the allotments.'

'Show me. Inspector Faversham has a map.'

This was opened out and spread on the table. After perusing it for a few moments Collins jabbed at the spot with a finger.

'Was that where the children found it?' Patrick asked Faversham.

'Yes, roughly, perhaps a hundred yards away.'

'I walked along holding it for a little way, didn't I?' Collins was showing every sign of wanting to be helpful. 'Thinking. Then I chucked it away.'

'Have you any idea how the bag was brought from woodland near Billingshurst?'

'No.'

'So you were aware that it was lost there then?'

'I didn't say that. You're trying to trick me.'

'But you did know it had been brought from the woods.'

'No, why should I?'

'Wasn't the story all round the village? How a lady visitor had been abducted in a trailer belonging to the proprietor of the riding stables and that it had been found burnt out in the woods?'

'Yes, but I wouldn't connect the bag with that.'

'But, man, you saw the name on the chequebook and credit cards — you said you examined them. Ingrid Langley, the well-known novelist. You're not telling me that, after giving her name at the riding school and to Jessica Campbell, the entire population — including you — didn't know who she was.'

Collins went white and then red.

'Tell the truth,' Patrick said quietly.

'OK,' Collins muttered after half a minute of sullen silence. 'I saw her name and realised it was hot property. That's why I threw it away.'

'But you didn't *find* it on the riverbank, did you? There's no earthly reason for it to have been there. Ingrid left it in the trailer but it was not burnt so someone must have removed it before it was set on fire. I suggest that the someone was you.'

'You're way out,' Collins said defiantly.

'We were having a laugh about ferrets last night,' Patrick said, coming round so Collins could see him.

'Ferrets?' Collins shivered as though suddenly cold.

'Your hands stank of ferrets just now,' he was told genially. 'You were poaching over in the colonel's woods, weren't you? You heard all the shouting and the old boy blasting off with his shotgun and, being a nosy Herbert, sneaked close. You're good at that.'

Collins shot a look at Faversham as if to appeal for help. He didn't get any. 'So I've got ferrets,' he mumbled.

'You arrived at the scene just in time to see Ingrid and her colleague making their escape from what they thought was criminal attack. Later, when the colonel and his men had gone, you went into the trailer because you wanted to know what was going on. I expect you had a flashlamp of some kind. In its light you saw Ingrid's handbag in the straw. You took it home, removed what money there was and threw the bag away on the riverbank.'

Collins made no answer to this. A look of mulish obstinacy had settled on his sharp features.

Patrick commenced to pace up and down behind him. 'If you hid and awaited developments or were perhaps forced into hiding by the colonel's men milling about . . . There now. There's a thought. You might even have still been in hiding when the real thugs returned to destroy the evidence.'

'What evidence?' Collins asked. 'I don't know what you're talking about.'

'Doesn't he?' Patrick said to Faversham. 'No, he doesn't, does he? Well, Pete, it looks as though the trailer was borrowed to move the murdered man's body. The corpse was strung up by the neck like so.'

Collins shrieked. For on the word 'so' Patrick's long fingers had encircled his neck. Inspector Faversham and I also started violently, my pencil making a large squiggle on the paper.

Patrick unclasped his hands – they had exerted no pressure

whatsoever – and loosened Collins's collar. 'How many of them were there?' he asked in fairly unfriendly fashion.

It still seemed as though Collins might pass out from the shock. 'In the colonel's bunch?' he asked hoarsely.

'No. Those who came next.'

'They'll know it was me who grassed on them,' Collins whispered. 'I'll get done over.'

'You'll be given police protection,' Patrick told him, adding. 'That's a promise,' after a nod of verification from Faversham.

Silence.

Patrick said, 'But only if you co-operate *now*.' He was standing to the rear of Collins again and now, suddenly, took a sharp intake of breath. Collins, anticipating a blow from behind, flung himself forwards on the table, his head beneath his hands. When he emerged from this position, slowly, half a minute later, he discovered himself face to face with his tormentor, Patrick having taken my seat. Without looking I knew the expression in my husband's eyes was quite, quite horrible. Not at all sane.

Collins's mouth moved but no sound emerged.

'I can't hear you,' said Patrick, his own voice a whisper.

'There were two of them,' Collins croaked.

'Go on.'

'A – a really big guy and another, smaller one. The smaller one had a bit of a limp. But it was dark. I couldn't see much. The only light there was came from the car.'

'What kind of car?'

'I couldn't see. The headlights were pointing almost straight at me and I was scared they'd see me in the ditch.'

'If the headlights were anywhere near you you'd have seen nothing at all.'

'Honest – '

'You don't know the meaning of the word. Tell the truth.'

'It was a red van,' Collins said after a short silence. 'It might have been one of those ex-Post Office ones.'

'Describe the men.'

'The big bloke was really big ... about six foot four. He had dark hair. He shouted a lot at the other bloke.'

'What did he say?'

'I couldn't hear, really. I wasn't close enough. No, honest
... I'm a bit hard of hearing. There didn't seem to be any real
gist to it. Just telling him to hurry. Swearing mostly.'

'No names?'

'Not that I heard. But they didn't seem to like each other
enough to use names.'

Patrick gave the other a few seconds' respite from the
relentless, dreadful stare while he sat back, thinking. Then he
said, 'Did you get the impression that they might not know
each other all that well?'

'Yeh ... it could have been like that. The little guy just ran
around doing what the other bloke told him to. Like a hired,
stupid sort of – '

'Describe him to me,' Patrick interrupted.

'Like I said ... he had a bit of a limp. About fifty-five. Not
too clean.'

Faversham said, 'Coming from you, that probably means
he was inches deep in muck.'

'What else?' Patrick persisted, ignoring the interruption.

'His hair was so dirty I couldn't tell what colour it was. It
hung over his neck. Bald on top, though ... like those
pictures you see of the old monks.'

'I've seen him,' Patrick whispered. 'Outside the pub last
night. Hanging about in the car park.' He grabbed one of
Collins's wrists. 'Swear to me. Look me in the eye and swear
you don't know his name.'

'Please, guv,' Collins whimpered, trying to move his wrist
in the iron grip.

I waited for those long, wiry fingers to tighten. I had once
seen a man's wrist broken like this. No real effort was
involved, he would merely shift his thumb a little so it acted as
a lever. As easy as cracking walnuts in his fingers at
Christmas.

Jerkily, Collins said, 'I don't know his name. He works on
a farm just outside Longcoombe. Old Barton's place.'

'The RSPCA know *him*,' Faversham said succinctly. 'Wait
a moment and it'll come to me.'

Patrick released his hold.

'Munro,' the inspector said. 'Duggie Munro. Once did a
stretch for taking an axe to someone during an argument. I'll

111

put out a call and get him brought in.' He left the room.

'What did the men do when they arrived by the trailer?' Patrick said.

But Collins was not happy. 'They'll know it was me. That big bloke ... he'll come after me. He's the sort you have nightmares about.'

'So let's get him behind bars,' Patrick said. 'What did they *do*?'

'Can I have a fag?'

'When the inspector comes back. I don't smoke.'

'It's all right for you!' Collins burst out after pondering for a few moments. 'You get back in your big car and drive away. You don't have to live with the fear for the rest of your life. Just a morning's work, isn't it? Put the heat on me and then go home for a nice lunch.'

Probably unwittingly, he had hit a large nail right on the head. For the people whom Patrick normally interviews in the course of his work rarely face violent retribution. And, if guilty, of course they are duly removed to places where they are quite safe from any attack. Police protection could be promised, but for how long? What if the big man was not arrested?

Patrick smiled a trifle ruefully, reached inside his jacket and placed his Smith and Wesson on the table. Predictably, Collins gaped at it.

'Pete,' said Patrick. 'Among other things I am one of the prime minister's bodyguards. I am a bloody good shot. Tell me everything you know about these two men and I will personally sleep outside your bedroom door until they're found.'

'Not for always, though,' Collins declared.

'No. Information can be given to the papers that you've come forward with very useful knowledge. We'll set a little trap.'

Perhaps because he could see that his interrogator was losing patience, and mindful of that grip on his wrist, Collins started talking. It seemed to be a great relief to him to do so. This was not surprising for, as Patrick had been convinced, he remembered what had taken place in some detail. He also had an idea that the big man worked as a warehouseman at an electrical wholesalers on an industrial estate outside Pulborough.

Collins continued, 'The bloke with the limp – Munro – fetched a can from the van and went into the trailer with it. I got a whiff of petrol. He nearly fell over, he was in such a panic, what with the other one shouting at him to hurry. He couldn't even strike a match for a bit, he was so nervous. Then the straw inside the trailer went up with a whoosh and I ducked right down in case they saw me by the light of the fire. I didn't show myself again until I'd heard the van drive off.'

'What about the bag, though?' I asked.

'Oh . . . yeh. Munro brought that out with the empty can. But the big bloke yelled at him and he threw both of them back. But the bag hit the edge of the trailer and went into the undergrowth. Neither of them noticed.'

'So when they'd gone you retrieved the bag and then ran like hell.'

'To where I'd left my bike . . . yes.'

'I'll have the money back if you don't mind,' I told him. 'And the key ring with the St. Christopher medallion on it. It isn't gold. Just my dad's and he's dead so its rather precious.'

'You'll have it,' said Collins in a low voice. 'Honest –'

'You don't know the meaning of the word,' I butted in angrily.

'Munro was hanging around waiting to be paid,' Patrick said to Faversham a little later. 'I saw him when we went in the pub but he had disappeared by the time we left.'

'So you think he was waiting for those two men you saw?'

'Looks like it, doesn't it? Have they been traced?'

'The car they were driving belongs to a Leytonstone businessman. He didn't fit either description. When leaned on a little he admitted that someone had "borrowed" it but had brought it back the next day . . . early this morning. He seemed scared silly.' Faversham cleared his throat with a growling noise. 'Protection racketeers, I shouldn't wonder. It's being followed up.'

'Have you had any luck finding the secretary whom Hurst sacked?'

'Not so far. She's moved from the address Hurst gave us and hasn't left a forwarding one.'

'Is that the same address he gave you?' I said to Patrick.

'I'd forgotten about it,' he confessed. 'Hell, I should have sent it to HQ.' He found the slip of paper in his wallet. 'Miss Lindsey Davies, 16 West Avenue, Marshlands Road, London W8.'

'That's it,' Faversham said. 'Moved out a couple of months ago.'

'No leads, no luck,' Patrick grumbled. 'I vote we go and raid the Campbells.'

Chapter Eleven

Always alarmed when my spouse becomes bored with inaction, I rang the Campbells' number and was highly relieved to find Jessica at home. Even though she now knew I was involved with the murder investigation, she unhesitatingly asked me round that afternoon.

'No problem,' I reported. 'Not the manner of a lady with anything to hide.'

Patrick merely gave me a death's-head smile.

'Interviewing Collins was very difficult for you, wasn't it?' I commented as I was leaving for my appointment.

'Of course it was,' he replied irritably. 'Faversham's groundwork saw to that. He really expected me to go in there and hang the guy up by the heels. Besides, I quite liked Collins. The world could do with a few more of them, complete individuals who rely on nobody and just get on with their lives, even if their way of earning a living gets them into trouble now and then.'

'Were any charges against him withdrawn?'

'I saw to it,' he said grimly. 'Just pray that they pick up Munro and his buddy or you might be sleeping on your own for a while.'

'I don't suppose I'd notice,' I said and swept out.

I was so busy congratulating myself on this grand exit and the putting across of his lack of affection that I didn't stop to think he might still have every intention of carrying out his plan.

Jessica received me in very friendly fashion. 'Well, of course I didn't say much to you at our first meeting,' she said, showing me into a sitting room. 'That would have made me look a horrible gossip. Anyway,' she added with a light laugh, 'I'm quite sure Jan will have made it clear what sort of woman I am. You've probably come to find out how much of it's true.' She sat down beside me. 'I'll ask Grace to bring in the tea in a minute.' Another laugh. 'If you'd seen me half an hour ago you would have *died*. My daughter is horse-mad too and bought this poor little Shetland at the market. It's teeming with lice. I was shampooing it with some stuff from the vet and I think there was more on me than on Toffee.'

She organised the tea and, while we waited, told me about the history of the house. It had been built on the site of a moated dwelling mentioned in the Domesday Book and excavations by the local archaeological society had found the remains of an earlier habitation, a tiny Saxon fort thought to have been conquered by the Romans at about the same time they overran Maiden Castle in Dorset.

'It makes you feel funny sometimes,' she concluded. 'Knowing that people died violently right under your feet.' She gave me one of her straight looks. 'Forgive me for asking, but did you get those bruises when you fell off Warwick?'

'News travels slowly *sometimes*,' I said with a grimace. 'No, I stuck my nose in where it wasn't wanted and someone knocked me flat.'

One elegant hand holding the teapot came to a halt in mid-air. 'That's frightful!' she exclaimed. 'Is the entire subject *sub judice* or can you tell me about it?'

So I told her, leaving out the most recent revelations from Collins.

'Libby really is a dear,' Jessica commented when I'd finished. 'Her temper gets the better of her sometimes but she'd never – but never – get mixed up with anything illegal. Let alone murder!' She cocked her head, listening. 'Did you hear a horse whinny?'

'No,' I answered truthfully.

'I hope no one's outside. Brandy always whinnies when he sees someone. Mostly because he's greedy, I'm afraid, and asking for titbits. Tum rules.'

'Tell me about the Hursts,' I requested.

She sipped her tea for a moment and then set down the cup.

116

'They're flash. Like people who have won a lot of money on the football pools. That sounds so snobby and I'm not saying for a moment that we're aristocrats. Far from it, Rowan and I come from very ordinary families. I think it was the Hursts' parties that really upset everyone — carloads of city yobs screaming through the village throwing bottles at people. They all *despise* us. It's only become really bad lately — when they first moved in everything was quite normal. I went round there to introduce myself to Jan. I'm not a do-gooding sort of person but I know how, frankly, bloody it can be when you're young and move into the country where you don't know anyone.'

'Was she friendly?'

'Yes, she appeared to be quite grateful that she had someone to talk to. That first Christmas we had them both here and introduced them to a few people. But I could never get on with Miles. He always seemed to have a faraway look on his face when you were talking to him as though his thoughts were elsewhere. I think what happened finally is that they got so bored with the social life here that they imported their fun from London.'

'Jan does seem to have a dreadful down on you.'

She pulled a face. 'I'm not surprised. We had a huge row after her brother took a shot at one of our dogs. After that she seemed to think I was responsible for all the bad press they were getting.'

'Why did he try to shoot the dog?'

'Silly old Dixie was in their garden. We were walking the dogs over the hill — roughly where I met you — and flushed a rabbit. Away she went — for miles. Jan's brother hated dogs and tried to pot her in the rose bed. I don't think I've ever seen Rowan so angry and, believe me, he has an awful temper.'

'Did Jan ever mention — before you fell out — that her brother was writing a book?'

'What on earth ...?' she began and then regained her composure. 'More tea?'

'Thanks,' I said, giving her my cup.

'He might have been,' Jessica said in offhand fashion. 'I mean, everyone's at it these days. The Official Secrets Act's been tossed out of the window.'

'We don't know *exactly* what the book was about.'

She coloured. 'Oh. I just assumed it might be one of those revealing-everything MI5 tales. Spies in high places, sort of thing.'

Behind her the door opened and, catlike, Patrick walked in. I rather felt that he had dressed for the occasion; pale-blue slacks and matching cashmere sweater, white moccasins. And somehow, using that kind of alchemy that I've never been able to fathom, he was, right now, displaying as much malice as a four-week-old kitten.

'You were listening and came in right on cue,' I said, and Jessica turned to see whom I was talking to.

'The fencing man!' she gasped. 'Oh, of course — someone said there were three of you.'

I was wondering what was in the small package he had under one arm.

'That was sneaky,' Jessica said to me.

'Ingrid had no idea I was coming,' Patrick assured her. 'May the burglar sit down?'

'You seem to be a better burglar than you are at fencing.' Understandably, she had gone a little pale. 'Well, as you're here . . .'

'Much better,' he acknowledged, flopping into a chair.

'That was in the wall safe!' Jessica cried, noticing the package.

'Alas,' said Patrick. 'I'm not to be trusted at all.'

'So now you're going to arrest me.'

'I have no powers to arrest anyone. Tell me . . .'

'What?' she snapped nervously.

'Is there any more tea in the pot?' he enquired, giving her a winning smile.

'I simply don't understand you,' Jessica said when she returned from asking her daily help to make more tea. 'You have in your hand evidence that you obviously came looking for and you're . . . well . . .'

'Charming?' Patrick suggested sardonically, withdrawing the typescript from its wrapper. 'Perhaps I'm trying to dispel a notion that I'm one of Westfield's colleagues. *Spy Triad*,' he read. 'By Kimberley Andrews. Is that her real name?'

118

Jessica said, 'I don't think I have to answer your questions.'

'By refusing to help us you're implicating the girl in the murder. Is she a friend of yours?'

She pursed her lips.

'Let me guess. Her real name is Lindsey Davies, Miles Hurst's one-time secretary. Sacked for incompetence.'

'Is *that* what they told you?'

'I can only repeat what I've been told until informed more correctly otherwise.'

'You're a right smartarse, aren't you?'

'A charming smartarse,' he replied, with another smile.

'What are you going to do with the book now you've got it?'

'After I've spoken with your husband — who no doubt arranged its removal from Bitterns — I'll probably give it back to the author. She might tell me how Westfield came to get hold of it.'

'I can tell you that. He sent a couple of thugs to demand it from her.'

'To stop her sending it to a publisher?'

'Of course.'

'Why?'

'He must have thought she based the story on his own activities. I don't know, I haven't read it.'

'But you and your husband were perfectly prepared to break into Bitterns to get it back for her. Why not go to the police if — '

'They threatened her, that's why,' Jessica interrupted. 'The two men who took it from her. Rowan's never been the sort of man to knuckle under to that kind of thing so he said he'd try to get it back for her.'

'How did you know it was at Bitterns?'

'She received an anonymous letter containing quite the most unspeakable threats if she went to the police. Lindsey recognised the typewriter as the one she'd used at the office. Something to do with the upper-case A.'

'Surely that was no guarantee that the novel was at the *house*?'

Jessica sighed. 'Rowan was very angry. As I said just now,

my husband has a dangerous temper when he's upset. He had a feeling it might be and was in the kind of mood where he would have ploughed up their garden to find it.'

'So he broke in, found the novel in a briefcase in Miles's study and brought it home.'

'You obviously know he did so I can hardly deny it. Although how you found out, God above – '

'He left the title page beneath the desk. Perhaps he dropped the whole thing on the floor. When did he carry out this little sortie?'

After a long silence Jessica replied. 'Last Thursday.'

'Ah,' Patrick said. 'His reticence is now understood.'

'So what happens now?'

'As I said, I'll have to talk to him.'

'I should imagine he'll only consent to talk to the police.'

Patrick got to his feet and hummed a Sousa marching tune under his breath.

'I don't mean the local police either,' Jessica continued. 'He has no faith in them at all.'

The quiet 'oompahs' progressed down the long room and then returned. 'There were fingerprints found within the house that Inspector Faversham hopes were left by the murderer or his accomplices.'

'I didn't know about that,' I said.

'Nor did I until this morning. Grant let it slip.'

'Rowan didn't kill him,' said Jessica.

'The Hursts are making a lot of noise in your direction,' Patrick pointed out. 'The sooner I interview your husband, the better. When will he be home?'

She glanced at the clock. 'At about seven. But if you leave it until about eight-thirty he'll be in a better mood than before dinner.'

'Does he still have any connection with the military?'

'You'll have to ask him that.'

Patrick's eyebrows rose.

'Some units are secret,' Jessica said. 'They don't talk about any sustained contacts even with their families.'

'Really?' Patrick murmured. 'How exciting.'

*

120

'There are so many undercurrents in this case,' said Patrick, viciously stabbing a new potato with his fork, 'that I'm drowning in them.' He put the potato into his mouth and chewed gloomily.

'But we do have the typescript of *Spy Triad*,' I pointed out.

'I had a quick look through. There seems to be precious little to do with spies in it. I suppose I'll just have to find the time to read it properly.'

'So what have we got that's *fact*?' I said. 'A man is murdered and his body left in his sister's bedroom probably some distance from where he was killed. The actual spot hasn't been located. His body was transported in a pony trailer belonging to a woman who seems to have gone into hiding. Are the police actually looking for Libby?'

'No. Mainly because of the bee Faversham has in his bonnet about the prints. At the moment they're not thought to be a woman's.'

'Everyone seems to have hated Westfield. He upset just about the entire population of Longcoombe if one can believe what one's told.'

'The episodes with the dogs can be laid at his door but the Hursts threw the parties.'

'I appreciate that. And we now have the problem of those two men who were obviously looking for us. Surely if that man Munro was hanging around outside the pub he told them what we looked like — ferret pie or no.'

'It wasn't Munro who attacked you — it was the other bloke. Munro doesn't necessarily know what we look like. And he didn't look particularly bright. One thing — ' and this with a broad grin — 'he won't have placed Daws as one of MI5's very own. I bet our Richard's still trying to get those whiskers off.'

'Where *is* he, by the way?'

'Working from a country estate that takes paying guests. In other words having a few days off.'

We had finished our meal and were about to leave the hotel restaurant when Daws and Steve came in together, having met in the foyer. Patrick, realising that Steve would feel awkward dining on his own, ordered more coffee.

'I got your message,' Daws said to Patrick. 'I take it this would-be novel is pretty sensitive stuff.'

'It wouldn't appear so, sir. Lots of corpses and people having it off. Mind, I haven't read it properly yet.'

There was an eerie moment while they gazed at each other, Daws, I'm convinced, wondering whether his subordinate was engaged in some kind of joke.

'Perhaps you'd better let me have it,' said the colonel eventually. 'Not now, later will do. What a pity – I really thought we were on to something interesting.' He brightened. 'You don't suppose something's in *code*?'

'He didn't write it,' Patrick told him. 'Sorry, but I couldn't leave too comprehensive a message with your country-house receptionist. No, it seems that the author was Hurst's secretary.'

'But she wouldn't have insight into *Westfield's* work!' Daws exploded.

'No. I think the sooner someone finds this girl, the better. She must have some idea why he wanted it.'

I said, 'Perhaps Westfield didn't. Perhaps the book's all about Miles Hurst and dubious business deals. Or, at least, things she found out gave Lindsey Davies the ideas for a plot.'

'It's possible,' Patrick said, looking at Daws. 'But that doesn't explain why it's called *Spy Triad*.'

Steve cleared his throat. Then, when everyone had looked at him, he said, 'I've got the lowdown on those two jokers in the pub.'

'Surely they weren't at Bitterns today?' Patrick said quickly.

'Oh no. No one was at Bitterns. They all went out. No, I nodded off and nearly fell out of the tree at four-thirty and they were still out so I called it a day and went to see what Grant could tell me.'

'Four hundred lines for sleeping on duty,' Patrick said. 'What did you find out?'

Steve took a piece of paper from his pocket. 'The darker of the two's name is Brad Harperley. He's into prostitution and protection rackets in the East End. The other one was his minder. Harperley is in partnership with a man called Harry Pugh and Pugh's friends refer to him as Harry the Fuse

122

because he once electrocuted a guy on purpose. The police want them both behind bars very, very badly but only ever seem to be able to grab the small fry.'

'But why was Westfield *killed*?' Daws said in some desperation. 'What on earth these people had to do with him I just cannot imagine.'

'And by whom?' I added. 'Rowan Campbell? One of the mafioso we were talking about just now? The author's boyfriend?'

'One of a hundred folk who loathed him anyway?' Patrick said with a grim laugh. 'Hell, what a mess. Perhaps Campbell can throw some light into our darkness.'

We could hear Rowan Campbell shouting as we approached the house.

'Remain calm,' Patrick said. 'Don't antagonise him. If he had wanted to kill Westfield it would have been with neat knifework, not by beating out the man's brains.'

'Unless he wanted to make it look as though someone else had done it,' I remarked sarcastically.

'That depends on his IQ,' was the mild reply as he rang the doorbell.

The door was immediately snatched wide, Campbell obviously having been waiting behind it. His anger was a tangible force. He hefted Patrick over the step and into the hall, where he skidded desperately on the polished floor as he tried to keep his balance. My arm was then grasped and I was hauled in likewise but perhaps with not so much violence. The door slammed.

Miraculously still upright, Patrick said, 'We might of course have just been collecting for the church roof.'

'*I* might just put you *on* the church roof,' Campbell said. 'After I've given you a hiding for breaking in here and frightening my wife.' He appeared to have every intention of carrying this out and had all the advantages, being taller, heavier and younger than Patrick.

'I didn't lay hands on your wife,' Patrick said, very quietly. 'And if you *are* by any chance acting as military adviser to a certain colonel round here who has created a little army to deal with poachers and travellers who invade his property . . .'

a graphic indrawing of breath through the teeth '. . . then perhaps you ought to resign, laddie.'

Campbell went up very close so that his face was only inches from the man to whom he was speaking. 'I'm not. And there's no way he would drop names.'

'You're lying. He didn't have to mention anyone by name. He just said that he had impressive help. From the way he said it I took it to mean that he meant help from *the* regiment. The folk at Hereford don't approve of private armies. They might not like the idea of you endeavouring to dust up a major who was once in 14th Intelligence either.'

I saw Campbell swallow but otherwise he didn't move.

'So are we going to sit down and talk like civilised people or do we have to go through the whole distressing business of you polishing this nice shiny floor with your backside?' Patrick asked, politely but still through the teeth.

This didn't seem to me to be the kind of remark that would lower tension.

'On the other hand,' Patrick went on, 'if you're the hit man who was hired by the God-fearing folk in this village, you might not fancy the idea of talking at all.'

'Me?' said Campbell. 'Hired? I'd have killed the bastard for nothing.'

'That's what I thought. And there is the complication of a few so far unidentified fingerprints in Bitterns that are probably yours. Now, are we going to talk?'

His fists bunched, Campbell groaned and then swore.

It was a silent group that went into the sitting room, Jessica entering from the direction of the kitchen where, I guessed, she had been hiding.

'I don't remember your name at Hereford,' Campbell said, giving Patrick back his ID card. He spoke grudgingly but had obviously come off the boil.

'Well, no, 14th Int. only do part of their training in that locality. Besides, it's over ten years since I was playing Tarzan and trying to stay out of the way of instructors using live ammunition.'

'There was a Gillard killed out in the Falklands.'

'No, that was me. They discovered when they took the bits

from the plastic bag that the right leg was the only thing not breathing.'

It was silent again while Campbell's gaze drifted over Patrick. Then he said, 'I'm in trouble, aren't I?'

'Yes. Why the hell didn't you contact the police right at the beginning?'

'Because I'd have been in the slammer as soon as I opened my mouth.'

'You can't expect them to ignore breaking and entering. And now you've kept quiet it'll look even worse when they finally discover you were in the house on the night of the murder.'

Campbell put his head in his hands for a moment, wrenching his fingers through his thick fair hair. Jessica, sitting next to him on the sofa, put an arm around him and gave him a quick hug.

'You've given them the typescript, I take it,' Campbell said.

'No, it's gone to my boss. He's not interested how I came by it.'

Hope gleamed in the other man's eyes.

'The army doesn't look after its own when murder's the game,' Patrick said.

'Look, I didn't kill him.'

'Then prove it. Talk. Tell me why Westfield wanted the novel so desperately. Tell me the present whereabouts of the author. I want to know everything about last Thursday night. Start with that if you like.'

He might enjoy playing soldiers and have a bad temper but even though now thoroughly scared you could see the calibre of Rowan Campbell. He clasped his big capable hands together as though to keep them quite still, then looked Patrick in the eye and said, 'Westfield was MI5. That's no secret. He was also a bastard — and I don't mean the kind of bastard you can handle or ignore. Him and the Hursts are birds of a feather. When Jessica said you were coming back I admit I flipped a bit. I imagined you'd be friends of his — you know, the garden full of blokes in uniforms with no badges. I know what goes on. I've been involved, haven't I? I know the resources given to people with the real power. For all I knew you were going to hang this killing round my neck.'

125

Patrick said, 'You have my word that is not the case.'

'Despite what you said just now I've a feeling you don't think I killed him.'

'Westfield wasn't killed at Bitterns and I can hardly see you going to the trouble of transporting a stiff when you went to look for the typescript. And it's hardly likely that you'd put the murder weapon in the church afterwards. According to the vicar, most of the people in this end of the valley are dedicated pagans, you included. It wouldn't have occurred to you, not even to create a red herring.'

'In the *church*?' Jessica gasped.

'It hasn't made the local press yet,' Patrick told her. 'Now ... last Thursday.'

'I didn't go upstairs,' Campbell began.

'First of all explain how you bypassed the alarm system.'

'That's easy. It was switched off.'

Patrick frowned. 'Go on.'

'I got in through the kitchen window. They sometimes leave the top one open for the cat. I'd been in the place once or twice and knew that the system didn't involve infra-red beams, just pressure pads in places beneath the carpets and triggering devices on the windows and some of the interior doors. They've had the pressure pads taken out recently because the cat kept setting it off. I know that because our daily's the sister of theirs. Grace gossips a bit.'

'How were you hoping to get in through the window without setting off the alarm?'

Campbell grimaced. 'Luck. I was hoping I could reach in when I opened the large window and pull out a wire or something. As it was I got in a bit of a blue funk and forgot all about it until I'd opened the window a short way. But nothing happened. There's not a lot else to tell. I climbed in, checked that the alarm was switched off and then went into Hurst's study. It seemed a good place to start. There was a briefcase on the floor by the desk. I opened it and what I was looking for was inside. The worst moment was when I dropped it and the loose pages went all over the place. I had to put it back in order and check it was all there. It seemed to take hours.'

'What time was this?'

126

'When I left it was nine-thirty-five.'

'Why the hell didn't you wear gloves?'

'God, I didn't know someone was going to be *murdered*!' Campbell shouted. 'I didn't think Hurst or his damned brother-in-law would have the nerve to call the police if they discovered that the thing was missing. Then it would have come out that it wasn't theirs in the first place.'

'And you didn't go upstairs?'

'I've just said I didn't.'

'Did you see anything that struck you as unusual?'

'Like what?'

'Anything. You'd been in the house before. Was anything different from your last visit?'

'Nothing that I could see in the light from a torch. The fact that the alarm system was switched off was the only odd thing I noticed.'

'Shall I make some coffee?' Jessica ventured a trifle nervously.

'I could do with something stronger,' her husband muttered.

'Coffee first,' Jessica decided. She went out.

'Has anyone ever approached you?' Patrick said. 'With a view to taking out Westfield?'

Campbell shook his head.

'You're quite sure about this?'

'Yes. But there can't be many people in this village who didn't hope that something nasty would happen to him one dark night.'

'Why, because of the parties? Because he killed a few local dogs? There must have been more to it than that.'

'Because of his *contempt* for us all. He used to practically shoulder people off the pavement into the road. When he drove he used to carve you up. He ignored the speed limit through the village. I've seen pedestrians have to run for their lives. God, even thinking about it makes me bloody seethe. I'm glad he's dead – whoever killed him did Longcoombe a favour.'

'What relationship is Lindsey Davies to you?'

Campbell was still speaking in quick staccato sentences but now looked very tired. 'None. She's the daughter of a school

127

friend of Jessica's. Both her parents are dead — killed in a plane crash. We're the only people who can keep an eye on her, really. It was through us that she got the job with Hurst — at that time we were on fairly good terms with them.'

'Did she ever go to any of the parties?'

'Not likely. She's not that kind of girl.'

'Someone said that a girl was raped one night.'

Campbell paused fractionally before replying. 'Yeah, that was supposed to have been Sandra Mason — sister of that woman who runs the riding school. God knows if it's true. Sandra went to London to work shortly afterwards.'

The doorbell rang and we heard Jessica's light footfalls as she crossed the hall.

'I'd like her address,' Patrick said, adding, 'the present one, if you don't mind, not the one she left a couple of months ago.'

'I don't want her harried,' Campbell replied with a hint of his original aggression.

'I was thinking along the lines of protection by Special Branch until we get to the bottom of this,' he was told. 'But someone'll have to talk to her, even if it's only to ask her if she can describe the men who took the typescript away.'

I had heard male voices in the hall and with a sinking feeling beheld Inspector Faversham as he pushed open the door of the room. He had several constables with him. In short, he required Campbell to accompany him to the police station to help him with his enquiries. Sergeant Grant had apparently mentioned Patrick's latest line of reasoning — the possibility of a local hit man with military connections — and Faversham, who had a very good memory, had recollected that Campbell had at one time provided the law with his fingerprints after a burglary in his own house. This of course had been to eliminate him from the detection processes.

'It was a long shot that paid off,' Faversham finished triumphantly.

'I really trusted you for a little while,' Campbell said to Patrick as he stood up.

Whether Patrick saw Campbell tense or whether a wild look came into his eyes I'm not sure, but he suddenly lunged forwards and grabbed him by his sweater. 'Fool!' he barked

128

in his army-command voice. Then, quieter, 'Only fools run. Co-operate.' He shook him, for flight was still uppermost in the other's mind. 'Co-operate! There's nothing to connect you with this murder.'

'You're wrong there,' Faversham said as Campbell was bustled out. 'It looks as though the handle of the murder weapon was wiped. But there's half a thumbprint visible. It's Campbell's all right.'

Chapter Twelve

Jessica was so stunned that she was staring down the drive even though the car taking her husband away was out of sight. But when a man stepped from beneath the cover of a clump of rhododendrons she started violently.

'It's all right,' I assured her. 'It's Steve. He's with us.'

She turned to face Patrick, standing in the hall.

'I have no control over the police,' he remarked quietly, anticipating the accusation.

'Can't you do *anything*?' she asked, a dejected droop to her shoulders.

'There's very little I can do at the moment — other than look for fresh evidence.'

'But Rowan trusted you — he's part of your world. You *must* do something to help him.'

All this was very harrowing for him but he could do nothing then but murmur that he would do his best and bid her goodnight. He must have heard her start to sob as he went to the car for he paused and then walked on, a little faster.

'So how *are* his prints on the hammer?' Steve said when I had explained, Patrick driving very fast and talking to Daws on the phone.

'Search me,' I said.

'They've been away for a couple of days,' he went on thoughtfully. 'Haven't kept in touch with the latest developments.'

'So?'

'Was the word "hammer" mentioned when you were questioning him?'

'No, I think Patrick just referred to it as the murder weapon. Why?'

'Well, if it wasn't mentioned he might have forgotten that he'd used a hammer he found lying around to reach in the window to pull up the catch of the bigger one. His arms aren't as long as the major's.' He shrugged. 'Only a fragile theory.'

'It's a good theory,' Patrick said, having finished his call. 'I was working along those lines myself. And he might have omitted to tell us that he called in at that garden shed on the way for something heavy with which to break a window if necessary. Even if he didn't know what the murder weapon was, it would be an incriminating thing to admit to. It would sound as though he was contemplating violence if challenged.'

We took the next turning right, a manoeuvre which brought it home to me forcibly that I hadn't fastened my seat belt.

'I've told Daws I'd like to talk to Pamela Westfield,' Patrick said. 'She lives not far from here, just a few miles north of Steyning. He said he'd meet us there, which surprised me rather — he must be at a loose end.'

'Did you give him Lindsey Davies's address?' I asked.

'Yes, he's going to arrange for her to be kept an eye on and brought down here if necessary.'

'Do you have to drive *quite* so fast?' I said a couple of minutes later.

'I want to get there before Daws. Really, I think *four* people turning up is too many. The poor woman'll think . . .' But he didn't finish the sentence, just shrugged angrily, no doubt remembering Jessica gazing after us, the empty house behind her.

I put into words things that had been going through my mind for most of the day. 'You think Libby's involved with the murder, don't you?'

'I'm still not sure. It was her trailer. It looks as though her sister was raped at a party although we still don't know for sure. Now she's made herself scarce. But is it because of the men we saw in the pub whom she's obviously frightened of or because we were bound to ask awkward questions?'

'A mite ready to spit people on pitchforks,' Steve recalled.

'Not a woman to cross,' Patrick agreed. 'And we mustn't

131

forget either that Westfield was supposed to have killed her dog.'

'No one seems to suspect the Hursts,' I complained. 'I've a funny feeling about them.'

'Not of *murder*,' Patrick said, slowing down in preparation to turning right on to the A24. 'I agree that they're shady and seem to know shady people. I'm beginning to think that Westfield was involved with something not at all legal. But until we know a lot more we can't lay his death at the Hursts' door.' He looked at me quickly. 'What does the writer's intuition tell her?'

Patrick has a very healthy respect for my 'funny feelings'.

I was silent for a while and then said, 'Perhaps it's this. So far, almost right from the start, Westfield's death has been regarded from the angle of a horrible man getting what was coming to him. Everyone hated him. Almost everyone we've spoken to had a motive. Not for one moment has he been thought of as a victim. Murdered people ought to be thought of as victims — whatever they were like when they were alive.'

The car slowed a little. 'You're teaching me my job again,' Patrick said and he was not being sarcastic. 'Go on, elaborate on that train of thought.'

My mind was very clear. 'If you sort of step back and take a completely different look at this, assume that he's innocent of just about everything but hating dogs because one once badly bit his wife, then suspicion goes straight to the Hursts — or, at least, to Miles. We know *he* has connections with criminals — it was to *his* house that those men went. Jan Hurst is very nervous, almost as if she's under some sort of pressure. Her brother's body was placed in her bedroom. Why? To frighten her? To prevent her talking? Suppose her brother had discovered something about Hurst. What pressure was being put on *him*? People say how he had no consideration for others. Perhaps he was so beside himself that he was on the verge of breakdown. And why was he at Bitterns such a lot if he and Miles didn't get on? Hurst told you himself that it was a case of cordial dislike. Patrick, your own intuition is very good and the first thing you said to me about Miles was, "I don't like him, he's snaky." '

132

'If he was guilty he would have fled the country after the murder, surely?'

'He might be trying to unfreeze assets, or is arrogant or stupid,' I retorted.

'You sleeping across Collins's door tonight?' Steve said into what had been a long silence.

'Looks like it,' Patrick replied morosely. 'Munro and partner seem to have vanished. I'll check again with Grant when we've finished here.'

The sun was very low in the sky now, shining across the Sussex Weald through a thin mist on the horizon. Magnified hugely as it slowly sank, a redly blazing ball, it flushed the westerly sky a delicate pink, reflecting pale rose in cottage windows. Usually I see a setting sun and think of other times, other sunsets, the occasion when I gazed across a beach in Wales and failed to recognise Patrick kicking a football on the sand because I had expected to find him in a wheelchair after, finally, having to have the lower part of his right leg amputated. Now it seemed as though the world was but a mirror to a blood-tinted sky. All I could think of was murder.

'Are you still feeling unwell?' Patrick asked me as he swung the car into a tree-lined lane.

'I'm all right,' I mumbled.

The village of Westfield consisted of a neat cluster of cottages, a stud farm and a tiny church, the latter, sadly, with its windows boarded up and its wrought-iron gates padlocked together.

'You know where the house is,' Steve stated in surprise as we turned into an almost hidden opening in a huge beech hedge.

'Daws gave me directions,' Patrick said. Then he braked hard.

The telephone wire to the house was lying in a large loop across the drive.

'I'll go,' said Steve as Patrick got out of the car.

'Stay here. I want you to stay with the car every time you come with us anywhere from now on.'

I put this down to worry about severed brake pipes, not that he was still brooding over Terry's death and had a horror of bombs.

133

'It's been cut,' said Patrick, getting back into the car.
I said, 'Are you sure? It could have caught on a high vehicle and snapped.'

'I'm sure,' he practically snarled at me. 'I can tell the difference between cutting and breaking.' He reversed the car back into the main road, there wasn't space to turn. 'Stay here,' he said again to Steve who had had his mouth open to suggest otherwise. 'When Daws arrives, tell him we've gone in. That's if I haven't reported back to you by then.'

'Perhaps I should have stayed in the car,' I said as the pair of us walked down the drive. 'Surely Steve's more use to you than me if there's trouble.'

If it had been anyone but his wife he might have given me a 'don't bother me with stupid comments now' look. As it was, he said, 'He's so weak still he can't even lift a cup of tea without his hand shaking. I prefer you unarmed to a bloke with a gun who might shoot me in the back by accident.'

We reached the cut wire, which Patrick again examined. 'Cut,' he said to himself. 'The loop probably caught on something like a milk float which pulled it out of the hedge. Otherwise we'd never have noticed. We haven't noticed,' he said, more loudly, to me. 'This time we *are* collecting for the church roof.'

'It's boarded up,' I pointed out.

'Because the roof's got holes in it,' he said with a fleeting and quite unfathomable grin.

The house came into view as we rounded a curve in the driveway. It was a typical Sussex dwelling, built sturdily of red brick and flint with a little timbering from an earlier structure at one end, all beneath a red tiled roof.

'The curtains are closed,' I said. 'Surely no one at home would shut out such a wonderful sunset.'

'Perhaps she's away and left them closed as a sign of mourning,' Patrick suggested, not sounding at all sure.

Any 'funny feelings' I might have had were now evolving into stark apprehension. Now we had fully rounded the curve we could see that two cars were parked on the mossy setts at the side of the house, one a small foreign saloon, the other a Jaguar. In front of them, blocking them off, was a red ex-Post Office van.

'We continue,' Patrick said without moving his lips over-much. 'If someone's keeping watch and they've seen us it'll make them highly suspicious if we turn back. The woman's life might be in serious danger if it's the same two who hijacked you.'

He rang the doorbell. No one came.

Patrick didn't hesitate. He plunged off round the side of the house down a slippery brick path. A gap between the side of the house and the end of a privet hedge that bordered a vegetable garden was bypassed rapidly as, gun in hand, he went through a thin part of the hedge a few yards into a row of celery. I waited until he whistled a soft 'all clear' and caught up with him by the back door. This yielded very rapidly to a small tool that he carries on a key ring in his pocket, a strong wrist actually breaking the lock so that a piece of metal fell on to a stone floor inside.

Once inside Patrick snapped on the light switch for it was very dark, the blinds being down here also. Then we stood very still, listening.

I became aware of a small sound. A tap dripping? No, the sink was dry. A freezing shiver went all the way down my spine. Blood dripping?

'What's that noise?' I whispered.

'The kitchen clock,' Patrick muttered and went through an open door into a passageway.

I hung back a little. One doesn't crowd a man expecting ambush around every corner. The passage was gloomy and I almost fell over a huge oak chest at one side of it. Then we went round a right-angled bend and were immediately in a long living room. Dim illumination was provided by a couple of small lamps.

There was a stone fireplace at each end of the room, magnificent carved coats of arms over the mantelpieces. The ceiling was high and beamed and, as might be expected in such a setting, the walls were adorned with ancient weapons. But there was nothing ancient about the shotgun that was being trained on us by a man standing before the fireplace at the end of the room farthest away from us.

He was, I was sure, the man who had attacked me in the pony trailer. Another man, a grubby-looking individual holding what looked like a pickaxe handle, started to limp in Patrick's direction but stopped when he saw the gun. Munro, I thought.

'Are you from the police?' called a woman who had been standing to one side of the fireplace. 'Only these men are protecting me,' she continued before Patrick could reply. 'Please put your gun away.'

'Mrs Pamela Westfield,' said Patrick, raising his gun hand slightly, palm opened so that the weapon now pointed towards the ceiling. 'No, we are not from the police.'

'Who are you then?' asked the man with the shotgun.

'My ID card's in my top pocket.'

'Stay just like that. Put the other hand up as well.' He jerked his head at Munro. 'Go and get it. And the gun.'

'They'll go if I ask them to,' said Mrs Westfield.

'Shut up,' said Munro, baring discoloured teeth at her.

'Special Branch?' Patrick wondered aloud. 'Or did you get them from one of those agencies?' He clicked his tongue disapprovingly.

Munro raised his stave as if to hit Patrick with it and then, belatedly, realised that his situation was that of a man walking into a dragon's lair armed with a toothpick.

Patrick gave him the gun, swung it down side on so that it made annihilating contact with his temple. The shotgun-wielder hesitated until Munro fell, to give himself a clear field of fire, but by then it was too late for him also. His weapon dropped from numbed hands, the breech smashed, showering him with wood and metal splinters.

'There are no laurels to be earned in frapping the really stupid,' said Patrick in absent-minded fashion, stepping over Munro. He tucked his gun back in the holster and went to Mrs Westfield. 'My apologies that the mental processes were slow in realising you might be in danger.'

The one who had had the shotgun regained his balance and yelled, 'Bastard! The sort who hits cripples and — '

He didn't finish what he was about to say, and I took Pamela Westfield into the other end of the room and persuaded her to sit in a chair with her back to what was, I'm afraid, the enactment of pure revenge. My husband is not vicious, but neither is he the sort to allow a man who has

136

struck his wife to get away lightly. At least, that is what I told myself, all the while aware that a certain amount of man-handling was going on and also that, these days, since he was blown up by the grenade in the Falklands, I make a lot of allowances for him.

'A cup of tea, I think,' said Mrs Westfield when there was, at last, silence from the other end of the room. She looked up at me, smiled and then blew her nose, wiping away a few tears.

'I'll do it,' I told her. My kidnapper might be six foot four but he was now prone in front of the fireplace, a bit like a bear rug.

Patrick came over. Before he could say anything, Pamela Westfield said, 'Major, I knew who you were as soon as you entered the room. Thank you, a million thanks. I really thought, for one ghastly moment, that you were both going to be killed.' She turned to me. 'Forgive me. You must be Ingrid. The pictures of you on the jackets of your novels never do you justice.'

We were both slightly nonplussed by this recognition and our puzzlement became slight alarm when she leapt to her feet.

'Steady,' said Patrick. 'It's safe now.'

'Poor Madge!' the lady exclaimed. 'Here we are talking and she's still tied up in the bedroom.'

Madge — equally indomitable, it seemed — was an old friend of Pamela Westfield. She was far more concerned and angry about her ruined tights than grazed wrists where she had been tied tightly to a chair. It was she who began to recount their ordeal.

There had been a phone call, a man's voice telling Pamela to unlock the door or it would be kicked in. He had further warned that he was holding one of her grandchildren hostage and the child would be killed if they resisted or tried to get away. The line had then gone dead.

The women had discussed what to do — in level-headed fashion, one could only assume, watching them drink a reviving cup of tea — and had decided not to resist, thinking, wrongly as it happened, that whoever it was would only

137

demand money. There had been no time for them to have even told a neighbour, two men bursting in only about a minute after the call. Madge had immediately been bustled upstairs and tied up, they were not interested in her. Pamela had been questioned at length about what her husband had recently told her in connection with his brother-in-law. She could not help them, she and John Westfield had not lived together for over a year.

'We didn't shout our separation from the rooftops,' Pamela said quietly when she had finished giving us her part of the account.

'Whom *did* you tell?' Patrick asked.

'Just close friends like Madge. And the department, of course.' She smiled bravely. 'That's when it was no longer deemed necessary for Special Branch to carry on watching over me. Sergeant Waring stayed with my husband — perfectly correct, I suppose.'

'So where was Sergeant Waring on the night he was killed?' Patrick asked incredulously.

'Oh, John didn't take him to Bitterns with him. That would have really been too much to expect.'

There was no opportunity just then to ask her to elaborate because Daws and Steve walked in through the front door. Patrick had already taken word to Steve.

'The beast burned her with his cigarette,' said Madge to the room at large, lighting one herself and blowing a large cloud of smoke in the culprit's direction. 'I say, aren't you going to call the police?'

'Eventually,' Daws replied grimly. He went to Mrs Westfield and I got the impression that had they been alone he would have taken her in his arms. 'Pamela, are you sure you're all right?'

'Quite,' she told him, smiling.

Patrick said, 'Have you established whether they had in fact got hold of this child?'

'All lies,' said Pamela. 'They were so sure of themselves and that I'd snivel and whine that that was the first thing they said. They thought it really funny that they'd fooled two silly old women.'

I was still analysing the astounding hunch that Colonel

Richard and Pamela Westfield knew each other quite well, or at least, were friends in the not so distant past. If so, she was hiding it far more successfully than he. I found myself looking at him with different eyes. The Daws of some years ago must have been a very good-looking man. Even now his fair hair is thick, although going grey at the temples. He carries his tall frame like a military man and, like Patrick, is on the thin side.

Steve was regarding the two men, who had been trussed up with lengths of washing line. 'I take it we're going to endeavour to extract a little information.'

'Naturally,' said Daws. 'Is there somewhere private?'

By private he meant a place where no sounds connected with the questioning would be heard by the women.

'The garage?' cried Madge enthusiastically.

'Do you need a note-taker?' I enquired, bracing myself, because I knew full well what the prisoners faced.

'No,' said Patrick immediately, thus confirming my suspicions that no quarter would be given.

'Sherry,' Pamela decided when the men had gone. 'I don't feel very noble,' she went on, glass in hand, a minute or so later. 'Will they beat them badly?'

'No,' I said. 'Daws will leave it to Patrick and then no questions will be asked afterwards. There won't be a bruise on them.'

'But he'll hurt them if they don't talk.'

'Like hell,' I muttered. 'Don't think about it. Any information they get might prevent someone else going through what happened to you.'

'He was right, though,' she said in a faraway voice. 'There's nothing clever in bettering stupid people.'

'They should bring back the cat,' Madge asserted. 'And the birch. It would be surprising how people would find their wits when those were on offer.'

'No,' Pamela and I said together, and I wondered if Madge would change her mind in a short while.

When the three returned, Patrick a little pale, Daws gave him a stiff tot of whisky from a drinks trolley without asking and, on an afterthought, poured one each for Steve and himself. Then he downed his in one and went out to use the phone in Patrick's car.

139

'We all need some food,' Pamela said. 'Come, Madge, old thing, to the kitchen.'

'It's not safe for them here,' Patrick said when just the three of us were in the room. 'Daws is going to take them to a safe house in London. He's escorting them personally.'

'I think,' I said, 'that he and Pamela are old friends.'

But he wasn't really listening and had sunk tiredly into a chair.

'Was it difficult?' I asked.

'Bloody,' Steve said. 'He had to wring each word out of them a syllable at a time.' He glanced at Patrick quickly. 'I don't think if it'd been just the major and I we'd have carried on so long somehow.'

'What he means,' Patrick said bitterly, 'is that Daws ordered me to ensure that they weren't hiding *anything*. Perhaps I don't have the stomach for interrogation of that variety any more. Perhaps I'm going soft.' He shot to his feet, rammed his hands in his pockets and took himself off to the other end of the room. 'If that sounds like insubordination . . .' Here he rounded on is. 'Hell, it probably is – the reason I'm reputed to be not at all in the officer mould.' And then, with a quite crazy light in his eyes, he swore with shudder-making intensity for at least two minutes.

No, I hoped, no cat or birch. Someone, a man like Patrick who goes home to wife and children, has to use it on the convicted.

'Is Hurst implicated now?' I asked when he seemed to be at peace with the world.

'Oh yes. But the evidence of those two alone would be shot to pieces in court by a good barrister. We've got to *prove* it. The only thing not established is motive and the part that damn novel plays in all this.'

'Fill us in on the rest,' I requested, aware that talking about it would force him to marshal his thoughts and calm him down.

Daws reappeared at this point and listened impassively. I would imagine he finds Patrick's concise summing-up of assignments more than a little useful. Having read some of the colonel's own reports on cases and been struck by more than

140

a passing similarity to the wording, I wondered if he was memorising what was being said.

'According to Munro and the other one, Browning, they were hired by Plummer, Hurst's chauffeur, to help him with certain tasks,' Patrick began. 'They themselves had nothing to do with Westfield's murder – that was Plummer, they insist on that. But they did "borrow" Libby's trailer for the night to move the body.'

'To try to put the blame on her?' I enquired.

'They don't know about whys and wherefores but it might have been to leave a few red herrings around. I'm coming round to the idea that Rowan Campbell might have been intended to be in Bitterns that night. All we know right now is that Plummer then ordered Browning and Munro to keep a watch on us. When Browning saw you go in the trailer, Ingrid, he panicked and without waiting to confer with Plummer decided to deal with you on his own. Munro apparently saw him drive away the Land-Rover and trailer and thought he'd taken leave of his senses. He followed. Then of course one bungle led to another and they decided to get rid of the evidence.'

'Plummer must have received his orders from Hurst,' Steve said.

'We must assume so – or rather set out to prove that he did.'

'Where do these guys from London fit in?'

'Our pair don't know. What they do know is that they've been threatened with a nasty end if they talk at the hands of people who've had plenty of practice at such pastimes. Where they're going they won't have to worry about that for a while. I think our next task now is to read this novel that all the fuss seems to have been about and see if either it'll give us a lead as to motive or an insight into what Miles Hurst is actually up to. We've also got to make sure, of course, that there hasn't been any kind of security leak. Perhaps, while we're doing that, the author can be brought from London so we can ask her a few questions.'

'I'll leave that up to you,' Daws said. 'Please bear in mind that *we're* really only interested in the security angle.'

*

141

It was well after midnight by the time we finished going through *Spy Triad*. I had been reading – some ten pages behind Patrick – on the bed in our hotel room and must have fallen asleep for I was suddenly aware of him shaking me awake.

'I'm none the wiser,' I told him, bad-temperedly shoving the untidy pile of sheets of A4 in his hands.

'No spies,' he sighed. 'A rather purple detective story pure and simple. Brainy and sexually frustrated heroine thaws ditto, ditto police inspector and together they solve beastly murders. Lots of car chases and people going over cliffs. The crooks were going to hold up a bank and the plucky pair foil them. End of story, she in his arms while he ignores a bullet through the shoulder. I discovered I could never ignore bullets anywhere.' He yawned. 'It's no good – we'll have to talk to the girl.'

There was a loud knock at the door.

'The fuzz,' groaned Patrick. 'You can tell by the mailed fist.'

It was Faversham, alone.

'You appear to have been concealing evidence,' was his opening remark.

'We did agree that my priority was national security,' Patrick said wearily. 'You mean the penny dreadful, I suppose. Take it. Light the fire with it if you must. We've just wasted two solid hours reading it through.'

Faversham listened to this impatiently and then said, 'Rowan Campbell has admitted breaking into Bitterns on the night of the murder to try to retrieve a typescript belonging to a friend. I would have appreciated you telling me that you'd done precisely the same thing a few days later.'

Frostily, Patrick said, 'Inspector, the title page of that novel was on the floor in Hurst's study for three whole days and none of your people found it.'

'Major – '

'Campbell clutters up this case,' Patrick interrupted. 'Be a good chap and let him go. Concentrate on the two pin-brained thugs we gave you earlier. Have you brought Plummer in for questioning yet?'

'Not to be found,' said Faversham. 'The Hursts aren't at

142

home either. But it must be pointed out that Plummer has a good alibi. He was at a martial-arts club in Brighton. Several people have vouched for him. Not only that, the officer who took his statement was struck by his helpfulness — a genuine wish to co-operate. And I would like to remind you that Campbell's thumbprint *is* on the murder weapon.'

'Martial arts?' said Patrick silkily. 'That sometimes goes hand in hand with collections of weapons, handbooks on survival in the wild and a general likelihood to go mad and create massacre.'

'Like soldiers, you mean?' Faversham asked.

For once, Patrick was lost for a suitable reply.

Chapter Thirteen

Lindsey Davies seemed to be almost overwhelmed with excitement at being brought from London in a car with two armed men from Special Branch in order to be questioned by a senior member of MI5. Ushered into Inspector Faversham's office the following morning, she surveyed us with eyes that positively glowed. No, I inwardly berated myself, it was not she who was naive but I, Ingrid Langley, who had forgotten what it was like to ache to be accepted as a writer. I did not attempt thrillers when I started writing but I suddenly realised how Lindsey must feel, all at once projected into the world she was trying to create in words.

To begin with she thought that Faversham would be doing the questioning, for the inspector was sitting at his desk. When the introductions were made and the budding author's attention drawn to the dark-haired man sitting quietly in a corner, she looked distinctly disappointed.

Patrick chuckled, genuinely amused, her mind utterly transparent to him. After indicating a chair placed almost opposite him he said, 'Only colonels and above are allowed to wear a monocle and black leather gloves.'

'You're teasing me,' she said, a lift to her chin as she seated herself.

'Of course, I always tease pretty girls. Now, I want you to call me Patrick and be aware that I shall tease you mercilessly.' He leaned over, took the typescript of *Spy Triad* from a corner of Faversham's desk and gave it to her.

'Can I keep it now?' asked Lindsey a trifle breathlessly, hugging it to herself as one might a small child.

'Of course.'

'Do you think it's any good? I suppose you've read it.'

'I'm no judge,' he told her. 'But it's a good exciting read.' He shifted his chair slightly to face her. 'D'you mind my asking how old you are?'

'Eighteen — nearly nineteen.'

'And you understand all about libel and that kind of thing?'

She coloured, probably because of his steady scrutiny. 'Yes.'

'Are all the characters' names in this story purely fictitious?'

'Yes. I just open the phone book when I want someone's name.'

'Have you any idea why anyone should want to remove that typescript from your possession?'

'No.'

'Why did you call it *Spy Triad*?'

Lindsey looked at him in utter bewilderment. 'I thought it quite a good title.'

'But there are no spies in the story.'

'But — but of course there are! I thought you said you'd read it.' She balanced the folder on her lap and opened it at random, flipping through. 'Darien was a spy. He was getting secrets from his brother-in-law in MI5 and . . .' Her voice trailed into silence. 'But this isn't it!' she cried. 'This is *Dead Before Noon*, a thing I wrote years ago. Yes, I remember now — I typed new title pages for some of my work. I must have put this back on the wrong one.'

'So you gave the men the wrong story and *Spy Triad* is in London.'

'It must be. Oh, dear, I'm terribly sorry.'

Patrick gave the girl another searching look. 'Tell me,' he murmured at last, 'to your knowledge was Miles Hurst getting secrets from his brother-in-law, John?'

'Not to my knowledge,' she answered carefully.

'Why were you dismissed from Hurst's employment?'

She blushed bright red this time. 'I'm afraid my typing wasn't as good then as I made out. And I said at the interview that my shorthand speed was sixty words a minute. That was an exaggeration, too.'

'You're very frank,' Patrick said with a disarming smile. He was still smiling when he added, 'Now please be perfectly frank about the rest.'

'I have been,' Lindsey protested.

Patrick leaned forwards. 'Lindsey, my child, this is my job and I've broken far better liars than you.'

Somehow she dragged her gaze from his and looked at me beseechingly. This is one of the reasons I am present at a lot of interviews with the young and impressionable, acting as a refuge from his relentless questions. More often than not a little sympathy is the catalyst that brings out truth.

'He doesn't mean you're not telling the truth because you're some kind of criminal,' I said gently. 'It's just that fear makes people not say all they should. But you mustn't be frightened — people will guard you until this business is finally sorted out.'

There was a short silence while she stared at me. Then she blurted out, 'It — it didn't seem to be wrong at the time. But then, afterwards ...'

'When you'd got it all down on paper?' Patrick prompted quietly.

But when she spoke it was to me. 'It seemed really exciting when I found out about it. Just like a plot for a book. I think I admired Mr Hurst until I thought about it a bit more clearly. For a while I thought he was clever. And then I found out more.'

'Yes?' I said.

'He was blackmailing him — Mrs Hurst's brother.'

'To obtain information?'

'Yes.'

'How did you find out?'

'He must have left the dictating machine switched on when he was talking on the phone. It got all mixed up with some letters I had to do. I heard him say something like "Well, you know what'll happen, John, old man, if you don't deliver the goods this time. The gutter press'll have a field day." Something like that. It was then I realised how horrible he was.'

'Have you any idea what he had against his brother-in-law?'

146

'Some photographs — I think they were taken at a party.'

'Ah, yes, the parties,' Patrick said softly, relaxing back in his chair. 'But before we get on to that, have you any idea of the nature of the information that was given to him?'

'I didn't put it in the book,' Lindsey mumbled. 'I didn't dare. I said it was defence secrets and that the crook was a spy. That sounded more interesting, too.'

'No doubt,' Patrick said dryly. 'But in boring real life?'

'You're nasty,' she whispered and folded up around her beloved story in a pathetic huddle.

I shook my head at Patrick. After all, she was very young. That kind of approach would *not* do. I got up to go to her side but he had already done so, an arm around her thin shoulders.

'I'm nasty,' I heard him say in an undertone into her ear. 'Sorry. Shall we have some coffee before we go any further?'

After a few seconds the girl uncoiled. 'No, I'm all right. I'd rather get it over with.'

'Fine,' Patrick replied lightly. 'Then tell me what the information was.'

'I've no proof.'

'Don't worry about that. Looking for proof is my responsibility.'

She bit her nails for a moment. 'I think it was all to do with contracts for government construction projects. Things like work on naval dockyards, prisons and army barracks. I have an idea that it involved details of what firms were tendering so that Mr Hurst could tender lower.'

'Eureka,' said Patrick peacefully. 'Oh, brother! The possibilities are endless if you think about it. Presuming that Hurst had his brother-in-law screwed right down, it wouldn't just be info about tenders. Designs for new prisons to be sold to parties interested in getting inmates out of same, barracks and Ministry of Defence building plans to be flogged to terrorist organisations keen on planting bombs. Lindsey, that kind of thing *is* defence secrets.'

'Westfield had access to all that?' Faversham said.

'You've hit the right word. Access. Among other things he was involved with contracts for secure installations and the construction and design thereof. Inspector, I suggest you organise a search warrant. Two, perhaps — one for Bitterns

147

and the other for the offices in Petworth.'

'Anything for a lead,' Faversham said, getting to his feet.

'Do you have pictures of those two hoods from London?'

The inspector handed over a couple of photographs, one of Harperley, one of Pugh, and Patrick showed them to Lindsey.

'Have you seen these two men before?'

The door closed after Faversham.

'The dark one, perhaps,' Lindsey said hesitantly.

'Not the other one?'

She shook her head.

'The dark one . . . did he come to the office?'

'No, I never saw him there.'

'So it was at Bitterns. I didn't realise that you sometimes worked there.'

'Just once or twice . . . when we were very busy.'

'Was he at the parties?'

'I don't know − I didn't go to them.'

'Weren't you invited?'

The reply came very quickly. 'No.'

'Come now,' Patrick chided.

'I knew what sort of thing they'd be,' she said defiantly. 'I hate parties like that.'

'But you weren't invited?'

'No.'

'Tell the truth, Lindsey,' he whispered.

She found the willpower to close her eyes, shaking her head from side to side as though it hurt. 'I'm not saying anything else about that. Whatever you do to me − even if you hit me − I'm not saying any more.'

I raised an eyebrow at Patrick and he nodded grimly. Yes, we had to find out what had really happened.

'Lindsey,' Patrick said very gently. 'You were working for a man who I think enmeshed everyone in his influence and intrigue. From what you tell us and from things we've already found out, it would appear that he is involved in criminal activities and knows people who are criminals. It might sound a little dramatic but since John Westfield was killed it seems that half the village has been dragged into a web of suspicion and hatred. It is impossible that you, Hurst's secretary, could

148

avoid being involved. I suggest that you were flattered when your employer asked you to a gathering of friends one evening and that you went. I also suggest that you can't forget what took place. Nightmares have to be talked out, child, or they take away your sanity.'

Large tears were welling from beneath Lindsey's tightly closed eyes but she said not a word. Patrick drew his chair up close to her and took one of her hands.

'I can imagine what happened,' he said. 'There's no need for you to tell me much. It was wonderful, wasn't it? – an invitation to a party in a large country house. You put on your best dress and had your hair done in a way that made you look a little older and a woman of the world. But when you arrived you were disturbed to see that most of the other women present were tarty to say the least. People were drinking heavily and, you suspected, were even taking drugs. There was very little to eat. You asked for only wine or fruit juice but as the evening wore on – and you didn't want them to think you a fool if you left – you began to think that your drinks were being laced with some kind of strong spirit. It all became very confusing and what you can remember after that makes you feel horribly ashamed and gives you nightmares. Right?'

A tiny miserable nod.

'People had sex, didn't they?' Patrick went on. 'Perhaps in ways that revolted you. Some of them took part in filthy ceremonies when perhaps a small animal was killed and its blood smeared on people. They might have even put some on you and you were so under the influence of whatever drugs or drink you had been given that you thought it all great fun. Lindsey, you did nothing *wrong*, it was their way of dragging you into – '

'I'm one of them!' Lindsey suddenly cried. 'That's what they told me. "You're one of us now," a woman said. "Whatever you do, wherever you go, you'll always be one of us."' And she wept then, huge sobs that shook her slim body.

Apparently absent-mindedly, Patrick kissed the fingertips of the hand he was holding. 'Was that the party where a girl was raped?'

149

'I'm so ashamed I'll die if you say any more,' Lindsey sobbed.

'You're not one of them or you wouldn't be ashamed,' Patrick said, studying the small oval fingernails. 'Who raped her?'

'We all did in a way,' said Lindsey. 'We all held her down and . . .' The rest was lost in sobs. Then, 'She was only a local girl brought in to wash the glasses and clear up.'

'Only?' Patrick queried.

She looked up, shocking us with her haggard appearance. 'Only meaning she was ordinary. Not one of the prostitutes. I don't think she was really very intelligent.'

'I see. Go on.'

'Miles raped her first. Then all the other men . . .' Her face crumpled into more weeping.

'Did Westfield?'

'No. He wasn't there.'

'Were photographs taken of anyone present?'

'I don't think so.'

'Were you yourself subjected to any kind of assault?'

'I'm not sure. I think I passed out or something. They were burning incense and it was making me feel awful. Then I woke up on the floor and Miles was bending over me.'

'But you'd know, wouldn't you, if you'd been sexually assaulted?'

Silence.

'Would you rather I went away and you talked to Ingrid about it?'

'No. I'm all right. I don't think I was. But some of my clothes had been taken off.'

He patted her hand and stood up. 'That'll do for now.'

'I felt really dirty afterwards,' she said in a small voice.

Patrick gazed down at her, seemingly quite at a loss for words. Then he took from around his neck the silver cross and chain he has worn for as long as I can remember, opened her clenched fingers and dropped it into her palm. 'That might help. It's the sort of thing that usually does. Just a couple more questions . . .'

'Yes?' said Lindsey, looking at what he had given her.

'You wrote *Spy Triad* before the party you attended?'

150

'Yes.'

'Have you any idea how long Hurst had been blackmailing Westfield?'

'No, but even when I first worked there he did everything Miles said. He always seemed ill whenever I saw him. I didn't like him very much but I felt sorry for him.'

After a pause Patrick said, 'I can only think that someone saw a sample of your work — perhaps on your desk if you'd been doing some writing in your lunch hour, perhaps in the wastepaper basket — and noticed words like "MI5" or "security leak" or some such thing and thought you were keeping an account of what was going on.'

'I'm glad I told you what happened,' Lindsey said unhappily. 'But I'll never forget — I'll think about it all my life.'

Patrick touched her elbow so that she rose to her feet. 'Come and have coffee with us and say yahboo to the gremlins of bitter memory. I have a colleague with a tin leg whose back looks like a relief map of Mars where some thugs beat him with their belts. Some mornings he doesn't want to get out of bed because everything hurts and the world looks black. Then he kicks the gremlins in the teeth and puts the kettle on. Be like that. Better than that, write it all down. I know a lady novelist who gets rid of all her nightmares by putting them in her books.'

'I'd like to meet them both,' Lindsey said when Patrick had gone to find Inspector Faversham.

'You already have,' I said.

Later there was a briefing. In Faversham's office assembled Daws, Steve — who had been working closely with him endeavouring to build up a clear picture of the information that had been available to Westfield in the course of his work — Faversham, Sergeant Grant, Patrick, one of the Special Branch men who had escorted Lindsey and who had been subsequently 'borrowed', a couple of plain-clothes constables and me.

For the benefit of those who had not been working closely on the case, Faversham first briefly outlined the facts that were known and then went on to summarise what had been discovered during investigations. There was an interruption

151

while he was summing up, someone to tell him that Browning and Munro had been driven to the spot where they had delivered a hired car towing the trailer to Plummer and a quick search in a nearby copse had resulted, amazingly, in the discovery of the site of the murder and also Westfield's car, covered with branches. At this point the inspector suggested that the briefing of the 'raiding party' be delayed for a while to enable him to put his full team to work on this latest development. It was agreed that we would reconvene at six-thirty that evening.

The day seemed endless.

'Both of Miles Hurst's premises have been under close surveillance today' was Faversham's opening remark after apologising for keeping us waiting, the time being a little after six-forty. He smiled wearily. 'I must be getting tired − I'm sure you were all fully aware of that.'

Daws cleared his throat. 'If I may say a few words ...?'

'Certainly, colonel.'

'I don't propose that my people get under your feet any further in this matter. I received a phone call a few minutes ago and it's important that I go straight back to London. With your permission I'll leave Mr Lindley to take care of any sensitive evidence that comes to light. The motive for Westfield's murder seems to have been fairly well pinpointed and you appear to have strong evidence against at least one person. There is absolutely no point in my keeping key staff here now.'

My spirits soared. Home for the weekend, a meal for two at our favourite restaurant in the Barbican in Plymouth, a long lie-in on Sunday morning, cuddles with Justin, a chance to wander round the garden.

'That is perfectly acceptable to me,' said Faversham.

'I want a detailed report from you,' Daws said to Steve. 'On my desk first thing on Monday morning.'

'Yes, sir,' replied Steve quietly, his face grey with exhaustion.

Patrick said, 'Sir, have you any objection to my accompanying the inspector tonight?'

'Yes, major, I have,' said Daws, 'Several.' His tone suggested that he did not expect to be cross-examined on what

152

these were. However, Patrick's response to this, an infuriating small polite smile worse than a thousand arguments, forced him to bark, '*Well?*'

Patrick feigned shock at being shouted at. 'The case interests me, sir, that's all.'

'And there might be a little rough stuff if the occupants of the house return,' Daws added heavily.

Patrick beamed at him. 'That too, sir,' he conceded.

'No.'

'I had already decided to withdraw Mr Lindley from service on the grounds that he's not fit,' Patrick continued calmly.

Daws glared at Steve, who manifestly was not fit, so much so that Grant felt it necessary to draw out a chair for him and loosen his tie. Someone was sent for a glass of water.

'Very well,' Daws said slowly. 'But I want you out of here at midnight. Phone me at home with an interim report.'

Already furious with Patrick, I became absolutely beside myself with Daws. There was further discussion for another few minutes, of which I heard not a word. And then the room emptied, everyone going to prepare for their own part in the night's sortie. Steve went out with Grant at his side. He had not been pretending.

'I'm invisible,' I said to four very plain walls.

Patrick put his head round the door with the frown of a man who had forgotten to pick up his briefcase. 'Are you coming?'

'I'm invisible,' I said again. 'Perhaps I don't exist.'

He came in. 'Daws knows you go everywhere with me.'

'Pet rocks go everywhere with some people,' I observed truculently.

I was taken in a passionate embrace. 'Obsidian the beloved,' he moaned breathily in my ear. 'Igneous wonder. Grit of my conglomerates. Shale of my metamorphics.' A lingering kiss. 'Oh, dream of my molten silicates.'

I began to feel a lot happier.

153

Chapter Fourteen

This rare mood of inspired lunacy on the part of the man from MI5 took hold among the assembled representatives of law and order but, mercifully, was tempered into a feeling of keen anticipation for the activities ahead. At least, this is how I read the situation. Me? I was half-seriously composing my resignation letter. For, while I appreciated that every case was different, if my role had degenerated into little more than note-taker and I was to continue to play a completely passive part – the powers that be, i.e. Patrick, having decided that I was to be unarmed except in emergencies – then they could do without me.

In truth, I did not want to return to Bitterns. I accepted, I think, that on my first visit either a strong imagination or some chemical substance, or both, had contributed to a most peculiar experience. At the same time I was very strongly attempting to repress the idea that I had come under the influence of something evil and quite inexplicable. After all, if one accepted the supernatural beliefs of the Christian religion – which I was still endeavouring to do, if only for Patrick's sake – it was surely not totally impossible for utter and complete evil also to exist and be used by unscrupulous people for their own gain.

The house, I knew, had been searched when Westfield's body was first found. But looking for clues after a murder and the hunt for evidence against the householder can be two quite different things. This time not so much care would be taken with the Hursts' possessions and if a wall sounded hollow or there appeared to be recent alterations to cupboards ...

As we left the police station we met Rowan Campbell, who had just been released. He looked the other way when he saw us but I detained him with a hand on the arm. For a moment I thought he would shake himself free and continue walking.

'Are you being charged with anything?' I asked.

'Not yet,' he answered in hostile fashion.

'You should have mentioned taking the hammer with you,' Patrick said.

'It's easy to be glib when you've never dared do anything but toe the line,' Campbell snarled at him before striding away.

The one who has hardly ever toed the line gave me a twisted smile. 'Are you ready?'

'As only a lava flow can be,' I told him.

Even Faversham seemed to have shed his usual lugubriousness − his mood now probably the nearest he would ever get to being bouncing and jolly − and was waiting for us with Sergeant Grant in an unmarked car. No sooner had we seated ourselves than he let out the clutch and we were away, swerving through the other vehicles parked in the yard at the rear of the building.

'What kind of profile is this going to have?' Patrick asked when we were on the open road breaking all the speed limits.

'Not high in the sense that I have members of the tactical firearms unit with me,' Faversham shouted over his shoulder. 'Because I haven't. What you should have asked first is if the Hursts are home. Well, they are − arrived half an hour ago. They can't suspect a thing. Plummer's with them too − drove them in the Roller.'

There had been other delays after the briefing so it was just after eleven-thirty-five when the car swung into the drive of Bitterns. A thin drizzle was falling, giving a weird halo to a huge full moon shining in a clear sky to the east.

Patrick said, 'Perhaps we'll be fortunate enough to catch them dressed up in their wizards' and witches' outfits.'

Faversham parked the car. 'Practising witchcraft hasn't been illegal since 1951.'

'I was thinking from a purely *entertainment* point of view,' Patrick told him. 'I've always wanted to be turned into a toad.'

'You speak for yourself,' Faversham muttered, hauling his bulk out of the car. 'Grant, see that the dogs and handlers stay outside. I only want them if someone makes a break for it.'

'There's only the Roller parked here,' Patrick said, thinking aloud and sounding slightly disappointed. 'Just the three of them then.'

'The police can arrest the London mobsters,' I pointed out.

'Yes, but to have bagged the *lot* . . .' He took my arm and hitched his through it. 'We hang back, lodestone mine, and allow the law to get on with its mailed-fist-and-boots thing. D12 should not — Hello, is that our large friend Plummer trying to get away?'

It was indeed Plummer. He had run from what appeared to be a side door and had shoved several policemen to one side, kicking at one who fell. There was considerable confusion and a lot of shouting.

'His car's at the side there!' Patrick shouted. He swung round. 'Surely the fool . . .'

I turned and also saw the patrol car that had just been parked across the gates, blocking the drive. Behind us, Plummer was starting the engine of his car. It roared, headlights suddenly blazing.

'He'll get away,' I heard Patrick say above the din. 'He'll ram that car out of the way and — Bloody hell!' he exclaimed. 'Am I really the only bloke with a gun?'

Apparently he was. I made myself scarce in a clump of lupins, bobbing down just at Plummer's car came at us. He drove straight at a dog handler who was crouching on the grass at the side of the drive and I heard a dreadful scream as the dog was hit. Then there was nothing but the glare of the lights and, silhouetted against them, Patrick, down on one knee, his Smith and Wesson grasped two-handed.

The first shot, astoundingly, hit the front tyre farthest away from him, causing the car to veer to the right. The next took out the windscreen. Plummer plunged out of the vehicle before it stopped moving and ran towards the entrance.

'Stop or I fire!' Patrick yelled. But there was too great a risk of hitting someone else.

Plummer swerved a couple of times but kept running. He was right upon the patrol car by this time, the two constables in it flinging open their doors to intercept him. By the time others had converged Plummer had punched one to the ground and had hold of the other, slamming him repeatedly into the side of the car. He was about to deliver a vicious blow to the man's body when he was chopped down from behind with tremendous enthusiasm by the Special Branch man, Hammond.

'That all happened a bit fast,' Hammond was saying when I arrived.

Patrick took the pair of handcuffs held out to him by the constable who had been rescued from Plummer and clipped them on the captive's wrists. 'Where were you?' he asked, straightening up.

'I'm not exactly *permitted* to do that kind of shooting,' Hammond said. 'If he'd had a gun and —'

I cannot repeat what Patrick said to him.

'Did you get him?' called the dog handler as we approached the house. He was crouched down stroking the dark shape on the ground.

'Like a side of beef,' Patrick replied. 'Is the dog dead?'

The man flicked on the torch he was carrying. 'Breathing just now,' he said dully. 'Yes,' he added, after briefly examining the German Shepherd. 'Not breathing now. I knew he was finished. All that blood coming from his nose like that.'

'Life's a real bastard sometimes,' Patrick commented as we walked away.

'I accept no responsibility for the actions of my staff!' we heard Miles Hurst shout as we walked through the wide-open front door. He was standing by the large fireplace in his living room, a hunted expression on his face, Jan by his side nervously pulling at her mohair sweater.

'We want to question him in connection with your brother-in-law's death,' said Faversham when Grant, just ahead of us, had confirmed the arrest.

'Was it necessary to indulge in these heavy tactics?' Hurst asked before the inspector could continue. 'Really, I do think that —'

'And I also have search warrants both for this property and for your office in Petworth,' Faversham cut in.

'This has nothing to do with me,' Jan wailed, wringing her hands.

'Did you know Plummer had a criminal record when you employed him?' Faversham asked Hurst, ignoring her.

Defiantly, Hurst said, 'Yes, I did. Someone has to give these people a chance, don't they?' He was darting glances around the room as he spoke and every time he heard heavy footfalls upstairs, or other sounds of rude disarrangement of his possessions, he winced. 'What on earth makes you think he had anything to do with John's death?'

'Why did he run?' Faversham countered.

The searching and questions went on for two hours, a small team having already been dispatched to the office in Petworth. Nothing of any interest was found. By this time Hurst's solicitor had arrived and had placed himself between Faversham and his client in such a fashion that I feared for the inspector's mental health.

'Orgies,' Patrick mused aloud, kicking his heels in the hall. He had just returned from searching through filing cabinets at the office. 'Where did they hold such things? In the living room? In a cupboard under the stairs? In the attics? Where, for God's sake?'

'You forgot to ask Lindsey,' I said.

He glanced at his watch. 'Oh, well ...'

When he came back from using the phone he said, 'She didn't really mind being woken up. She's not sure. It all started off in the living room with drinks ... just as I thought. But she can't remember if what followed took place in the same room. Isn't even sure what was dream and what really happened. Only that it was lurid, there was lots of choking smoke that made her feel dizzy and everyone was shouting and singing. I'm beginning to think they were all on some drug-induced trip ... LSD or whatever.'

'A house like this should have cellars,' I said.

'Cellars,' Patrick echoed and then unaccountably went upstairs. He returned after a minute or so with Grant and the two set about rolling up the long Wilton runner in the hall. Nothing was revealed but more of the stone flags one could see at the edges. At this point Patrick, sitting thoughtfully on

158

the roll of carpet, had another idea. Grant and I followed him into the kitchen.

In the centre of the floor was a circular woven grass mat. When it was slid to one side a trapdoor was revealed. It was not particularly obvious for the top was covered in the same patterned vinyl as the floor. It was locked.

'We needn't bother Hurst for the key,' Patrick said, a kind of mad grin on his face. 'Eye of newt and wing of frog,' he intoned, bending down, the lock-picker's tool in his hand.

'Wish I had the kind of mandate you do,' Grant said enviously. 'I don't mean a licence to kill — just being able . . . well, to do things like this.'

The delicate-looking fingers were holding the tool as might a surgeon wield a scalpel. 'The perks,' Patrick said with a chuckle. 'To be able to force a lock without first filling in a form in triplicate. But I do have to justify my actions afterwards. It's afterwards that any tears are shed.'

'Go on,' said Grant softly. 'People in your position . . .'

The lock clicked open.

'Are crucified afterwards for errors of judgement,' Patrick whispered. 'Could you handle that, sergeant?' He laughed. 'Who knows what we'll find under here — cabinet ministers in compromising situations with peers of the realm, perhaps? At least, this time, we do have a search warrant.'

And then, most definitely, the joking stopped.

The current of air that wafted into our faces as the trapdoor was raised smelled of mould and dampness. I thought of dry rot and rising damp and then forgot them and found myself brought to mind of decay and putrefaction instead. We went down the short ladder into the darkness and it was like descending into a grave.

'We need a light,' Grant muttered.

'There's a switch,' Patrick told him.

A low-wattage bulb illuminated a passageway. The stone walls oozed moisture and here and there were patches of a slimy-looking greenish growth. The heavy wooden beams over our heads, supports for the floor of one of the ground-level rooms above, looked rotten in places. Our feet boomed hollowly on the sweating floor as we made our way towards a door we could see at the other end of the passage, slightly

159

ajar, a faint chink of light shining through the gap.

When we reached the door, Grant, who had been leading the way, stopped. Patrick squeezed round him and pushed the door open wider. It grated back on rusting hinges.

'This is the place,' I said, looking over Patrick's shoulder.

'This is the place,' he agreed. He found another light switch just inside the door and put it on. Then, glancing round, 'Such out-of-use words spring to mind: profanity, blasphemy ... I'm glad my father will never see this.'

The pale greenish light that had been the only source of illumination until the lights were switched on shone through a skylight in the roof. This was directly above what I can only describe as an altar on a raised dais at one end of the room. The cross on it was made of some black substance and inverted, a large red eye painted in the centre. The eye seemed to follow me wherever I went in the room.

There were several rows of chairs arranged as they might be in a small chapel with an aisle down the centre. But it was the paintings on the walls that took all the attention: people and animals contorted as in a nightmare, garish colours, all the pictures of unspeakable obscenity. Many of the figures were of obvious biblical origin, the scenes depicted certain to provoke in a Christian beholding them rage, nausea and shock.

'Patrick ...' I began, really frightened of what he might do as he looked more closely and the utter disbelief in what his eyes were telling him turned to something else.

'I gave my cross to Lindsey,' I heard him whisper.

I said the first thing that came into my head. 'It's the people wearing them who matter.' Out of the corner of my eye I saw Grant move over to the door and wondered if he was thinking the same as I was, that Hurst's life might need to be protected.

The explosion of ferocious temper did not materialise. Instead, Patrick went to the altarlike table, slowly, like a man in a dream, wrenched the inverted black cross from it and, again slowly – but not because of the effort for, just now, such things were no effort – bent the solid metal until it was a shapeless mass. The eye popped out of its setting and rolled across the floor and, not even seeming to notice what he was doing, he ground it to dust beneath his heel.

I discovered that I was shivering.

'We search this place,' Patrick said woodenly, dropping the twisted metal on the floor, 'Sergeant, there's no need to look so worried. The thought that I'd have to lay hands on you first has already stopped me wanting to wring Miles Hurst's neck.'

We found Libby's body behind the altar.

She lay in a pathetic huddle, her wonderful red hair covering her face. But that was all that was covered for her body was naked and there were wounds of a kind that were in keeping with the pictures on the walls of the room.

Grant had been kneeling by the body and now shot to his feet. 'That bastard's upstairs playing the upright citizen. God, I'll – '

Patrick grabbed his jacket as he went by, bringing him to an abrupt halt. 'You'll go upstairs quietly and soberly and report what we've found to the inspector.' One of the time-honoured Gillard shakes. 'My mandate says that, while you may *endeavour* to stop me taking someone to pieces, I can definitely box your ears to prevent you from doing the same thing.'

'Yes, sir,' said Grant in a whisper and was released.

'Poor sod,' Patrick said when Grant had gone.

I went to the nearest chair and sat down. Although this meant that I felt a little less faint I could not banish from my mind the dreadful, obscene images of Libby's last moments. Almost certainly she had died right here in this room. Horribly.

'There's no need for you to stay down here,' Patrick said, his voice tight with anger.

Mutely I shook my head. I was still shivering uncontrollably and was not sure whether it was my imagination or the room really was full of whispers, the voices of creatures and beings not quite seen until they were called by name.

Patrick came over and sat by me. 'Is that no or no?' he asked.

'The sensation of evil ...' I started to say but could not continue.

'It's nothing that a good priest and a bucket of whitewash can't cure.'

161

I was still sitting there when Grant came back with Faversham and a good many other people besides. Except for one or two who gave the wall paintings startled glances, no one really noticed anything but the body. That was how it should be, I told myself dully, here were policemen doing their job.

After a while the Hursts were brought down and confronted with the body. Jan had not wanted to come, I had heard her shouting and screaming as she was made to climb down the ladder. Her husband also shouted, protesting that he never came to this part of the house normally but that a local club used it for meetings, he had no idea what they *did*.

It was at about this time that I began to wonder if Hurst was playing for time. There were even more people present now, several from the forensic department, a photographer who was taking pictures of the body from every conceivable angle, more plain-clothes police, a doctor.

I stood up and looked around for Patrick but he was nowhere to be seen. The strange thing was that I could not remember him leaving the room. This should have warned me that something was wrong but all I did was to reseat myself and watch and wait.

Hurst talked and kept on talking, all the while standing by the door. Faversham let him get on with it, half listening and at the same time conferring with his assistants. In a dreamlike way I saw him stagger a little and a couple of men loosen their ties.

'Hot down here,' someone muttered.

It wasn't, it was very cold.

In my weird unattached and uninvolved way I saw the air in the room take on a greenish hue. People were moving slowly now and no one noticed when the photographer, focusing for yet another shot, keeled over slowly, hitting his head on the dais step as he fell.

And I just sat and waited for them to go down like a row of skittles.

Hurst had gone. I could do nothing about it. For to me it seemed as though the murals had come to life, writhing and slithering from the walls to take their places among us. Nobody else appeared to see them, not even when a naked

162

courtesan who had previously been entwined with a donkey on the wall, draped herself over Faversham as he and Grant slid to the floor.

Anger got me to my feet. Anger at seeing the fear in the eyes of a young policewoman on the other side of the room as she clutched at the doorpost for support. Then she too slumped down.

We were all being gassed.

Someone shouted.

The sound came from above and I seemed to swim towards it through a green sea.

Then came the unmistakable roar as a shotgun was fired, both barrels of the sawn-off variety.

A man screamed. It went on and on and then was choked off as though his throat had been cut.

I was by the ladder, only realising that I had been holding my breath when I found myself gasping for air. The gas swirled around the rungs of the ladder. Trying to climb it was most peculiar as my legs would not obey and were just useless appendages on the end of my body.

Somehow, I reached the top. I knew that if I did not get into the fresh air I would pass out. Finding Patrick and staying awake were more important than anything so I didn't stop to look at the dead man, Hammond, lying in an ever-widening pool of blood in the kitchen, I just staggered out through the open back door and into the night.

Silence.

No, on my knees on the grass I could hear my own gasping breathing. I held my breath and nearby heard someone moan. Out in the darkness of the garden a shape moved and I jumped to my feet with a small shriek of fright as it came towards me. It slowed and, as it moved into the light streaming from the house, I saw that it was the surviving police dog, leash trailing, dark eyes crazy with fear.

I grabbed the leash and it immediately went off at a run, towing me after it. 'Seek,' I said inanely, when the dog paused, whimpering. Then I saw that it was walking on three legs, the fourth dangling uselessly. We sat there, dog and I, on the lawn, my arms round the animal as it sang a moaning song of misery and loss into my ear.

163

I'm not sure how long we stayed there. The gas probably took its effect on me and I became unconscious. I was not aware of the passing of time, only, eventually, of the dog licking my face and a pale light in the eastern sky. It was like waking up to find that you're the only person left alive in the whole world.

But was I awake? Or was this dream or even death?

It was reality. As my senses cleared I saw that the light in the sky was still a bright moon. Out of the house ran four men wearing gas masks. I flopped down on the grass again, a tight hold on the dog's collar so that it had to keep still. Through half-closed eyes I saw one of the men pause and survey the garden. He took a couple of steps in my direction. Then one of the others shouted at him and he ran off. A car screeched away, and another, perhaps a larger vehicle.

Silence.

It was quite clear now what had happened. While everyone's attention had been on searching Bitterns, questioning the Hursts and then on the discovery of the body, a gang of armed men had raided the house. But why had the Hursts returned to their home in the first place? Confidence that the police would discover nothing to connect them with the murder? As bait so that hostages could be taken? It seemed to be the latter, for Patrick had disappeared.

Chapter Fifteen

Several factors were responsible for Patrick not being kept as a hostage. One of these was that he was wearing the same kind of clothing — dark-blue sweater and trousers — as the police that night, another that even under pressure he is a master at hiding his true identity. Ineptitude on the part of the men who had grabbed him also played a part, that and the fact that he was transported in a separate vehicle to Jan and Miles Hurst, a van which had brought the gang from London. So there was no one to recognise him and make the decision that here was a far larger fish than the one they were already holding. In view of these points he was merely used for the purpose for which he had been taken, as a messenger who would witness certain things first-hand.

The messenger was taken to a house in the East End of London — a different destination to the Hursts — and there was made privy to a business transaction that had taken place between Hurst and Harry Pugh, the Welshman known to be an associate of Brad Harperley. Harperly had gone into a new line of business, the plan being that hostages important to, and even working for, the system of law and order were taken and sold to whoever required them as insurance against prosecution. At least, that was the idea. Pugh's right-hand man spoke with the messenger, giving the latter the impression that the bosses were bored and if the idea brought in a little ready cash so much the better. If not, the hostage in the present trial was regarded as expendable and the cost of failure was the price of a bullet.

After this conversation the messenger was taken to see the

hostage to ensure that he was well aware of the bleak conditions of his existence. This experience proved too much for him and some kind of rescue was attempted, resulting in one of the hostage's captors suffering a broken nose and another a broken wrist and dislocated shoulder. Patrick was not killed for this unwise behaviour, merely beaten senseless and dumped on a piece of waste ground just off Railway Avenue, Rotherhithe.

I received all this information from Daws. Not all the details over the phone, just that Patrick had been found and taken − after a hospital check-up − to his tiny flat near Gower Street. The rest of the story came out when I met the colonel at his office, where I had had strict instructions to report first as he intended to accompany me.

It was a relief to find that Steve was with Patrick and also that the latter's appearance did not suggest that he had been beaten as badly as Daws's account had led me to believe. True, he was endeavouring not to move overmuch and one side of his face was badly bruised. Our eyes met as I entered the living-room-cum-bedroom and it was not the look of a man in the depths of pain and despair. I know because I have seen Patrick in that condition on more than one occasion.

'Tears?' he chided softly when I had my arms around him with great care. 'No need for tears now.'

'That's a most odd thing to say,' I said, trying to find a tissue up my sleeve.

'Then cry for Hammond who still hadn't learned to ask questions afterwards of people with shotguns.'

It was as if we were on our own in the room.

'Something's happened,' I said. 'You have that look about you when you're going to tell me something awful.'

'No, not awful ... just ...' He shook his head, the right word escaping him.

'Please tell me.'

He took a deep breath but caught it, wincing. 'I was taken to where they were holding a hostage. The hostage's life depends on Hurst being left alone. It's a business deal between Harry Pugh and Hurst and has cost Hurst a hundred thousand pounds.'

'The colonel told me most of that.'

166

'I know. But I haven't told him everything, I thought I'd wait until we were all together. To have the best bargaining power and save time — in other words to get their money quickly when Hurst is safe in South America or wherever — they've starved the hostage fairly carefully and given him the kind of rough treatment to ensure that photographs of him will have the desired effect with the police. Also to make him crack up a little, another spur to a satisfactory conclusion for them. Looked at totally dispassionately they've done a good job. In fact I hardly recognised him.'

'Recognised him?' I repeated. 'You mean it's someone you know?'

'Yes, Terry.'

'Meadows!' exclaimed Daws. 'Man, are you sure?'

'I'm sure,' Patrick replied.

'Did he know *you*?' Steve asked.

'Of course. He was acting a bit crazy but I got the impression he's OK underneath.'

'But -- but the body in his car,' I stuttered, quite unable to think straight.

Patrick said, 'I wasn't enlightened on that. But the kidnap might have gone wrong. He might have grabbed a gun being held on him and shot one of them. If so, they possibly heaved the body inside the car and set it on fire to avoid identification pointing to anyone else.'

'Is he very weak?' I asked.

Patrick gave me a very straight, honest look. 'They beat him when they feel like it with whatever's handy. A dog lead, walking sticks, things like that. They gave him a going over while I was there — to prove the point. That's when I lost my temper.'

'Risky,' Daws muttered.

'He's naked,' Patrick continued, staring steadily at the colonel. 'You can count his ribs. He looks as though he's in Belsen.'

'Are you sure no one suspected that you knew each other?' said Daws after a silence.

'No. Otherwise I doubt whether they'd have let me go. Hurst might have put them right now but then again I doubt it.' He smiled wanly. 'He might not connect me with a cop in possession of a strong Dublin accent calling himself Detective Sergeant O'Shea.'

'D'you know where they took you?' Steve wanted to know.

'I was guessing when I said the East End. It felt like the East End somehow. But they won't be there now. The house was derelict and probably due for demolition.'

'This will have to be thought out very carefully,' Daws said.

'What reaction was there from the police?' Patrick enquired, sitting down, biting his lip as he did so.

'None. For the simple reason that I haven't yet said anything. Frankly I'm more interested in getting Meadows back alive than apprehending a gutter rat like Miles Hurst. Sometimes I find myself wishing I was still working on a war footing. At least you can then send people behind enemy lines to blast scum like that from the face of the Earth.'

Patrick raised an eyebrow in my direction. Coming from Daws this was strong stuff.

'There's no reason – ' Steve started to say, but Daws cut him off.

'No, Lindley. And you're not even old enough to know what a war footing means. Forget the Falklands,' he went on testily. 'I'm talking about months – no, years of intelligence and counter-intelligence carried out under conditions that today's servicemen could hardly imagine.'

No one argued. Daws is a veteran of Malaya.

'I don't think there's any choice but to play this straight,' the colonel was saying when I re-entered the room with coffee and biscuits. 'It'll be out of Faversham's hands now, I shouldn't wonder. I'll get on to Brinkley first and find out how they're going to play it.'

Inspector John Brinkley is D12's liaison officer within Scotland Yard. He and a senior colleague, Commander Dickson, arrived twenty-five minutes after Daws had made a phone call.

'There's no question of negotiating with them,' said Dickson, seating himself. 'Criminals who gas the police unconscious are immediately regarded as terrorists.'

'Exactly the words of the Home Secretary to me,' observed Daws, who had made further phone calls. 'However . . .'

Brinkley gave Dickson an 'I told you so' look and said, 'I had in mind some kind of undercover operation but that

168

seems to be out of the question now.' He took a small but bulky envelope from his document case and gave it to Daws. 'That arrived on the editorial desk of one of the more noisome members of the gutter press. They want to print – they're going to print. I still can't fathom why they sent them to us first.'

'Too many people suing them for libel lately,' Dickson said and sniffed. 'Probably getting a bit twitchy.'

Patrick, looking over Daws's shoulder, swore quietly.

'Pictures of Terry?' I asked.

'Too right,' Steve muttered from the other side of the colonel.

'This kind of thing makes me feel quite, quite murderous,' Patrick said. He handed me one of the photographs at random.

Some things are bearable. Looking at someone you know being hurt so that they are snarling like an animal is not. I gave the picture back and managed not to cry. Dickson was looking at me as if I had no business to be present even though I had been introduced as a member of the team. I decided that he didn't like women.

'He appears to be in some kind of wooden building,' Daws said. 'You can see planking behind him.' He brooded for a few moments. 'I'll be honest with you, gentlemen. The Home Secretary has given me three days to find him, no longer. Then you can do everything in your power to arrest all these people.'

'In writing?' Dickson asked a trifle sarcastically.

'No doubt there's a communication on the commissioner's desk now,' Daws told him. And then, seeing that he was really angry, added, 'Commander, I needn't have said a word, photographs in Fleet Street or no. I don't *have* to come trotting to you with this kind of problem.'

'What I'd like to know,' Brinkley said, always one to defuse situations, 'is how they knew Meadows was a good catch.'

'What *is* a good catch?' Patrick said. 'A bobby on the beat? Of course he is. I suggest that Harperley and Pugh have planned better than we've so far given them credit for. They might have asked someone in the Soviet embassy if they had any ideas. Nothing like causing maximum embarrassment to MI5 and earning a little ready cash.'

169

I said, 'For embarrassment read roubles. People like Harperley and Pugh aren't really interested in national security.'

'I'd go along with that,' said Steve. 'So far we've assumed he's never done a thing to deserve being on anyone's hit list. We forgot the Russians — D12 has spoilt quite a few of their plans. They probably gave Pugh Terry's name.'

Dickson laughed, without any real humour, offensively. 'A bit like being passed over for promotion, eh, colonel? You're in charge but they take one of your underlings instead.'

To him Patrick said, 'Co-operation or not? Backup for three days or not? Do tell us and then, when we inform the underling's family that he's alive before they read it in the papers, we can add, if necessary, that the police officer in charge is an obstructionist bastard because of a fit of pique.'

'No doubt I shall receive orders to co-operate,' Dickson said icily.

'That's not good enough. Throw your whole heart, mind and soul into this or forget it. If you won't let us have the best you've got, then I have plenty of connections with the military who would be only too pleased to assist.'

'You have no authority to do that,' said Dickson.

'He has,' Daws observed. 'I'm afraid you must rather ignore our army rank from the point of view of *firepower*.'

The commander rose to his feet. 'I'll await orders and then contact you.'

Daws said, 'I'd rather know now, if you don't mind.'

Dickson smiled thinly. 'Then the answer's no unless I'm otherwise directed. You have three days.'

The door of the flat closed quietly.

'Late of the Anti-Terrorist Branch,' said Brinkley apologetically. 'I get the impression they preferred the enemy without.'

'Not the sort to be won over by calling him an obstructionist bastard,' I said to Patrick.

'An extremely forthright and accurate description nevertheless,' Daws asserted.

Brinkley said, 'On my own I can't do an awful lot but Special Branch owe me a few favours. They want action after Hammond's death, too.'

Discussion went on for a long while, the flat turned for the time being into headquarters. At just after twelve-thirty, when several decisions had been made, Patrick and I left for Reigate. Informing Terry's family before the early editions of the evening papers appeared was of paramount importance.

'You don't seem too bad,' I remarked tentatively when Patrick said that he would drive.

'Half a bottle of aspirin works wonders,' was the brisk reply. He smiled. 'You'll probably think I'm a bit gone in the brains if I say I didn't feel a thing when they beat me up. But it's true. I don't think Terry did either when they gave him a going-over. We were both on a strange high. I wanted to laugh — walking on air. Especially after putting two of them out of action.'

'So we mustn't let him down,' I said, haunted by how Terry must have felt when Patrick was taken away.

In many ways Mrs Meadows reminded me of Elspeth, Patrick's mother. Quiet, very capable and content to stay in the background when their menfolk are around. The kind who so thoroughly infuriate the shriller feminists and whose ready shoulders the latter rush to cry on in moments of crisis. Avril Meadows was most certainly getting on with life, greeting us warmly, her smile only fading when she looked at Patrick more closely.

'Major!' she began sympathetically.

' 'Tis but superficial,' he assured her. 'And apologies for turning up at lunchtime without giving you a ring first.'

'So this isn't one of those visits to check that the bereaved family are coping?' she said with remarkable lack of bitterness.

'No,' said Patrick. 'I've come to make things better and much, much worse.'

By the time the papers were on the streets, another package had been delivered to the editor of the publication with this unique scoop. It contained more photographs, Terry's watch, his signet ring and a lock of his hair. The hair had been pulled out. Surprisingly, this last item caused the proprietor of the paper, who had been informed, to contact the police immediately and pledge the support of his entire empire to work for the safe release of the hostage. When Dickson realised that this support meant private planes, helicopters and any amount of money to hire men, weapons and whatever was needed, he declined politely and mobilised every unit that could be spared. Then he received orders to do precisely that.

Brinkley contacted Daws with this intelligence, admitting to having had a blazing row with Dickson prior to the proprietor's phone call and having been threatened with dismissal. Daws had immediately offered him a job with D12, whereupon Brinkley had rung off, stammering his thanks and intimating that he would kick Dickson's backside if it would bring results.

'The police must make *some* kind of statement,' Patrick said, after taking a call from Daws. We were in the BMW heading back towards town after driving around the East End for half the night trying to identify the place where Patrick had been taken. He had heard trains and, where the blindfold had lifted slightly, glimpsed chalked pictures on the pavement, an alley with a single light that was faulty, flashing on and off, at the rear of a Chinese restaurant.

'And soon,' I added.

'Absolutely. Even if it's a pack of lies.'

'But they won't,' I protested. 'They won't even *appear* to be doing a deal with Harperley and co.'

He grunted. 'Well, tonight was a complete waste of time, that's for sure.'

The police had more luck. One of the constables who had been overcome by the armed gang at Bitterns and hospitalised with a suspected fractured skull recovered consciousness and remembered the number of the van. This was immediately traced to a back-street garage business in Bethnal Green. The owner being 'away', the workshop was broken into and the van removed for examination.

Patrick and I had eaten a quick meal at the flat — fish and chips — and then slept where we were, fully clothed, on the sofa. We awoke at four-thirty to discover that someone was in the kitchen, making tea. It was Daws, to whom we had given a front-door key. Daws, obviously, had not slept at all, bringing in three steaming mugfuls on a tray before sinking wearily into a chair, his eyes red-rimmed. He looked, shockingly, an old man.

'This is for you,' he said to Patrick, giving him a brown envelope. 'Delivered by hand to the home of our editor some time after two this morning.'

Even though the writing was shaky I could see that it was Terry's.

'You read it,' Patrick muttered, handing it to me.

I slit open the letter carefully, using a knife, in case he had written anything on the inside of the envelope. It contained two sheets of cheap, lined writing paper. ' "Dear Patrick," ' I read.

'When did the lad ever call me that?' Patrick whispered.

'Listen!' I said angrily. 'His life depends on you concentrating on this. "Dear Patrick. Writing this is my idea. It is not being dictated to me but a big guy is holding a knife near my throat in case I put in any hidden messages. There seemed to be no harm in telling them that the bloke they'd grabbed was you and that you're my boss. They mean business and I don't know how long I can hold on. This thing leaks and I feel pretty bad all of the time, as bad as when ... " '

'Go on,' Patrick said.

I sniffed. 'There's a sort of squiggle on the paper there. I think the bastard must have hit him. Terry goes on: "When Hurst is out of the country they'll release me. Yours, Terry." '

'Leaks?' Daws queried. 'It hasn't rained for a while now.'

'A damp cellar, I expect,' Patrick said.

'With planking up the walls?' I said.

'A damp shed then. What difference does it make? We still don't know where the hell he is.'

The photographs that had arrived with the second communication were worse. No newspaper could have published them, a naked man being held down by the hair while others kicked him. I folded the letter slowly, the ghastly images burning into my mind.

The newspaper editor rang the flat at seven. Yet another letter had been delivered, he thought in the hostage's handwriting but addressed to himself. It was an offer. Terry would be released immediately if Patrick would take his place. He was to wait on Hammersmith Bridge on the south side, that night, at ten-thirty. There was a postscript in different writing to the effect that the hostage's captors were afraid that

173

he might die on them. They wanted more time.

'The young fool,' Daws said mildly when he had relayed all this to us. 'He saw no harm in telling them who they'd grabbed. This is the damage he's done.'

'It's worth a try,' Patrick said.

'No,' said Daws with an air of finality. 'You know too much. Think who they could sell you to.'

'With backup, though,' Patrick argued. 'I could be followed by undercover people all the way.'

'No,' Daws said again. 'I'm not even going to consider it.'

The air of mutiny, albeit respectful, drove Daws to utter a last warning.

'Major, you are not only in charge of the prime minister's security arrangements outside London but privy to the kind of information that would have the KGB dancing in the streets. And please don't try to tell me that you're quite good at keeping things to yourself because you know as well as I do that time conquers all, even you, and so do truth drugs. I'll say it again — no.'

Patrick stared at the floor. 'If you say so, sir.'

'Give me your gun.'

When Patrick looked up his expression was of shock only. He said, 'They kept it.'

'I see,' said the colonel, rising to his feet.

'It's the truth,' I told him.

'Hardly a fact I was going to brag about,' Patrick said.

Daws took his own Smith and Wesson from the shoulder harness and laid it on the table before him. 'You've disobeyed orders before. It's vital that you don't this time. If you forced me to stop you I'd aim low, but that's hardly a consoling thought for you, is it?' Without waiting for any reply he then made a phone call and all the while he spoke the look in Patrick's eyes became stonier. But he did nothing that would have forced Daws to take action.

Two armed military policemen duly arrived and Patrick was placed under house arrest for twenty-four hours. I was ordered to either stay with him or return home to Devon. I went. No one had forbidden *me* to do anything.

174

Chapter Sixteen

'I wish you'd tell me what you have in mind,' Steve said, as the car crested a rise and began to drop down into a valley. The village of Hinton Littlemoor, where Patrick's father is rector, lay before us surrounded by a mosaic of green, yellow and gold fields in various stages of being cut for silage.

I outlined a few ideas I had and he gazed at me as though I had taken leave of my senses.

We had arrived at Bath Station at eight-fifteen and had been fortunate to find the office of a car-hire company just being opened. The mood of the sleepy young woman trying to find the right keys had not matched mine and I am afraid I was less than polite. But every second wasted was a second of Terry's added misery.

'Did you get your gun from the safe?' Steve asked.

'My middle name is Annie,' I replied, adding, 'It sometimes pays to be thoroughly underrated. Those two hulking goons weren't going to let Patrick so much as go to the toilet without leaving the door open but they wouldn't have dreamed of watching me getting changed in the bedroom. That's where the safe is — behind a picture on the wall.'

The Gillards were having breakfast. John opened the door to us, his apparel and demeanour suggesting he was looking forward to a day in the garden. It was clear that neither he nor Elspeth had recognised the identity of the hostage so much in the news, Terry's name not having been released.

'I see what you mean,' Steve said to me out of the corner of his mouth as we followed John down the hall and into the kitchen.

'He looks like Terry,' Elspeth whispered, looking at Steve, after she had embraced me warmly.

'I'm after another lookalike,' I said, my attention on John as he went over to the sink to fill the kettle to make more tea. From the back the resemblance was uncanny, he even had a slight halt to his gait due to a touch of rheumatism in his right leg.

Over tea and toast I broke the news to them, showing them a couple of not too distressing photographs. Elspeth passed them quickly to her husband and I marvelled again at the likeness between father and son, seeming to see John properly for the first time. The long delicate fingers were the same, now with a tiny tremor as he beheld what was in front of him.

After a silence John said, 'And you've no idea where this boat's moored?'

'Boat?' I breathed.

'Oh yes,' replied the one-time marine consultant and naval reserve officer. 'These pictures were taken down in the hold of quite a large wooden boat. By quite large I mean something in the region of eighty to ninety feet long. You can tell by the size and shape of the timbers.'

'Care to guess which type of boat, sir?' said Steve.

'Probably something like a ketch. She's had some work done on her, too, by the look of it. There – that picture – the planking behind his head is new. Good workmanship. There are not too many vessels around like this. You need to get in touch with small yards on the Hamble and places like Buckler's Hard. I think I'd even be prepared to stick my neck out and say it's a gaff-rigged ketch.'

Steve said, 'Terry said in the letter that it leaked. That's what he meant – they've shoved him in the bilges.'

'*In* the bilges!' Elspeth agonised.

'There *must* be a hold of sorts,' John said. 'There now,' he went on, 'coming to me was a good idea, wasn't it?'

'I came to you for another reason,' I told him. Then I simply could not go on and probably only Elspeth would have known why.

'We'll go in the church and say a short prayer for Terry,' John decided. 'And then you can tell me how I can help.'

It is strange how a man does not have to don robes to

176

become a priest. With real men of God — I had already decided — their true vocation falls around their shoulders like an invisible mantle as soon as they so wish. Thus it was with a priest we entered the church, a person to whom — the prayer for Terry offered and my request unhesitatingly granted — I could talk at length about my own difficulties in believing as he and Patrick believed.

'Behave as though you did,' he concluded, smiling. 'The rest usually follows.'

At ten-twenty-five that night it seemed much too good an idea and I wasn't even sure whether we had had in our company until a few minutes ago the trendy clergyman, name of Possil, a role he fitted so well dressed in his son's clothes, or Commander John Gillard, RNR (retd.).

'Are you sure he hasn't any means of identification on him?' Steve enquired.

'Absent-minded,' I answered, forced into being laconic from sheer nerves. 'Left his wallet at home.'

Steve and I were seated in the car of one of his department's pseudo-British Telecom vans. The hazard lights of the van were switched on and, to the rear of it, one of Steve's assistants worked under a red-and-white-striped awning. I had noticed that he hadn't even bothered to raise a manhole cover, merely had a mass of multi-coloured wires and a lamp. We might have to make a quick getaway.

Ahead of us on the bridge John lounged against the parapet, occasionally glancing at his watch. It was getting dark and I had asked him to stand directly beneath a street light. Just out of the bright glare even I could not have said whether it was Patrick or his father.

'Methinks the major won't be too overjoyed at you dragging his dad into this,' Steve said.

'He's in no real danger,' I countered. 'I impressed on him that as soon as they leave the area where a priest might conceivably expect people to be taking him to an evening poetry reading he is to query it. By then we'll have the number of the vehicle which picked him up.'

'They might smell a rat,' Steve persisted.

'That's why John's not going to allow them to take him all

177

the way. A plant would sit tight until the place of arrival.'

My heart began to thump when a car approached slowly and stopped between us and where John was standing on the bridge, some thirty yards away. Then I saw that it was full of Japanese waving their arms and maps at the driver. It drove off, a small capsule of utter chaos.

'Suppose they call him by name?' Steve said.

'Possil's slightly hard of hearing,' I snapped.

We waited and ten minutes went by.

'They're not biting,' I said. 'Perhaps they've been watching the bridge for hours and saw the car that brought him.'

The car in question was still close by, with the bonnet up, its driver ostensibly adjusting the fan belt.

'Oh, God, I hadn't thought of that!' I exclaimed.

A refrigerated meat lorry had drawn up and John was talking to the driver.

'No priest in his right mind would expect to be picked up for a poetry meeting in *that*,' Steve remarked gloomily.

John was giving directions and moments later the truck pulled away from the kerb and drove off.

'Super person, the major's mum,' Steve said reflectively. 'Absolutely convinced Terry will be OK. When we left she was airing blankets for the spare-room bed so he can stay with them to recover. She said she'd get your little nipper up with his nanny for a few days too. Said Terry was really fond of him.'

'He is,' I said. 'More to the point, though, Elspeth is a matchmaker and has a notion that Dawn is more than a little fond of Terry.'

The traffic was thinning now, the very lack of it seeming to expose my little charade for what it was, amateurish, pathetically amateurish.

'Hardly a good match, surely?' Steve murmured, watching an approaching car.

'Just because Dawn's a nanny it doesn't mean she spends all her spare time crocheting dishcloths and making jam,' I retorted. 'Terry might have had fluffy sort of girlfriends like Alison but when he finally settles down it'll be with someone like Dawn.' The word 'finally' really came home to me then and I wanted to scream and cry and bang my fists on the windscreen. Terry's life was in my hands and everything was going wrong.

'This looks like it,' Steve said.

But it wasn't, just another foreigner trying to find his way and slowing down to read road signs.

'I don't suppose they'd release Terry immediately,' Steve mused. 'They'd make sure they had the right substitute first.'

'No such luck,' I agreed.

'That's Hurst's Roller!' Steve said suddenly. 'Get your head down!'

My heartbeats seemed as though they might choke me now. 'He must be driving it himself,' I said from somewhere near the floor. The police had taken Plummer straight into custody so he had not been driven away with the Hursts.

'He's slowed down and is scanning the bridge,' Steve reported. 'There's another guy in the front with him.'

'He'll *know* it isn't Patrick,' I wailed. 'And he'd expect Patrick to recognise him.'

'Keep your hair on. John's playing it cool and staying where he is while they give him the once-over. They can't possibly see his face from where they are. He's moving forwards. No, damn, they've driven away.'

For a moment I felt just relief.

'They might have been acting as scouts and be contacting someone to pick him up.' Steve grabbed his radio and ordered the man tinkering with the car across the road to be ready.

Several more agonising minutes ticked by.

Then a taxi drew up. John got in it.

'That's worse!' I stormed. 'You can't get in a taxi by mistake.'

Steve shouted and the man working at the rear threw the equipment and himself in the van and slammed the doors. We set off, heading south, tucking in behind the car. By the entrance to Barn Elms Waterworks the taxi turned round, so Steve contacted the car driver and told him to carry on for a short distance and then turn and follow us. I hung on tight as the van did a hair-raising U-turn in the road and set off after the taxi.

'If it's a real taxi he won't expect to be shadowed,' Steve said.

179

'What will John *say*?' I fretted. 'You're just not thinking straight. A taxi can only be traced to a taxi firm. They've outwitted us already.'

'Unless John goes with it all the way to where it's taking him.'

'Steve, he mustn't! He'll be in terrible danger!'

We went back across the bridge and turned towards the east in the direction of Kensington. Without deviating at all the taxi crossed Knightsbridge and we almost lost it at Hyde Park Corner. It wasn't the only taxi on the road, of course. After heading down Constitution Hill it went along the Mall, through Whitehall and thence to the Victoria Embankment.

'Forever east,' Steve muttered, grimly jumping red lights in order to keep our quarry in sight. 'I'm closing – if we lose him in the back streets of the East End ...'

Almost as if telepathy was at work, the taxi began to weave and dodge in the narrow roads near Cannon Street Station. Steve called up our following car, ordering the driver to overtake us. This took place and we dropped back a little in an attempt to allay any suspicion on the part of the taxi driver.

At last we emerged in East Smithfield and I sighed with relief. But virtually straight away the taxi and car in front of us plunged into a maze of roads in the area of the docks. We twisted and turned, Steve reduced to swearing, going, according to the map and compass, towards Wapping.

'Rogue car on our tail!' Steve said all at once, grabbing the mike of the radio.

With a straight stretch of road ahead, the vehicle behind overtook us, the car in front and then the taxi, braking violently in front of it across the carriageway, forcing the taxi to a halt.

'Get there!' I yelled, quite unnecessarily for Steve had his foot hard down on the accelerator.

My spirits soared, for we were there. When I tumbled out, my gun in my hand, the driver of the long, low, dark car was only just by the taxi and about to open the door.

'Don't move or I'll shoot!' I shouted and he turned and looked at me.

'Very impressive,' said Patrick and opened the door of the taxi. He added, upon discovering that John was perfectly all

180

right, 'No one plays ducks and drakes with my father's life.' In the circumstances he was speaking remarkably mildly.

'How did you know what was going on?' Steve asked.

'You told the bloke in Transport your plans,' Patrick said. Then to the taxi driver, 'Out!'

'All quite in hand,' John said, annoyed. 'We've been discussing this quite amicably. The destination is *Wave Dancer* in St Katherine's Dock and he was ordered to take a roundabout route. It's Maritime Heritage Week. I should have remembered that.'

'She sailed at high tide,' said the master of a restored schooner, returning from another boat with his arms full of cans of beer.

'Can you tell us anything about her?' Patrick asked, showing his ID card.

'No, not a lot. She's only been here a couple of days and the couple with her didn't seem to want to know anyone.' He put down his burden on the gangway. 'There was a right row earlier on tonight, though. You could hear it going on even below decks.'

'Between the man and woman?'

'No, between the bloke and a couple of guys who arrived in a car.'

'What was it all about?'

'Well, I couldn't hear every word, you understand, but it seemed that the bloke on board was insisting on sailing and they didn't want him to. I heard him shouting that if they'd got the times all wrong that was their funeral.'

'Did you only see the man and woman on board – not another man as well?'

'Just the two of them.'

We thanked him and went back to the car to contact Daws. Surprisingly, Patrick was not *persona non grata*, the colonel having ended the house-arrest order at ten-thirty sharp, its purpose having been served. We were told to drive to Tilbury and there board a police patrol boat which would be waiting for us.

'It'll be touch and go if they hope to head him off,' John

said, still very firmly with us. 'If he goes downriver on engines with the tide he'll do at least twelve knots.'

'Why sail like that?' Patrick said to no one in particular. 'I appreciate that he needed all the water he could get to manoeuvre a boat like that out of the lock, otherwise he'd have had to wait until the next high tide, but why did he sail just *then*?'

'Perhaps he panicked,' I said, putting my worst fears into words. 'Decided it was too risky.'

'So will dump the incriminating evidence overboard?' Patrick asked grimly. Then, obviously determined to meet a coming awkwardness head on, he said to his father, 'Nothing would give me greater pleasure than having your company on the boat, but these people are armed and very dangerous. If anything went wrong I'd never be able to look Mum in the eye again.'

I could imagine John's aching disappointment.

'Surely Ingrid isn't staying with you?'

'It's her job,' Patrick pointed out gently.

'I see,' John said shortly. 'Very well.'

Steve's colleague with the car was ordered to take John back to our flat, and Steve was to make arrangements for the van to be collected. Then the three of us got into Patrick's car.

Anticipating the question, I said, 'Your father thought I only went with you on social sort of assignments. Exactly what Daws had in mind when he asked you to fix up a female working partner. Remember?'

There was no reply, I had made a mistake. All that was on Patrick's mind was a young man drowning.

On the outskirts of Tilbury we were stopped by a police car. There had been a change of plan. The car was to escort us to Southend, where we were to board a coastguard launch. *Wave Dancer* had made far better progress downriver than anticipated. Then we were off, Patrick with a rare opportunity to see the needle of the speedometer at the interesting end of the dial.

There was no pleasure to be gained, of course, not on such a mission. And even with the needle registering ninety-five, the flashing blue light in front almost mesmeric with its intensity, there was no real sensation of speed. Perhaps I was

182

tired but it seemed to me that we were rushing down a tunnel of darkness in pursuit of that light. A little like dying, perhaps.

At Southend Pier the launch was waiting for us, bucking and rolling in a steep, choppy sea. I went gratefully into the shelter of the wheelhouse but Patrick stayed on deck with Steve. The following hours would be pure misery for him; like a lot of soldiers he suffers from seasickness.

In the event, the period before dawn was misery for everyone, for somehow, in that wide expanse of water, the *Wave Dancer* eluded us.

'She could be anywhere,' Steve shouted over the noise of the engines. 'You could lose a frigate in the Medway. Or she might have put into Sheerness, Whitstable, Herne Bay — it's anyone's guess.'

We were about to return to Southend when a call came through from a Trinity House supply boat off Margate that she had nearly rammed a ketch that was showing no lights. The officer in charge of our vessel opened the throttles and we set off in pursuit. But among the many ships in the Straits of Dover we could find no trace of her.

At five-thirty the next morning we entered Newhaven Harbour, the boat short of fuel, all on board her utterly weary. Sitting in the harbour master's office, drinking a very welcome cup of coffee and almost falling asleep as I did so, I heard a phone ring. It was the West Sussex police with the message that *Wave Dancer* had been seen entering Brighton Marina, slowly and apparently on one engine. I gulped down the rest of the coffee. A car would take us there.

From the clifftop mainroad we could see the marina when still a fair way off and I was gazing down, trying to make out *Wave Dancer*, when we received the news that she had fuelled at a far jetty and cast off again before the police could reach her. Our driver, from the East Sussex force, jeered in disgusted derision.

When we arrived at the marina the ketch was still in sight, a small blob out at sea, heading west. With a sigh Patrick handed me the binoculars someone had lent him and I looked long and hard at the vessel moving away from us. I think it was one of the worst moments of my life.

183

'Does he owe you some money?' a man called from the deck of a fishing boat moored nearby.

'I owe *him* something,' Patrick said meaningfully.

The man, a walking scarecrow in what looked like several layers of sweaters, jeans and boiler suit, all with holes but seemingly not in corresponding places, climbed over the rail of his boat and approached. 'Sammy knows what plain-clothes policemen look like,' he commented with a gap-toothed grin.

'You saw the car we arrived in,' Steve retorted. 'Sammy had better bugger off and mind his own business.'

Patrick said, 'What are you doing in this poser's paradise, anyway?'

'The rudder gear threw a wobble,' answered Sammy. 'Even poser's chandlers sell cotter pins.'

'Scram!' said Steve, who had apparently taken an instant dislike to him.

'Where are you from?' Patrick asked.

'Shoreham.'

'Are you ready for sea?'

'Depends who's doing the asking.'

Sometimes Patrick does keep his temper but the look he bent on Sammy made the fisherman blench.

'Yes, I've fixed the problem.'

'Will you take us on board and follow that ketch?'

'What's the bloke supposed to have done?'

Patrick told him.

'You'll have to help me crew — the boy's gone to the shop to buy provisions. I said he could look round the town first.'

'No sweat,' Steve said and jumped on board.

It seemed to take far too long to get the *Mary Jane* underway but at last she was churning up the sandy water, her bow swinging slowly towards the open sea.

'We can catch her if you want to,' said Sammy with an unaccountable wink in my direction. 'She wasn't making much speed when I saw her. Only one prop by the look of it.'

The sea was calmer here than it had been in the strong easterly breeze in the mouth of the Thames and was now, of course, behind us, or, as Sammy would have said, astern. The *Mary Jane* wallowed along cheerfully, her captain smoking

184

cigarettes he rolled himself. They were so thin they resembled blackened twigs in the corner of his mouth.

'Feeling OK?' I asked Patrick, who was hanging on tightly as he had problems keeping his balance on the rolling deck.

'No.'

'The boy usually makes the tea!' Sammy bellowed through the wheelhouse door, looking straight at me.

'Tea might settle your stomach,' I told Patrick and went below.

The galley had never felt a woman's touch and, frankly, I had not the slightest desire to touch one square inch of it. But I poured a lot of boiling water over the inside of a blackened, greasy teapot and rinsed out several mugs likewise. There didn't seem to be any washing-up liquid. Or milk, for that matter. I yelled this news up into the wheelhouse above.

'That was one of the things he was going to get,' said Sammy imperturbably. 'There's some tins in the locker by the stove.'

I unearthed one of several large tins of evaporated milk from a mixed collection of stores and then stared at the encrusted tin opener, appalled. Both went into the locker, overarm, when I caught sight of a container of dried milk on one of the slat-fronted shelves.

The *Wave Dancer* was much closer when I struggled up the ladder with the tea, one mug at a time. So close that Patrick had warned against looking at her through binoculars in case someone on board was scanning the *Mary Jane*. He had asked Steve to busy himself with ropes and nets, a job that Steve manifestly thought necessary, the look on his face suggesting that all was not Bristol fashion.

'He's giving himself something to think about,' I said to myself, waiting until a particularly large wave had hissed beneath the hull before I went forward to give him his tea.

'Word's gone along the coast ahead of us,' Patrick said when I got to him. 'I've been in touch with the harbour master at Shoreham. The police have commandeered a private launch. They're going to cross the *Wave Dancer*'s stern, come about and then act out some kind of emergency. While the ketch's crew's attention is on her we'll approach from the starboard side and take her by surprise.'

185

'That seems a mite dramatic,' I said. 'Why not just simply order her to stop and go aboard?'

'Because there wasn't time for the police to arm themselves and these people might be dangerous. We're the only ones with weapons.'

It occurred to me that in a few minutes' time I might be giving Terry food and drink.

'Bloody boats,' Patrick groaned a moment or so later and went to the side, where he parted company with the small amount of tea he had forced himself to consume.

Steve drew me into the lee of the wheelhouse so that no one on the *Wave Dancer* could see us. 'There she is,' he said, pointing towards the land. When I had to admit that I could not see anything he gave me Sammy's binoculars. 'There – just in the entrance of the harbour.'

I obviously did not have a trained eye but at last picked out the twin stone walls of Shoreham harbour and a smart white launch surging through the green-grey water. As I watched it the sun came out and the sea was suddenly blue and sparkling, the soft lines of the South Downs in the distance coloured with fields of yellow rape. A lump came into my throat; such delights on a summer's day might as well be on another planet as far as we were concerned.

'Cheer up,' said Steve and gave me a hug.

'Are you married?' I asked, really to take my mind off everything else.

'With two children. Sarah's eight, David three.'

'I know Terry's in his twenties but now I've got Justin it makes it worse somehow – this ghastly worry. Does that sound stupid to you?'

'No. You feel responsible for youngsters, don't you? – when you're older. Whosever kids they are.' He took another look at the approaching launch. 'A real beaut,' he said on an envious sigh. 'I'd put money on that being the harbour master's own private little runabout.'

'Boring sort of coast, though,' I commented sourly.

'There's France,' he chided. 'Wine, sausage, cheeses . . . it makes my mouth water to think about it. Ingrid, when did we last *eat*?'

I couldn't remember and did not want to try. But I had to

186

admire his resilience, realising also that he was not so emotionally involved as Patrick and I.

The launch went astern of the *Mary Jane* in a wide arc and changed course so she was running parallel to both vessels. Slowly, and still quite a long way off, she began to overhaul *Wave Dancer* on the port side. She overtook her and someone could actually be seen to be waving from the deck. Then there was a loud bang, smoke poured from below and the man who had been waving went overboard. Apparently helpless, the launch drifted into the line of the course of the ketch.

'Wavy Navy,' Steve decided, crouching down with the binoculars so he couldn't be seen. 'Thunderflash followed by smoke canister.' He almost threw the binoculars at me. 'See the guy on the after deck doing a super imitation of severe burns and asphyxia?'

Just then the man who had been in the water struggled back on board and called to the *Wave Dancer* over a loud-hailer. 'Ahoy! Do you have a fire extinguisher?'

'She's heaving to,' Steve reported.

The *Mary Jane* picked up speed for a moment and then her engines were cut. Slowly the gap between her and ketch narrowed, the only sounds the sigh of the sea and halyards slapping on her masts.

'There's a chap with serious burns,' called the man on the launch. 'Put a Mayday over your radio, please — ours is where the fire is.'

Only about twenty feet of water separated us from *Wave Dancer*.

I looked around for Patrick but couldn't see him. Then I saw that he was in the wheelhouse with Sammy. Steve left our place of concealment and positioned a couple of fenders over the side.

Fifteen feet.

Steve had found a boat hook and, as we drew alongside, leaned out and caught hold of a mooring ring bolted to the edge of the *Wave Dancer*'s deck. It was the work of a moment to throw over a rope, follow it with himself and lash the two boats together. Having received no orders to the contrary, I went as well, not looking down as I crossed the narrow gap but hearing the fenders creaking and groaning as they were ground between the two vessels.

I went aft, stepped over the coaming of a hatch and descended a ladder. It was quite dingy below. I opened a door and looked into a cabin with double bunks. I left the door open; the light entering through a porthole streamed into the main salon, allowing me to see where I was going.

There was a large table seating about eight with bench seating along one side shaped to the curve of the hull. Forward of that was the galley. Nothing like the *Mary Jane*'s: a four-oven solid-fuel Aga almost filled it, just leaving enough space between it and the sink unit opposite for the cook and people to squeeze past to reach the main cabin in the bow. This had its own en-suite bathroom with shower.

I returned to the main salon, where I seized one end of the carpet that ran just down the centre and began to roll it up. Sure enough, beneath it was a hatch. The hinges looked well oiled and it was fastened, locked with a bolt inset into the deck so that the whole thing lay flush. I had pulled back the bolt when Patrick came down the ladder.

'I've brought a flash lamp,' he said.

But we didn't need it. We found a switch just below the hatch and it worked, light flooding into every inch of the hold beneath us.

It was empty.

Chapter Seventeen

It was I who climbed down the ladder into the hold, ears ringing with shock, unshed tears of disappointment choking me. Holding on to the ladder, for I was feeling very shaky, I looked around. There was nothing to see, just a large rectangular space full of nothing.

From above me Patrick said, 'Perhaps I'll just go and chuck myself over the side.'

'It's been scrubbed out,' I said.

'What makes you think that?'

'It's sort of evenly damp all over. There's a drain in one corner where the water could run into the bilges. Shut the hatch a moment, would you?'

Even though the light was on, the feeling of isolation when the hatch thudded down was quite awful.

'I thought so,' I said, when he had opened it again. 'It smells like a lavatory when there's no movement of air.'

'Surely the bilges would make it smell like that.'

'No. That's another nasty smell coming up through the grating in the corner ... like drains mixed with oil. There's another smell coming out of the decking, frankly, like a urinal.'

'I'll come down.' But he immediately wished he hadn't, going the most alarming shade of green as he fought to keep his balance on the slippery wood, the bilges sloshing beneath and sending gusts of stinking fumes through the grating everytime the boat rolled. Filthy brown water swilled up and back.

'Send Steve down,' I said.

'There's no point,' he managed to get out before rapidly ascending the ladder again.

'No joy, eh?' Steve called down. I was still gazing around helplessly, refusing to believe what my eyes were telling me.

'Can you get that flash lamp back from Patrick?'

'Honking,' said Steve, coming back with the lamp almost immediately. 'Beats me what he has inside him to honk up.'

With the flash lamp I examined closely every inch of the deck and sides of the hold. There were a few scratches and for one heart-stopping moment I thought that a group of marks were Terry's initials. I knew it was my writer's imagination at work but the hold was somehow echoing with a terrible cry for help.

'D'you think they threw him overboard?' I said.

'They're both hotly denying anything to do with kidnap,' said Steve. 'According to the bloke, they're delivering the boat to Oban where it's going to be used for cruises around the Western Isles.'

'So this has been just a hoax. To send us all rushing off in the opposite direction.'

'Looks like it.'

'Can't the police have a look down here? Surely even a few fingerprints might have —'

'Are you two coming?' Patrick called through the hatchway.

'Suppose they threw Terry overboard?' I persevered mulishly.

'What proof do we have? There's not a trace of him on the entire boat.'

'The police are the ones to look for proof,' I shouted.

'Ingrid . . .'

'You feel bloody terrible,' I shouted even louder. 'I don't bloody care. We can't give up now.'

'Look, their papers are all right and they're dead worried they won't make the Hamble for repairs before the *other* donk packs in. It does seem that we've deliberately been sent on a wild-goose chase.'

Probably recognising that I was about to go into one of my extremely rare rages, Patrick went away again.

'Coming?' Steve asked.

'In a minute.' All at once my anger had dissipated and I felt very, very tired. But also strangely clear-headed.

'That drain's partly blocked,' Steve said over his shoulder as he went up the ladder. 'It doesn't sound as though the bilges are *that* full.'

Without really knowing why, I went over to the grating. Crouching down I groped in the sliminess and got my fingers around the metal grid. Even though quite heavy it came up easily and I saw an oozing rag hanging beneath and somehow caught in it. Retching on the appalling smell that wafted from the bilges, I probed the cloth and felt something solid inside. I took the whole thing up the ladder and asked Steve to fetch me a bucket of water.

'What the hell's that?' Patrick asked weakly, leaning on the rail and looking as though he wanted to die.

I dropped the grid and whatever was attached to it into the bucket and stirred it around. 'It's one of Terry's blue lawn handkerchiefs,' I told him, moments later, struggling to untie it.

Inside was the silver name bracelet that Alison had given him.

The rage erupted. I snatched up the bracelet and dashed into the wheelhouse where lounged the individual who was in charge of the *Wave Dancer* with his slovenly-looking woman friend. The sailors from the launch had by now come on board and were having to listen to a series of snide remarks about how they were wasting the nation's money.

During the next few minutes, and when Steve had grabbed the wheel and given orders − after consulting Patrick − that the ketch be taken into Shoreham, and after I had been persuaded to let go of the man's collar and refrain from banging his head on his own chart table, the truth was beginning to emerge. The boat did belong to him and he had worked for Harperley and Pugh before, smuggling drugs from the continent. He had been given a further fee for leading us away from London.

More importantly, his 'guest' had been removed from his keeping by the two men with whom he had had the argument about the time of the tides at St Katherine's Dock.

*

191

Except for the time he had been taken to the derelict house in the East End of London, Terry had been kept on the *Wave Dancer* for the entire time since his capture. The *Wave Dancer*'s owner, Woods, now in custody and talking so fast his interrogating police officer could hardly believe it, had been paid a thousand pounds to keep his charge alive and no more. Woods hadn't dared ask who Terry was but hadn't believed his insistence that he was a policeman. He admitted he had hardly fed his charge at all, especially as Terry had almost succeeded in overpowering him twice, even with his hands tied together in front. Yes, Woods declared, he was a strong bastard all right.

This much we learned from Daws over the phone after a few hours' much needed sleep. We saw John on to a train for Bath and then made our way to the flat the colonel uses a couple of floors above his office in Whitehall. By this time it was eight-thirty in the evening.

'You've met Pamela,' said Daws, and I found it utterly charming that he had gone a little pink.

'Of course!' Pamela exclaimed. 'They rescued me from those awful men.'

'Permission to collapse into a chair, sir?' Patrick said, doing just that before Daws had time to reply.

'I called you here because there's bad news,' Daws said.

But for the slow, measured tick of his grandfather clock, there was utter silence.

'Miles Hurst and his wife were arrested at Heathrow half an hour ago.'

No one protested that the three days' grace had not elapsed. What was the point of protest when a criminal who fled abroad might be out of reach forever?

Quietly Daws continued, 'To feel anger is natural but bitterness and resentment have no place in the job in which we're all engaged.' When there was still no response he went on, 'Of course as far as the police are concerned this is very good news indeed. Hurst can have had no idea that his arrangement with his chauffeur, Plummer – ten thousand pounds for keeping quiet – would be conveniently forgotten by Plummer as soon as he was arrested. The story is coming out and, now that Hurst and his wife are in custody, I'm

192

confident the matter can be brought to a conclusion. They had documents in their possession when arrested — incriminating, Brinkley is sure.'

It would have been tactless then, with Pamela Westfield present, to discuss the part her husband had played in all this. His blackmail by Hurst and, presumably, Westfield's threats to expose him had resulted in murder. Libby also, I imagined, had been reckoned to be too dangerous to remain alive. I wondered whether bribes or menaces had been used to keep her and her sister quiet about the sister's rape. The latter almost certainly, I immediately decided; Libby had not been the kind of woman anyone could bribe.

'And now?' Patrick said, bitter notwithstanding. 'Meadows's headless body on a railway line?'

Daws got to his feet and strode over to the window, jingling the loose change in his trouser pockets.

'That's assuming Harperley and Pugh know the Hursts have been picked up,' I said.

'We've no way of knowing what they're aware of,' said Daws.

From his pocket Patrick took the almost dry pale-blue handkerchief and shook out what it contained on to the glass-topped coffee table. It made, wielded by an angry hand, a disturbing clatter and in more ways than one.

Daws said, 'Major, I feel as badly about this as you do. But short of asking the Territorials to take apart the East End, what do you expect me to *do*?'

'I promised him I'd get him out,' Patrick replied.

Rapidly, his movements giving away his agitation, the colonel garnered a bottle of whisky and several glasses. He brought these over and set them down on the table, saying as he seated himself, 'If you were me, what would you do?'

'I'd indulge in a little horse-trading. Send in my best man with a lot of readies and orders to find out who Harperley and Pugh's enemies are.'

Daws ferociously wrung the top from the bottle and then realised he had forgotten about his lady. 'Pamela, my dear, what will you have? You don't like this, do you?'

She rose with a smile. 'I saw a bottle of wine in the fridge — I'm sure Ingrid will join me.'

I smiled back. I don't drink whisky either.

'With what kind of mandate?' Daws enquired, pouring generously and not even noticing when Pamela put a bottle of Highland Spring water down in front of him.

'No limits,' Patrick said.

'Are you serious? Really thinking this through?'

'Of course. Otherwise half the underworld will adopt the idea. As well as looking out for the usual dangers, we'll have to be on the watch for any petty thug who's a bit down on his luck and fancies taking a valuable hostage. They've got to be taught that there's no joy to be had in taking *us*.'

'It might be too late for Meadows.'

'I'm being utterly impartial now. If it's too late it's too late.'

'I couldn't give anyone with that kind of mandate police backing.'

'It wouldn't be an awful lot of use.'

'There's another thing, too ... I had you placed under house arrest for good reason. I'd insist on you taking precautions in the event of being taken yourself.'

Patrick sipped the single malt appreciatively.

'No,' I said.

'Then he doesn't go,' Daws said.

'Someone else can go,' I pointed out. 'Someone not so valuable to the Russians.'

'Who?' Patrick asked. 'Steve? He's still not anywhere near fit for that kind of undertaking.'

There was a long silence.

Pamela came from the tiny kitchen with two glasses of wine and I took a large mouthful from mine, hardly believing what was being discussed.

'It'll be the end of D12's *present* efficiency if you're caught,' Daws said.

'Likewise if we have to work under constant threat of kidnap,' Patrick argued. 'I have no intention of being caught. I wasn't caught by anyone in my entire army career and I'm not going to start now.'

'Very well,' the colonel said, 'I'll show you the price.'

He had to go to his office safe a couple of floors below to fetch this and when he returned, very grave, he placed it on the table on a tiny Japanese saucer usually kept on a shelf with some of his jade collection.

'They'd have to offer me a drink,' Patrick said, eyeing it. 'I'm one of those people who can't swallow pills without liquid.'

'You wouldn't,' I whispered. 'You *couldn't*. It's against everything you believe in.' Love, marriage, his wife, our son didn't come into it, I knew that.

'You don't have to swallow it,' Daws told him. 'Just place it under your tongue. Ten seconds, no more.'

Patrick put the suicide pill in his pocket. So innocuous-looking, so small.

'First of all I'm going to take Miles Hurst's house apart brick by brick,' Patrick said later that night.

'Slowly or with artillery?' Steve wanted to know.

'In most respects you're very much like Terry,' he was informed crisply. 'Exhibit tremendous keenness if destruction's in the offing.'

The Hursts' arrest had been kept from the media in an attempt to prolong Terry's life. This we had learned when John Brinkley had phoned Daws just before we left. He had also reported that the papers Hurst had been carrying in a briefcase were sufficient to send him to prison without the murder charges. They comprised contracts, letters and copies of official documents marked 'Restricted' that Westfield had obviously sent him. A couple even had Westfield's signature.

My mind was strictly on my job.

'Nothing's different,' Patrick said to me all at once.

'Everything's different.'

'Look, I'm no more going to put this thing in my mouth than shoot myself with my own gun. OK?'

'OK.'

'Ingrid ...'

'Patrick?' I said and we gazed at one another like strangers.

'It sounds trite in the circumstances, doesn't it? To say we've drifted apart lately.'

'Yes,' I said. 'It does. Please let's get on with looking for Terry and talk about it another time.'

195

'You feel like Dr Watson, don't you? A helpless witness to what I get up to.'

'Your biographer,' I confirmed. 'As always your perception is breathtaking.'

Not seeming to care that Steve was present, he came and took me in his arms. 'When this business is over we'll go away together – have a holiday. I promise.'

'If you're not a corpse,' I replied, and he went away quickly and sat in the car.

'Sorry,' I said to Steve. 'Perhaps I should have mentioned to you before that Patrick and I have been married twice. I divorced him after the first ten years and we were apart for four.'

'The colonel mentioned it,' he replied with a wry smile. 'Are you ready?'

In the complete absence of orders from Daws, both Steve and I were tagging along. Neither of us had even raised with Patrick whether we should go or not and by now I was in an 'in for a penny, in for a pound' mood. I felt, dreadfully, that Justin's parents were squandering their lives with an appalling lack of responsibility as far as he was concerned. But then again, if young people like Terry couldn't go about their business in safety what hope was there for the country's children?

Perhaps this was why Patrick was doing it, I saw with a sudden flash of insight, and why Daws was allowing it to happen. In the dark of the car I touched the hand nearest to me on the wheel and gave it a squeeze.

'This isn't the way to Petworth,' I said a little while later.

'No, I've had a much better idea,' Patrick replied. 'The Hursts are being held at Hounslow overnight.'

He asked us to remain in the car, disappearing for a remarkably short time into Hounslow police station. When he returned I detected a certain amount of satisfaction and also something else that just then I could not put a name to.

'Did you get the information you wanted?' ventured Steve.

'No problem.'

'They let you interview Hurst?' I said, frankly surprised. It was, after all, just after eleven-thirty.

'The police *are* supposed to co-operate with MI5.'

'I know that. I just thought that there might be no one on duty with the right sort of authority.'

'No problem,' Patrick said again.

'So what did you find out?'

'About Pugh.'

'Pugh? Harperley's partner? The one called Harry the Fuse?'

'Yes. He has ambitions. Hopes to get top people under his control using blackmail and threats.'

I digested this for a moment.

'Miles Hurst is a very frightened man,' Patrick added. 'Weak, bent and very, very frightened.'

He would not be further drawn.

It became apparent as we headed back into the capital that Patrick had been given an address, for he stopped once to look at the map in the glove compartment. No further conversation took place until we drew up outside a large house just off East Heath Road, Hampstead.

'Well?' I asked, reasonably, I thought.

'It's his home,' Patrick said, gazing at the house. A surprising number of lights were switched on within, most of the curtains apparently open.

'A little guidance would be helpful,' Steve said as Patrick moved to leave the car.

'You heard Daws, didn't you?' Patrick said, mind obviously on strategy. 'Shoot anyone who tries to stop you.'

'You haven't a gun,' I said into the night air, across the roof of the car.

'Daws gave me his.'

He had gone a few steps towards the house when I said, 'Me as well?'

He turned. 'It's your decision.'

Since marrying Patrick for the second time and working for D12 I have had a horror of his walking away from me into a situation where my presence would have saved him from death.

I followed.

It was unnecessary, of course, for Patrick actually to issue orders. D12 personnel rehearse many times the entry into buildings, the assistants merely positioning themselves as the

197

leader indicates. In daylight this is usually by hand signals. At night, or in poor visibility, we rely on remembering certain sequences, numbered from one to ten. Would this, I found myself wondering, be a six or an eight? And would it have been a three if I had stayed in the car?

'Eight,' Patrick whispered and then, in utter silence, opened the front door with his set of thief's keys.

An immediate impression was that I had been here before. This feeling seemed to come from within to meet me on the doorstep. It was not a pleasant sensation and it took me a few seconds to realise that it was not the place that I had come across before but the unpleasantness itself. This was the aura that had emanated from Bitterns on the Monday of our first official visit.

All the lights were on in the hall. Steve went on ahead, gun drawn; Patrick was next and immediately dived into an open door on his left. He reappeared almost at once with a swift shake of his head and went into another room further along. Again he returned quickly.

There was an uncanny silence in the house. No music or the sound of a television, not even voices. But as at Bitterns I felt that we were being watched. Over all was some kind of brooding presence.

Steve mounted the stairs and I went with him, while Patrick remained in the hall, quite still, gun trained on the doors that led off at the rear of it. I was beginning to think that apart from the indefinable and menacing 'something' no one was in the house at all when a man came from what was obviously a bathroom. He saw Steve, grabbed for the gun that was bulging in his trouser pocket and opened his mouth to shout. In his panic and haste he could not wrench the gun out and Steve choked off the warning with his left hand while clubbing him down with the other. We dragged him into a bedroom and closed the door, locking it, the key, oddly, already being on the outside. No one else was upstairs.

Patrick raised his eyebrows at us as we rejoined him, Steve holding up one finger in reply. Looking at the men I could see that both of them were apprehensive. This was not just the stress normal when in a state of hyper-alertness. No, this was different.

In the kitchen, the first room we came to at the rear of the house, a man and a woman were sitting at a table drinking coffee. In absolute silence — for neither made a sound, such was the shock to them — both had their hands and ankles taped together and were gagged with tea cloths.

'Keep quiet and still and you'll be perfectly all right,' Patrick whispered, and I guessed that he had come to the same conclusion as I had, that the couple were servants.

Double doors with frosted glass panels led off the kitchen. A very large dining room lay beyond: a circular table seating ten or so, a modern fireplace with a gas log fire, a lot of white paint on the walls and woodwork, a light, bright, pleasant room. The paintings in gilt frames on the walls seemed to be by the same artist who had executed the murals in the basement at Bitterns. These were cruder, depicting scenes of human sacrifice among what looked like Aztec ruins. I did not gaze at them too closely, in fact hardly at all, my attention drawn into the next room.

For, silently, a wide door had slid back. We all stared at what was beyond and I thought I heard Patrick sigh. Two figures caught the eye first, Terry lying quite motionless on the floor and a man standing over him, gun in hand, pointing it at Terry's head.

'It's your gun, major,' said the man, Pugh.

The knowledge that it was Pugh and that Pugh had been at Bitterns on that Monday was placed in my mind as if by an outside agency. And suddenly I was made aware that Pugh had been behind everything ghastly that had taken place at Bitterns, had been the instigator of it all. Worse — looking into his eyes and recognising that they weren't quite normal — I knew that the events at Bitterns and what had resulted from them, murder, fear, rape and the unspeakable acts in that basement, he *enjoyed*.

Chapter Eighteen

The three of us laid down our weapons and two men whom we had not noticed until that moment stepped forward and picked them up. One of them was Brad Harperley, whom we had seen in the Speckled Hen at Longcoombe. The other was just a long-haired oaf, one of the small army of mindless thugs these two men employed.

'I love a joke,' said Pugh, pocketing the gun. 'He's dead.' He then kicked Terry in the side and there was no response.

'I'll remember that,' said Patrick softly.

Steve and I were shoved to one side of the room. I was now closer to Terry. It was difficult to remember him as he had been, looking at him now. No longer the lively, youthful personality within an energetic body vibrant with health. In fact I hardly recognised him at all; all that was familiar was the hand-tooled belt on his jeans. This was the only item of clothing he was wearing. His entire torso was covered with grazes and bruises.

'Bastard,' Steve said through his teeth.

Pugh said, 'I intend to do a deal. I'll keep the real prize and send the other three back to MI5. Major, you're worth a lot of money behind the Iron Curtain as a defector.'

As at Bitterns, it seemed to me that from this point everything became surreal. As Patrick stepped forward, looking at Terry and with an utterly unreadable expression on his face, an image burst into my mind. Pugh, whose eyes I found myself unable to look into, was utterly evil. And by contrast I remembered seeing Patrick, the clergyman's son, kneeling in the church at Longcoombe. It came to me that

200

what I was watching was not a man from MI5 confronting a criminal who had killed one of his men but an older, far older, conflict.

'Take a close look at him,' Pugh said and cuffed Patrick hard, causing him to sprawl on his knees at Terry's side.

It seemed hopeless but I said, 'Give him the kiss of life.'

Pugh laughed loudly.

'I've a feeling you fancy yourself as a Satanist,' Patrick said, trying to detect a pulse on Terry's wrist.

'You're in his temple,' Pugh drawled.

We were, I now saw, in a room about the size of the dining room next door. It had no furniture but for a chair on a raised dais at one end. Set into the high back of the chair was an eye similar to the one in the inverted cross that Patrick had destroyed at Bitterns.

I imagined when Patrick leaned forward over Terry that he was about to do as I had suggested. But instead of rendering anything that might be described as first aid he merely kissed Terry, on the mouth, lingering slightly before raising himself. The kiss had nothing valedictory about it, nor of sentiment, nor would, come to that, have sent shudders through the kind of military clubs he ought to belong to and doesn't. It was another kind of kiss altogether.

The result was shocking and almost instantaneous. Terry's fingers contracted like claws. His chest heaved and his arms flailed for a moment before coming to rest at his sides. His eyes opened.

Pugh had the gun in his hand before anyone could utter a word. Everyone, including me, was too stunned to move. I saw Pugh's right index finger tighten on the trigger, the weapon pointing directly at Terry.

The Smith and Wesson jammed.

Again Pugh tried to fire it and again it jammed.

'They do sometimes,' said Patrick. He then moved more quickly than I would have thought possible after that blow around the head, lunged forward and to his feet and caught Pugh by the wrist of his gun hand.

Pugh screamed horribly, as though burnt, and dropped the weapon.

Harperley and the other man were still staring stupidly,

waving around indecisively the weapons they had taken from us. Harperley seemed to come to some kind of decision but by then it was too late. Patrick shot them both.

'Sometimes,' Patrick said, gaze on Pugh.

Pugh backed away a little.

'This is where you do your stuff,' Patrick told him. 'Invoke all the terrors of Hell to come to your aid. Who knows, if you make a good job of it, Old Clootie himself might come rushing in and whisk you away on a cloud of sulphur.'

'He's just a filthy bastard,' growled Steve, kneeling by Terry and covering him with his sweater. I gave him mine as well, knowing that I should be searching upstairs for blankets. But I couldn't leave now.

Patrick put his gun away and searched in a pocket. 'See this?' he said to Pugh. 'It's a suicide pill my boss gave me in case you fancied selling me to the Russians. But it won't work on you, will it? Not after all those ceremonies with black chickens and naked girls.'

Pugh eyed the pill in the palm of Patrick's hand.

'Go on, take it,' Patrick urged. 'Swallow it down and laugh in my face.'

The other shook his head.

I knew then what Patrick intended to do. When driven to it he is capable of the unspeakable.

Pugh realised also. 'You wouldn't,' he said hoarsely.

With an inarticulate cry Terry struggled to his feet, shedding sweaters like a man angrily tossing off restricting bedclothes. Staggering over to where Harperley's gun lay on the floor, he stooped and then had the gun in his hand. A second later it was over.

Patrick took the gun from Terry's unresisting hand and gazed down at Pugh's body on the floor, a neat round hole between the eyes.

'He died just like anyone else,' Steve said.

'But we shouldn't have killed him,' I said quietly.

'No, we shouldn't have killed him,' Patrick agreed. Then, more quietly, to me alone, 'This isn't an execution squad.'

The debriefing was delayed for a week so that Terry could attend.

Looking at Steve, Terry and me over the tops of his half-moon reading glasses, Colonel Daws said, 'Before we go into the reasons why Major Gillard is not present I want quickly to go through this case as I know it.' He cleared his throat. 'Perhaps you'd be so kind as to interrupt me if I leave anything out or if you remember any details that you've omitted to mention. We'll start with your account, Meadows, but to save you having to repeat what you've told me already I'll read out the transcription and you can correct me if anything is wrong.'

This was thoughtful, for Terry — still baby-weak, able to hold nothing heavier than a pencil — had come straight from hospital and was in a wheelchair. Waiting downstairs were his family, eager to take him home.

'On June the 6th,' Daws began, 'you went out with friends, taking their young children to London Zoo. Later that evening and because it was the birthday of your friend's wife, you visited a restaurant near Henley.' He glanced up. 'I'll leave out all irrelevant details like the name of the restaurant and so forth.'

'It was a lousy meal,' Terry said. 'Don't ever go there, sir.'

'I'll make a note of that. Thank you,' said Daws and did, writing it in his diary. 'So,' he resumed. 'After you'd taken leave of your friends in the car park of the restaurant, you set off home. That is correct, is it? You were going home and not to your girlfriend's house?'

Terry grimaced. 'I had thought of calling in and apologising after the row we'd had. But it was pretty late by then so I decided to ring her the next morning.'

'Not prying,' Daws said airily. 'I was just trying to establish how the people who accosted you knew where you'd be. I can only think that someone was watching you in the restaurant and that they had a radio. Might have even been watching you for days. Were you aware of anyone?'

It had occurred to Terry that he was being thoroughly, albeit gently, hauled over the coals. He replied in the negative, warily but quite cheerfully, causing me to wonder if he had been expecting dismissal but had decided that Daws had settled for a carpeting instead. I found myself praying that this was the case.

'Then, when you reached Middleton Avenue,' Daws continued, 'there was a man ostensibly with a broken-down car who waved to you urgently to stop. You did so and, as you got out to go to his assistance, two other men who had been crouching down on the side of the car farthest away from you ran out. One had a sawn-off shotgun.' He glanced up. 'What precautions had you taken to protect yourself at this point?'

'None, sir,' said Terry after swallowing.

Daws allowed a steely gaze to rest for a few moments longer on Terry and then carried on reading. 'You were unarmed, of course. I appreciate that. I'm beginning to think we'll have to review the rules governing the off-duty issue of weapons for people of your grade. Now, you said that the man who had originally waved you down came at you with a spanner. You disarmed him, snatched the spanner from where he and it had fallen and threw it at the man with the shotgun. I can't see someone like the major doing that. Why not stick to accepted practice?'

Terry said, 'I thought he was going to fire it. So I threw the spanner at his head and jumped to one side at the same time. When he ducked I kicked him in the groin and got the weapon away from him. Then the other bloke jumped me.'

'And the shotgun went off.'

'Yes – killing the man who had first been in possession of it.' Terry glanced quickly at Steve and me, perhaps for a little support. 'God, killed is an understatement. He got both barrels – it blew him to hell.'

'He who lives by the sword ...' Daws quoted absent-mindedly. 'After this you're not quite sure of events because it seems that you were struck from behind – possibly by the man who'd had the spanner. You have a vague recollection of trying to bludgeon one of your attackers with the shotgun but hitting the car instead. Then nothing, you were rendered unconscious. It's not too difficult to piece together what happened. They threw the remains of the dead man in your car, possibly blasted him again with the shotgun, and then set light to it by some means or other, presumably with no other idea in mind than to destroy any remaining evidence of his identity. It was that action that led everyone to think you had been killed, not kidnapped.'

'What about all the blood and guts in the road?' Steve said.

204

'Did they shove Terry's car over the spot before they set it alight?'

'One can only assume they did,' Daws said. 'There's no point in going over the rest again — the subsequent period when he was kept on board the ketch — and before we come to the night when he was taken to Pugh's house I'd like to run through this business of Westfield's murder. First of all, though, coffee.'

'If you wouldn't mind, sir ...' Terry began before coming to an awkward halt.

'What's that?' the colonel asked, quite kindly, on his way to fetch the coffee jug from the hotplate.

Terry's fingers were tightly gripping the arms of his chair. 'About me, sir. I'm not too strong at the moment so I'd be grateful if you don't make me wait until the end until you tell me whether I'm fired or not.'

Methodically, Daws began to lay out Wedgwood Black Astbury cups and saucers. 'I can't be too specific about your future, Meadows, because at the moment I'm not too sure myself. It depends on what I can only call higher authority and also on a phone call I'm expecting shortly. But no one's talking of firing, rest assured on that.'

Terry, understandably, didn't look all that relieved.

'Dawn sends you her love,' I said to him, helping him drink his coffee. Terry was probably wishing the colonel had given him a plastic beaker rather than the most expensive teacup Wedgwood produce.

'Does she?'

I nodded, smiling inwardly at how Dawn's reaction to the news of his resurrection — wild laughter, sobs, rushing round hugging everyone and everything who would allow her — could be so neatly put into five simple words.

'May I — ?' he started to say.

'You don't have to ask if you can come to stay,' I scolded. 'Of course you can. Just as soon as you're strong enough.'

'Let's get on with this,' Daws said, reseating himself. 'Frankly, the murder of Westfield was a sordid affair. How the man ever became involved with Satanists, getting himself into a situation where he was being blackmailed, only he knew. His weakness, regrettably, seems to have been sex with

205

young women paid for their services. I find myself asking why he couldn't have gone to the usual establishments.'

'He was hooked on the ritual,' Terry said. 'I heard them talking about him.'

'Ritual?' Daws said.

'Even brothels have rules,' Terry explained, adding hastily, 'so I'm told. The girls at Pugh's place and Bitterns were paid but were doped so they didn't know what was going on, or what people did to them during the ritual.'

Daws's face screwed up with disgust.

'Pugh had everyone under his thumb,' Terry continued. 'Even Harperley, only he wouldn't admit it. Pugh was *bad*. He ruled everyone who came into contact with him. Mostly because of blackmail. One of his men bragged to me that Pugh had photos of half the crooks in London doing things they'd rather not be seen doing at his parties. Even crooks have mothers and wives. It was Pugh's main source of revenue.'

'The revenue from Hurst coming at first from his legitimate business,' Daws said, 'and then later the proceeds of his increased profits as a result of Hurst having dragged Westfield into it. Westfield gave Hurst not only inside information about tenders made for government contracts but also the details of the security arrangements at certain naval establishments. These were sold directly to Pugh who, no doubt, slipped them to his contact at the Russian embassy.'

I said, 'Westfield must have started to come to his senses, surely? Or Hurst wouldn't have had him killed. Everyone said how bad-tempered Westfield was — he must have been in a terrible inner turmoil.'

'I've an idea Hurst started to panic,' Daws said. 'From what the major told me about him and just the general impressions of this case, I should imagine that Hurst was all too aware that his own personal safety was the last thing Pugh would worry about. Hurst wanted out — as they say in films — and it was vitally important to him to tidy everything up behind him. He had the constant worry too that his one-time secretary, Miss Davies, knew everything that was going on. He might have even thought she was working undercover for the police. In a way we have to thank that young lady.

Unwittingly or not she threw a very large spanner in the works of Miles Hurst's life.'

'The night of the murder,' Steve said. 'Why was that guy Campbell so handy to be incriminated?'

'It seems to have been pure coincidence,' Daws replied. 'For all we know Plummer might not have made up his mind how to kill Westfield until he saw Campbell go into the shed looking for something to break a window. We must assume that Plummer was lying in wait for Westfield somewhere in the grounds.'

'Didn't Plummer have a good alibi?' I interrupted.

'More bribery and corruption,' Daws said, a twist to his mouth. 'He went nowhere near the martial-arts club that night.'

'Westfield wasn't killed at Bitterns,' Steve said. 'One can only come to the conclusion that Plummer overpowered Westfield, bundled him into a car and, having collected the hammer that Campbell had left on the ground by the kitchen window, drove out to the woods and murdered him.'

'That is exactly what Plummer has confessed to doing,' Daws said. 'Hurst had told Westfield he wanted to see him on the Thursday night and given orders that the trailer belonging to the riding-school proprietor be used to transport the body. Plummer knows little about the reasons but agrees that Hurst might have been trying to incriminate her as, although her sister refused to allow her to report the rape to the police — she was too scared, apparently — she had threatened to bring him to book.'

'It sounds as though Plummer's singing his head off,' Terry commented.

'Blaming Hurst for everything,' Daws said sourly. 'Saying Hurst had warned him if he didn't do as he was told, then he would be visited by certain people from London. Who knows, with a good lawyer a jury might even believe him.'

'Hurst was hoping that by arranging for the body to be brought back to his house he would be the last person to be suspected,' I said. 'I think he also did that to frighten Jan. She can have known nothing about a lot that went on. She said when we were there that a picture of her brother had been moved and that it meant his spirit was still in the house. Hurst must have done that.'

207

'Or Pugh,' Steve observed. 'D'you reckon he was in the house that morning?'

'Yes,' I said, after making myself think about him again. 'He wouldn't trust Hurst to handle MI5 all on his own. Hence a little something put in a cup that Jan was ordered to make sure went to me.' I recollected how Jan had fled from the house. Perhaps she hadn't been able to face me again. Or Pugh. Had he killed Libby?

Daws said, 'This man seems to have made a very strong impression on you.'

'He was the Devil incarnate,' Terry muttered.

Daws rounded on him. 'Meadows, I really do appreciate that you had a very bad time but to make such childish and emotive statements gets us nowhere.'

'Patrick thought he was the Devil incarnate,' I said.

Daws ignored me, saying to Terry, 'Is that why you shot him?'

'No, sir,' said Terry, chin jutting. 'I shot him in pure revenge.'

'No limits, you said, sir,' Steve said quickly. 'Your orders — '

'I'm fully aware what orders I gave,' Daws interrupted. 'Kindly keep quiet for a moment. Meadows, I'd like you to tell me why you suddenly decided — provocation apart — to take the law into your own hands. For, surely, Pugh was of no danger to any of you by that time.'

'I just did,' said Terry.

The colonel banged a fist on his desk, making Terry jump. 'Your entire future with MI5 depends on this, Meadows,' he said. 'Tell me the *truth*!'

Terry looked at me in what seemed to be panic.

'Tell him,' I said.

'Ingrid ...' Daws said warningly.

'It was because the major was going to ...' Terry started to say.

'Go on,' said Daws.

'He was going to make Pugh swallow the suicide pill,' Terry finished in a whisper.

Daws leaned back in his chair and stared at the ceiling. 'So you took that for permission?'

Silence.

'I'll rephrase that, then. If the major had not intended to do that you would not have shot Pugh?'

'No, sir,' said Terry after another silence.

'Major Gillard might have been bluffing,' Steve said, doggedly.

'He wasn't,' I snapped. 'Let's stick to reality.' My edginess was due mainly to the fact that I had no idea of the outcome of an interview Patrick had had with Daws two days previously or even his present whereabouts. This latter worry was lifted a couple of minutes later. Daws was taking Terry through the events at Pugh's house on that night before the shootings, when there was a knock at the door and Patrick entered.

'I though I'd come personally instead of phoning you, sir,' he said when he had seated himself.

Daws said, 'We were just getting to where you kissed Meadows.'

If he had intended to embarrass Patrick, he failed, for my husband laughed immoderately. It occurred to me that he might have drunk a couple of whiskies before facing what I suspected was a final decision.

Patrick said, 'I didn't know if he was shamming or had fainted or was in a coma. There's nothing like a bit of a shock under such circumstances. Ingrid gave me the idea. Give him the kiss of life, she said. But he *was* breathing . . . just now and then.'

Terry, who could so easily have slid into an easy death in that house, remained silent. He had obeyed the command that it had represented. Wake up *now*.

The colonel said, 'And then Pugh tried to shoot him with your gun. It jammed.'

'Yes, twice,' Patrick said.

'But it worked when you shot both of Pugh's men.'

'After it had been dropped on the floor. Yes. But understandable. Pugh had probably shoved it in a drawer.' Patrick shrugged. 'Dust, grit — who knows?'

The next question was asked innocently enough. 'Did it enter your head at any time that divine intervention might be at work?'

'Oh, yes,' Patrick answered. 'That's what being a Christian's all about.'

'Is that why you decided to kill Pugh?'

Patrick winced. 'That's an outrageous suggestion. No, those kinds of ideas come from people like Pugh. That was where I failed.'

'Do you still have that suicide pill?'

'No, I took it to a chemist.'

'Why?' asked Daws, surprised.

'To see if it was genuine. I think I wanted to know exactly what kind of footing I was on with D12. When he told me that it really was lethal, that was the moment I decided to do as you suggested and tender my resignation.'

'Surely it would have made no difference? You *had* been thinking of making Pugh swallow it.'

'I agree. And I wasn't even thinking of any situation where I might have been forced to take it myself. No, perhaps my appalling lapse came home to me at that point. I simply didn't measure up to the trust placed upon me.'

'Major, I have no choice but to accept your resignation,' Daws said quietly. 'If it makes it any easier for you I want you to know that I do it with the greatest regret. Despite what I said to you two days ago, your going will be a great loss to the department. But at the same time I am aware that you've sailed dangerously close to the wind before. There is no room in the department for those who allow their personal feelings to take over.'

'*I* killed Pugh,' Terry said, obviously quite devastated.

'I should have stopped you,' Patrick said. 'And at the time I don't consider that you were capable of behaving rationally. Make no mistake about that − provocation didn't come into it − you were momentarily off your head.'

But Terry shook his head, near to tears.

We travelled home to Devon in virtual silence. Officially Patrick was leaving D12 for personal reasons, there was no slur on his character and he would continue his position as head of the prime minister's security team. He had resigned once before from Daws's department, right at the beginning. But that had been because of misunderstandings within a newly created unit. There would be no question of reinstatement this time. And even if an offer was made I was sure that

Patrick would not take it. The crisis was too personal. I also had no intention of asking him if he intended to realise a personal ambition of following in his father's footsteps. Someone whose integrity — when not beside himself with fury in the face of cruelty, torture and greed — is of the highest will not contemplate such a step when aware only of self-disgust.

'I need time to think,' Patrick said when he had drawn up outside the cottage.

'Of course,' I said.

He turned in the driving seat to face me. 'Would you mind very much if I went away for a while — to think things out?'

'Whatever you say.'

'Don't be too unselfish.'

'Patrick ...'

He kissed my nose. 'What?'

'What'll happen to D12?'

'D'you really care?' There was an angry glint in his eyes.

'Only insofar as I like our Richard. D12 was his creation.'

'Will you carry on?' he enquired, deliberately not answering the question.

'No, I don't think so. There's no point now, is there? No, I'll stay at home and write. You'd prefer that, wouldn't you?'

'It's your choice,' he said, taking the keys out of the ignition.

I followed him indoors, wondering about the barely suppressed anger. But, once inside, he was unable to contain it.

'Not heaved out because I allowed a trigger to be pulled on an arch traitor,' he said tautly, mostly to Justin, who was making his way towards him on all fours, still preferring speed to hesitant progress on his feet. 'But for consenting to the death of a small-time crook.'

'Yes, you were wrong,' I said. 'But Pugh was of far more danger to people like that small one at your feet than all the traitors in history.'

Patrick picked up his son.

I had a sudden thought. 'Will Terry be prosecuted?'

'That depends on which way you look at it.'

'What on earth do you mean?'

He laughed dryly. 'Daws has given him my job.'

211

'Tea?' Dawn said, entering from the kitchen.

He did not go away to be with his thoughts. But, for a couple of days, it was almost as though he did. His physical presence was at home but he was mentally in a world of his own. He ate his meals, played with Justin, chopped sticks for the Aga, all with a faraway look on his face. Sometimes these activities would be arrested suddenly and the grey eyes would narrow for a moment. Once or twice he saw me looking at him and smiled in a vague sort of way.

'No, there's nothing for it,' Patrick said over breakfast on the third morning since our homecoming.

'What?' I asked, attempting to prevent my son and his boiled egg from getting into a state of complete anarchy. It was Dawn's day off and she was having a lie-in.

'I like the life,' Patrick continued, pouring coffee. 'It's in the blood, I suppose.'

'So?' I prompted.

'Think I might go private. Consultancy . . . security and so forth.'

'Spies?' I queried. 'Offering your services to government departments?'

'Might broaden out a bit. Take in industrial espionage and things like that.'

'Are you sure? Do you really want to resign your commission? That's in your blood too.'

'I can imagine the sort of thing my next posting will be,' he said with a wry smile. 'Licking stamps in an office somewhere on the Rhine. Or organising families' days at regiments stationed at Limbo Toto.'

'Why don't you wait and see before you make a decision.'

He handed me a cup of coffee. 'But surely you'd hate it if I went back to being an ordinary soldier. To keep together we might even have to go and live in a married quarter for a while.'

'I'd rather we were together,' I told him. 'Close. We haven't been lately.'

'All right,' he said and I was surprised at the relief in his voice. 'We'll wait and see.'